About the Author

I joined the American Air force when I was eighteen in 1952. I spent most of my time in boot camp taking the air cadet test. I passed but was booted out when they found out I had a speech impediment. I was sent to electronic school then to atomic weapons school.

Back then the weapons were stored in pieces for safety reasons. I was taught to assemble them and oversee their loading into the aircraft.

The main weapon, the Mark Six, was as large as a kombi bus and took three to four hours to test, assemble and load. They would only fit into B36 or a B52. The hydrogen weapon was much larger only a B36 could carry it.

I never counted or kept track of how many weapons I loaded. I only loaded two hydrogen weapons but at least three to four hundred atomic ones.

I never unloaded one and I never knew what happened to them. At that time at least ten armed planes were in the air close to the Russian border at all times.

Neither my family nor friends knew what I did. The Mark Six became obsolete in 1964 but I never talked about my service life until a few years ago.

I know that America had secret oversea bases because my outfit packed up ready to service one of them but we never did.

They could easily have another one in Australia, maybe it is still there?

I never thought or worried about what I was doing. I could not do anything about it anyway.

I was a good soldier and did my duty.

THE GREAT CONSPIRACY

Douglas Stewart

THE GREAT CONSPIRACY

Vanguard Press

VANGUARD PAPERBACK

© Copyright **2023**
Douglas Stewart

The right of Douglas Stewart to be identified as author of this work has been asserted by them in accordance with the
Copyright, Designs and Patents Act 1988.

A CIP catalogue record for this title is available from the British Library.

ISBN 978 1 80016 581 6

Vanguard Press is an imprint of
Pegasus Elliot Mackenzie Publishers Ltd. www.pegasuspublishers.com

First Published in **2023**

Vanguard Press
Sheraton House Castle Park
Cambridge England

Printed & Bound in Great Britain

NOW that I am old and know the end is not far away it is time to get rid of the burden that I have been carrying for many years. As a somewhat decent human being I would like to leave this world with a clear conscience.

During the cold war as a young man in America I served my country in the U.S. Air Force as an atomic weapons technician. I was a good soldier and did my duty without question. Near the end of my tour of duty I received a personal call from Air Force Headquarters to transfer to work on intercontinental missiles. You had to be highly skilled and of good temperament to join this outfit. Usually you had to apply and hoped that you would be accepted. But it meant that I would have to re-enlist for six more years and I was not about to make the air force my career.

After my tour of duty, I could not settle down and roamed around the country for years and roamed around the world and ended in Australia.

In order to travel I had to work and being very resourceful it did not take me long to learn new skills. Of all the jobs I did I liked cooking the best, especially baking breads and pastries

By the time I landed in Australia my resources were exhausted so I looked for some way to make some real money.

Being trained in explosives I did a tour of the mines in Queensland and Western Australia. It was a good move they pay you well to blow things up.

After years of working the mines, and a few near misses I retired to a small seaside town on the east coast. I am being vague on purpose to make it harder for anyone to find me.

Namely those government agents who come looking for people who expose their nasty secrets.

Along the way I taught myself massage and over time I gained a reputation as a masseur and sports massager. It occupied my time and gave me a place in the community.

You never know what faith has instore for you. A patient came in one day with a friend who was staying with him. They were about to go fishing when his friend slipped getting into the boat and strained his back. While he was recovering from his injuries over a few visits we found that we had a lot in common. He told me he was a major in the army intelligence corps.

Well of course I had to tell him that I was in the U.S. Air Force and worked with atomic weapons. He had a vague knowledge of atomic weapons and was pleased to learn more about them. I didn't give away any secrets because by then the weapons that I worked on were obsolete. Little did I know at the time what dire consequences that friendly conversation would cause me?

In the years that followed life was good. Most days I had the mornings to myself and would go down to the pier to *Fred's Coffee Shop* for breakfast. Fred had the lifestyle I had always dreamed of a nice café near the water making coffee and chatting with the patrons. But when I saw how hard he worked and the number of hours it took, I am glad that dream did not come true.

Fred and I became good friends. He made good coffee, during the busy summer season I would start early in the morning and bake bread, pastry and cakes for that day and help by cleaning tables and washing dishes. During the off season I would take over the shop so he and his misses could have a holiday. I got along very well with Fred but not with his wife. I am a loner and have never associated much with women.

AFTER breakfast and a chat with Fred, I would go down to my boat and go for a leisurely cruse around the lake. The boat was an old wooden half cabin fishing boat. It was a discarded hulk beached on the shore of the lake. The locals were going to burn it but I took it on as a project and over a few months restored it. All the other boats were tin or plastic but my little wooden boat had pride of place at the marina. I was never adventurous enough to take it out to sea just enjoyed cruising around the lake and up the river in it.

Most afternoons were spent in my practice. I only worked four days a week. Mostly by appointment, on the weekends I would roll out the Harley and go riding. Other times I would spend a few days on the boat. Overall, I had a good life peaceful, quiet and enjoyable life. But that was about to come to an abrupt horrible end.

ON a quiet day late in the summer I rolled out the Harley rode out to the highway and on to the city to do some shopping. We had good stores in town but occasionally you had to visit the city to get things the local shops did not carry. I had a good day in the city and a leisurely ride back to town. Pulled into *Fred's Coffee Shop* for a chat but he was busy, so I went on into town and stopped at the newsagent for the local paper.

As I left the paper shop and headed to my bike a stranger approached me and said, "Are you Mr Freeman?"

"Yes," I said thinking he was a potential patient.

"David Freeman?"

"Yes I am," I said.

"Would you come with me sir," he said.

"Why should I?" I said as I move toward my bike.

It was then I noticed another man standing between me and my bike.

"Don't ask questions, just come with us," he said.

With a man on each side of me we walked a short distance to a car.

"Get in," the same man said.

"No, I will not until I know what is going on."

"Don't give us any trouble; just get in," he said in an annoying but stern voice.

How can I get out of this? I was thinking. Two against one and they were bigger and stronger than me. Some locals saw me so I knew if anything would happen to me they would report it. They put me in the back seat and they both got in the front and drove off. Not a word was said as we drove downside road out of town. In a few minutes we arrived at the local airstrip, a grassy paddock with a windsock. It was getting dark and there was no one around. One of the men was talking quietly on a handheld radio. The other man, the one that did all the talking turned to me and said.

"It will only be a few minutes."

As if I knew what this was all about. I was thinking about jumping out of the car and making a run for it, wondering if they had guns and if I could dodge the bullets.

As I was thinking this, I could hear a loud engine noise. Then a large spotlight lit up the whole area. As I looked out of the car window, I saw a large helicopter landing in the middle of the paddock. When the dust settled the car drove up near the helicopter. A door opened on the side of the helicopter and three soldiers jumped out. The two men in the car got out and began to talk to one of them, he appeared to be an officer. Then one of the soldiers came over to the car and opened my door and beckoned for me to get out. He led me to the officer standing nearby.

"David Freeman? You are David Freeman? he said.

"Yes I am."

"I am Lieutenant Peterson. I am to take charge of you from here on. Would please get in the helicopter and we will be off."

Bewildered, I did not know what was going when one of the soldiers took me by the arm and escorted me towards the helicopter. Just then the man who had done all the talking came up to me and said, "Sir, would you give me your keys to your house and motor bike."

I must have looked rather bewildered because he said, "Don't worry we will take good care of them for you."

I handed him the keys and stepped into the helicopter, the door closed and we took off.

The inside of the helicopter was dimly lit and one of the soldiers led me to a bench along the side opposite the door. It was just a long metal shelf stretching from one end of the bay to the other with a lot of cargo straps hanging along the wall. The outside of the ship looked clean and shiny but inside it was just a big dirty hole. The floor was reinforced plate with a lot of tie-downs along it. I suppose to hold vehicles and cargo in place. Suddenly there was a loud screaming roar, the chopper began to vibrate and we were airborne.

WHEN I pulled up at the newsagent in town I took off my motorbike jacket and put it in the saddlebag. All I had on was a polo shirt and jeans on. The cargo bay was not heated and the door had cracks along the edges. The chopper vibrating and rolling like a small boat in a heavy sea, the noise was unbearable, and it was freezing cold. I was shivering, being tossed around and feeling airsick when a solider handed me a small cardboard box. It had two small round plastic balls in it. He put his finger to his ear, they were earplugs. What a relief. With the noise under control,

I tried to settle down and enjoy the flight. I had no idea how long we were in the air and there were no windows in the cargo bay, so I had no idea where we were. After what seemed like forever the engine noise changed and we began to descend and soon landed.

The cargo door opened and the solders jumped out. They had to help me down because I could hardly walk. The lieutenant came up to me and said.

"We will wait here for your transport, it will be better than this old chopper. When we got the orders to pick you up this was all that was available on such short notice."

I said, "I am freezing, airsick, hungry, and have to go to the toilet real bad."

"Not much I can do about that out here," he said.

It appears we landed at an airport because I could see at a distance a terminal building and beside it was a commercial airliner. I thought that was my transport and soon a car would arrive and take me there. But a few minutes later the plane moved away from the building and a little later roared past us on the runway and into the night sky. There goes my comfortable ride, though I will probably end up in the back of an army truck.

Not long after some lights appeared on the runway.

"Here we go," said the lieutenant.

Here comes the truck, I thought. Out of the darkness appeared this sleek looking long noised corporate jet with the round portholes along the side and the twin jets on the tail. The plane pulled up near us and the door opened. Down the steps came a tall slim good looking woman air force officer.

"Good evening, Lieutenant," she said. "Is this our passenger?"

"Yes ma'am, may I introduce David Freeman."

"Good evening, I am Captain Dalton. Please get on board, we are a little behind schedule."

I said goodbye to the lieutenant and climbed on board.

Wow: this was a real cooperate jet with large reclining seats and a bar and a kitchen.

"You must be a very important person," said the captain. "We were on our way to Canberra to pick up the Minister of Transport when we were diverted here to pick you up.

The minister was furious, he is demanding an explanation from the prime minister.

"Now before we take off is there anything I can do for you?"

"I am freezing, starving, and thirsty, also I have to go to the toilet real bad," I said.

She stepped to the fridge and took out a bottle of water and handed it to me.

"There isn't much in the kitchen just a few sandwiches. We were going to stock up at Canberra," she said. "Now we are about to take off so sit down and buckle up and when the green light comes on you can get up and use the toilet and refresh yourself. Help yourself to the sandwiches and whatever. I will turn up the cabin heat for you." When she got to the cabin door she turned and said, "We have to lock the cockpit door during flight, air force regulations. Oh yes, there are blankets and pillows in the overhead lockers. Hope you have a comfortable flight," she said as she closed the cockpit door.

As I sat down the plane began to move and in no time we were airborne. Before I could get comfortable the green light came on and I made a dash for the toilet. When I came out I went to the kitchen to see what I could find to eat. There wasn't much choice, I picked up a couple of sandwiches and found a couple bottles of beer. They were real sandwiches with meat, lettuce, tomato and pickle. After the meal, I settled down with the second bottle of beer and tried to relax.

Reclining in the large soft seat with a pillow behind my head and sipping on the beer I tried to make sense of what had happened to me but there was this annoying bussing that kept distracting me. Then I realized that it was the telephone at the side of my seat that was buzzing. I had fallen asleep and the telephone woke me.

"Good morning Mr Freeman, sorry to wake you but we will be landing soon and I thought that you would like to refresh yourself before we land," the captain said.

"Thank you very much I do need a shave," I said.

The toilet was very well equipped with everything but a shower. After a quick wash and shave I did feel a lot better. Now for a strong cup of coffee. I just made the coffee and sat down when the red light came on, we were landing. I looked out of the window but had no idea where I was.

As we approached the airport, I could see what looked like a military base it did not look like a regular airport. The plane landed and we taxied along the tarmac past the terminal and passed a line of hangers to a lone hanger at the far end of the base. We rolled up close to the hanger door. I thought it was strange to bring a plane under power so close to a building.

The plane stopped with its wing tip no more than a meter from the hanger door. The cockpit door opened and the captain stepped out. She moved to the outside door and said as she pressed the release button.

"Quick, Mr Freemen, step off the aircraft and straight into the hanger. It was nice meeting you. Goodbye."

I stepped off the plane and as I did the hanger door opened slightly and a soldier stepped out.

"This way sir," he said.

As I stepped through the door I could hear the jet moving away from the hanger and the door closed behind me.

It was a small hanger as hangers go, probably left over from WWII. At the back of the hanger was a group of five soldiers standing at a bench. On the bench was a coffee urn and a tray with sandwiches on it.

"Have a cup," one of them said.

As I was about to pour a cup, when a side door opened and two men walked in. The solders jumped to attention.

"As you were," said the captain as he approached me. "David Freeman, I presume? I am Captain Norman Williamson, and this is my aid, Sergeant Ian Jones. I am to take charge of you from now on. Hope you have had a pleasant trip so far."

"Captain, I said I have been kidnapped, shaken, frozen and starved and I don't know why or where I am."

"Don't worry, you will understand it all when you meet the Colonel," he said. "We are waiting for our transport; the chopper is out on a training run. It will be in about an hour. While we are waiting, we will get you out of those civilian clothes. Sergeant Jones, fit Mr Freeman with some gear, the good stuff."

"Yes Sir, what is your shoe size sir?" he said.

"Size ten will do." I answered as he walked away.

Just then the side door opened and a voice called out, "Captain, telephone."

"Excuse me?" the captain said as he walked away.

Instead of just standing there I walked back to the bench and made a cup of coffee and picked up the last sandwich. While I was having my coffee, Sargent Jones returned carrying a utility bag.

"Hope these are suitable, sir," he said. "There is a washroom through that door, you can have a shower and change into your new clothes." I was really enjoying the shower when Sergeant Jones stuck his head in the door and said, "Get a move on our transport is here and we are leaving right away."

I quickly dressed and packed my clothes in the utility bag. Had a quick look in the mirror on the way out, I looked like an old solider with grey hair. The uniform was of good quality, officer grade material. Even the shoes fit.

When I emerged from the washroom the captain was waiting for me.

"I was talking to the colonel on the phone. He cannot wait for an hour so I am pulling another chopper off the schedule. So, let's get on board. We have to leave right away before someone complains."

Outside there was a large helicopter waiting there. It was different from the last one. The captain, sergeant, and myself got on board. The engines roared and we were off. Sargent Jones climbed into the cockpit and returned with three pairs of headphones. That helped a lot to ease the noise. This was a troop-carrying chopper, it had seats along each wall and a double row down the center, about twenty in all. Then Captain Williamson said.

"It won't be a long trip, about an hour, then you will meet the Colonel. Relax and enjoy the flight."

There was a little turbulence as we crossed the mountains. The landscape changed from lush green to the grayish brown of the plains beyond the mountains. I sat there trying to make sense of what was happening but I only got more confused, so I gave up and decided to go with the flow. After a while the engine sound changed, the chopper lurched and we began to descend, I looked out the window and all I could see was scrub land. Then a modest farm appeared. A medium sized house, a small barn and some outbuildings. What is this? Where is the airfield or army base? What are we doing out here in the middle of nowhere? I was all the more confused.

We landed in a cloud of dust. Scrub, brush, grass, and dust flying everywhere obviously this was not a regular landing field. When the dust settled, we jumped out and moved away from the chopper which was immediately airborne and gone. We looked around but there was no one there to meet us, just the farmhouse in the distance. There was nothing else to do but to walk to the house.

By now it was mid-morning and getting warm. There were four cars parked near the house but no one in sight. We walked up to the house and went inside. There was a large table in the middle of the room and five men sitting around it. They were talking amongst themselves and one of them was talking on the phone. None of them looked up or acknowledged us but someone said in a loud voice.

"Colonel, your party have arrived."

Out of another room came Colonel Allen Martin. I recognized him immediately, but I knew him as a Major many years ago when he came to me with a sprained back.

He walked up to me and shook my hand and said, "Dave, it is good to see you. Glad you could join us."

"Did I have choice?" I said. "What am I doing here?"

Allen smiled and said, "Relax Dave, you will soon understand. Right now meet my crew, we have worked together many times and they are all very reliable."

"Gentlemen let me introduce David Freeman; now that he is here, we can make some sense of this situation."

They all started talking at the same time and I could not make any sense out of what they were saying.

"Hold on gentlemen," Allen said. "Dave has had a long hard journey to get here, he is tired and hungry. He will answer all your questions after he has rested and has been briefed.

Allen led me into the next room, which was the kitchen. He went to the fridge and handed me a bottle of water and a tub of fruit salad. Just what I needed. He tried to relax me with small talk but realized it was not helping. So when I finished, he said, "Come with me I want to show you something. A picture is worth a thousand words and I think it will answer all your questions."

We went out a side door across the porch toward one of the outbuildings. When Allen opened the doors to the shed, I just stood there and stared in amazement.

There hanging from a beam on a chain hoist in the middle of the room was an atomic bomb.

"Is that what I think it is," said Allen.

"Yes, it is a *Mark Six Atomic Weapon*," I said in disbelief.

"Now you know why you are here," Allen said.

"Why me? What can I do?"

"You are probably the only person in Australia who has any knowledge or experience with this thing," Allen said.

"This is too much, I need time to think," I said.

"Let's go back to the house," Allen said.

WE found a couple of chairs and sat at the table with the other men. I stared by saying.

"Gentlemen please do not think I am rude but don't expect me to remember your names, I'm not very good with names. Now down to business. First, I am a highly qualified Atomic and Hydrogen Bomb Fusing Technician with many years' experience working with the weapon out there."

"That is what we thought," Allan said. "I thought of you when we found it. We want you to help us dispose of it."

"That is a *Marx Six Atomic Bomb*. The younger cousin of the New Mexico Test and the Nagasaki Bomb. In its core is three thousand pounds or one thousand five hundred kilograms in the new scale of the most powerful explosive known to man at that time. That weapon has to be at least thirty-years-old, and you realize that the stronger the explosive the quicker it disintegrates so that weapon must be very unstable by now.

Also, it is hanging on a rotten beam that could give way at any moment and you know what that means there would be nothing left standing for about a mile in diameter and a great big crater where this farm was. So the first task is to stabilize the weapon. After that we can decide what to do with it. Now can someone tell me how it got here?"

One of the men said, "This farm is owned by a Norman Fowler. No known wife or family, but well known to the local police. Two nights ago he was stopped by the police for driving erratically and was arrested for drunk driving. They found a large amount of cash on him so they assumed that he was dealing in drugs and decides to search this place. That is how they found the bomb, the police contacted the army base and they called us. Mr Fowler will not talk, so we do not know where the bomb came from."

"Very interesting," I said. "I doubt that Fowler brought the weapon here. If he did he would have to hire a large van with a good suspension. A regular truck would have shaken the weapon so badly that it would have never made it here. So check out the hire companies to find out if he did hire a large van. As to where the weapon came from, well that is easy. During the cold war America had depots all over the world and it looks like they had one or more in Australia too. Also when they built a depot they did not build it for only one weapon. So gentleman there a lot more of the same out there, at least twenty or more and it looks like someone knows where they are."

Well that started a real heated discussion so I got up and headed for the door. Allen got up and followed me. He said,

"Now I know did the right thing bringing you here. I was going to bring in a truck and move the weapon to the army base to dispose of it. And that bit about the depot, that will really stir up the top brass. I can't thank you enough for helping us."

Allen went back to the group and I went outside on the porch.

Captain Williamson and Sergeant Jones were sitting on the porch sipping a cool drink.

"Well, you really stirred things up in there," the captain said.

"I just gave them the facts," I said. "I'm going to have another look, you want to come along?"

"Oh yes," they both said. We walked to the shed and opened the doors. They just stood there not speaking.

"You are looking at a *Mark Six Atomic Bomb*," I said.

THINK of a large egg about the size of a Volkswagen Kombi Van. The large end is flat, then it enlarges to the center then tapers off to the tail. The tail is also flat and has four large fins. On the flat front are two small doors that give access to the core. The doors also hold two small radars that determine what altitude to detonate the bomb. The center contains a large sphere of high explosive and the nuclear core.

But that is not what we were looking at. What we could see was a large silver sphere with a skeleton frame around it. Most of the body was gone, spread around the floor. The nose was gone and the tail, fins and most of the side panels.

"What was he going to do sell it for scrap?" the captain said.

"There is a lot more than scrap," I said. "I think he had something else in mind. But right now, we have to stabilize that thing. Look at the beam it is about to give way under the weight."

"Why don't you let it down with the chain hoist," the sergeant said.

"Look at what is stamped on the side of the hoist, 500 pounds max. There is nearly three tons on that it wouldn't take the strain. The only thing I can see to do is to sandbag it to prevent it from falling."

"Why not build a frame to support it?" said Colonel Martin, who had come up behind us.

"How long would that take?" I asked.

"A couple of days," he said.

"Look at that beam, it is ready to collapse at any moment, we haven't got a couple of days."

"Where will we get the sandbags?" asked Allen.

"Well, this is a farm there is plenty of dirt around and we can send someone into town to get some plastic bags. I would like to have that finished before dark," I said.

"Let's go inside and discuss it," said Allen

On the way back to the house Captain Williamson said, "While they are in town they could bring back some lunch, I'm sure we are all hungry."

"Look for some shovels," Sergeant Jones said. "If you cannot find any, we will have to get them in town."

THEY organized a trip into town. Sergeant Jones wanted to go but the colonel thought his uniform would start the locals talking. Two of the crew members left in one of the cars and the rest of us sat around the table to discuss the next move.

"Well," I said. "About all we can do today is make sure the weapon is safe. Once it is sandbagged, I will remove the detonators then I will be able to sleep tonight. There are thirty-two detonators around the sphere. It will take a little while to remove them but I should have it done before dark."

"Are there any other problems?" asked Allen.

"There is one more," I said.

"And what is that?" asked the captain.

"Security."

"What do you mean by security?" asked one of the men.

"By now the other people involved in this affair must know that Fowler has been arrested and they will come snooping around to see what the situation is."

"What other people?" someone said.

"Where did Fowler get all that money? How many weapons do you have between you?" I said.

They looked at each other and said, "None, what do we need weapons for?"

"A car could come up the driveway now and a couple of men could jump out and kill all of us and take their toy away and nothing could stop them," I said.

"That is pure Hollywood," one of them said.

"You really think so? Well think about this. That weapon out there isn't being stripped down for scrap, it is being downsized so it will fit into a small van or truck so it can be moved easily."

"What do you think they are going to do with it?"

"They plan to blow something up. Anyone who will do that will not hesitate to kill a few people who get in there way."

"Wow that puts a new perspective on the whole situation. What can we do about it?"

Then Colonel Martin spoke up.

"Don't panic gentleman I had already considered a situation like this could happen so I have ordered a company of armed solider here. They will arrive around nightfall about a hundred and fifty men complete with a field kitchen, so be at ease and get on with the task at hand."

About then, a car pulled up outside. The men were back from town with our lunch.

We took a well-earned break and ate our hamburgers. After lunch we organized ourselves into work groups. Sergeant Jones and the crew went looking for dirt for the sandbags. Norman and I went towards the barn and Allen went to make some phone calls.

"What are we looking for?" asked Norman as we entered the barn.

"We have to make the weapon safe, it has to be earthed, we are looking for some copper pipe and some copper wire. Also, we need some tools to work with."

"Wow look at the mess," the captain said as he opened the barn doors. "I think we will find everything we need in here"

In a short time, we had a coil of wire, some pieces of pipe and all the tools we needed and headed for the shed.

"We have to earth the weapon and then set up a static line. We have to earth ourselves before we touch the bomb, otherwise a spark could set it off."

We earthed the weapon and set up a static line along the wall near the entrance.

"Every time anyone comes in here they must slap the static wire to discharge themselves, one spark could blow us all to hell."

"I understand," the captain said. "Why didn't Fowler blow himself up?"

"No one will ever know. Let's clean up the area and get ready for the sandbags."

As we finished making a clean work area the car arrived with some sandbags.

"That was quick," the captain said as Sargent Jones jumped out.

"We found a sandpit just behind the hill over there, sir. A couple of trips and we will be done."

We unloaded the sandbags and the car was about to leave when a voice came over the car radio.

"Captain Slattery here, calling Colonel Martin, over." The captain answered, "Captain Williamson here, how are you Bill? Over."

"Hi Norm, we are just passing through the town, can you give us directions? Over."

"Continue on about twenty clicks. You will see an old white gate on the right side of the road, it's the only one around, over."

"Righto we will find it, over and out."

"Well, that was quick," said the captain. "Sargent take a car and go up to the gate and direct them in. I will inform the colonel."

They all left and I started packing sandbags under the bomb. When I finished, I went to the house for a cold drink.

I settled on the porch with a bottle of water when Allen came out.

"You look worn out, what have you been doing?"

"Just packing sandbags," I said.

"I won't have you wearing yourself out. The troops will be here soon, they can do that."

"I suppose you are right. Speaking of the troops, I don't want them anywhere near the shed. Have them camp somewhere out in the paddock."

"I thought the same way, I'll get organized. You take a break, that's an order," he said.

"Yes sir," I said.

There was a lot of noise outside as a convoy of vehicles came down the driveway and passed the house.

"The troops have arrived," Allen said. "You stay here, I will handle this."

I sat on the porch for a while with my drink trying to relax. A little while later Sargent Jones appeared and said.

"Mr Freeman, we are ready for you."

We walked around to the shed where a group of soldiers were waiting.

"You know what to do Sargent, I will just watch."

"Oh no," he said. "You tell me what to do and I will have the men do it."

I just smiled and nodded my head.

"You men listen up now," said Sargent Jones. "Mr Freemen is the expert here, you listen hard and do what he says."

I opened the doors to the shed and said, "Take a good look but do not go inside until I tell you to."

As they stood around the doorway I said,

"That odd looking thing hanging there is an atomic bomb. It must be approached quietly and with caution. Each time you enter the area you will slap that static wire you see there to prevent a spark. One spark could set it off and it would be the end of all of us.

Now you see that pile of sandbags there, your job is to carry them in there and stack them like the other ones are. One pile at the noise and one at the tail. Also, don't touch the thing because it may fall if it is moved. Have you got all that? Sargent Jones take over."

The sergeant had them go thru a dry run before they started. Each one slapped the static wire and walked around the bomb very quietly. It seemed to calm them down and in a short time the bags were neatly piled in place.

"Good work men," I said. "Now I need two volunteers we have to lift the tail and place a bag under there to secure this thing."

Four of them raised their hands.

"I'll take you and you, the strong ones. The rest of you can go and thank you. You have made my job a lot easier."

The two men lifted the tail against the bags in the front and I placed two more bags under the tail to make it more secure I made sure that it could not move then said to the two men.

"Good job, thank you. Would you like to help out some more?"

"Yes sir," they said. "This is very interesting."

"OK, pick up those remaining sandbags and line them along the wall over there. We are going to remove the detonators."

I removed five of the harder ones to reach to make sure they came out easily. Then I said to the boys.

"Would you like to have a go? OK, this is what you do. There are two wires to each detonator. You twist off the joint and then twist the detonator and pull it out firmly but gently. Don't drop it, it will blow your foot off."

With a man on each side and me underneath we soon had all the detonators off and laid out on the sandbags.

"Good job guys, now the weapon is safe as we can make it," I said. "I think we will call it a day."

I dismissed the men and headed back to the house. On the way Sergeant Jones caught up to me and said.

"The kitchen is up and running and we are the first in line. You head over and I will get the rest of the boys."

While we were eating, Allen said to us.

"You can sleep easy tonight, Captain Slattery has already organized sentries around the area. Dave, I want to talk to you later."

When I returned to the house Allen was on the phone, no one else was there. When he finished the call he said to me.

"Good job done today, you can take it easy tomorrow. I have been talking to the higher ups and they like the idea of destroying the weapon instead of dismantling it. The long-range weather forecast predicts a large storm in a couple of weeks. They think the bad weather will dissipate the dust cloud and no one will be the wiser. We are to sit and wait until they make up their minds."

"Well, that is an easy way out of the situation," I said. "But they don't have two weeks to decide. It will take at least a week to get things ready and get the troops out."

"I agree," Allen said. "I will inform them of the urgency of the situation. Also they want all of the discarded pieces, so they can examine them. You can do that tomorrow."

"That is all right but I don't have all the pieces," I said.

"What do you mean by that?" said Allen.

"There are some important things missing. For one the fuse is not there and also the nuclear core and so far we haven't found the explosive plug that fits in the front cavity. The weapon is useless without any one of these. It is hard to understand why they would go to so much trouble just for a ton and a half of explosives.”

“Maybe they don’t understand how the weapon works,” Allen said. “Something else to ponder over. That is enough for me, I am off to town. The crew has already left, they did not want to eat at the mess. You, Captain Williamson and Sargent Jones will sleep here tonight. There is one room each so take your pick, anything else before I leave?”

“There is one small problem,” I said.

“Can it wait until tomorrow? I am tired,” Allen said.

“It is only that we cannot find the trailer.”

“What trailer?”

“The weapon is transported on a large trailer. It is a rectangular frame with large balloon tires and it is painted bright yellow, you can’t miss it.”

“We will organize a search party tomorrow to look for these things. Right now, I am heading for town to put my feet up. See you tomorrow, good night.”

Later the boys came in and we decided which rooms we would sleep in and we soon retired. We were too tired to sit around and talk. It had been a long hard day for all of us. The bed was hard and lumpy and who knows when the sheets were last washed but I was tired and was soon asleep.

I woke up early before the others, it was a bright, fresh morning and I felt good. I did not want to think about the problems that today would bring so I went for a walk and headed towards the mess hall for breakfast. I didn’t think anyone would be there but there was a small crowd of soldiers there. I started with a cup of coffee then would go back for some food. I was sitting alone at a side table when the mess sergeant came over.

“Good morning Mr. Freeman, can I do anything for you?”

“Well that is good service, we never got that when I was in the air force.”

The sergeant smiled and said.

"I have been ordered by Captain Slattery to take good care of you, and when the captain speaks, we jump."

"Oh, I thought it was my good looks and charm that was the reason for the good service."

"Honestly, you are to get VIP treatment. So, what can I get you for breakfast?"

"I'm not a big breakfast person, just toast and some fruit will do."

"You sure? How about lunch?"

"Sargent, I will eat whatever the troops eat," I said.

"That is not VIP treatment, you have got to do better than that or the captain will think I am slacking off."

"All right I will be fussy, I don't like fluffy white bread and for morning tea how about some pastries with the coffee? And for lunch, a couple of nice sandwiches with meat, cheese, lettuce and tomato."

"That's more like it," the cook said. "Consider it done. We only have white bread now but I will bake a couple of whole meal loaves for you and some scones for morning tea. Leave it with me," he said as he left with a smile.

"What was that all about?" asked Captain Williamson as he came in with Sargent Jones.

"Seems I am to get VIP service," I said. "Stick close to me and you can have the crumbs."

They both laughed and they sat down for breakfast.

While we were eating, Norman said.

"We are organizing a cleanup of all the discarded parts. We will bring a truck to the shed and you can show us what to take."

"I know," I said. "I was talking about with the colonel last night. There are a lot of parts missing including the fuse all the way up to the trailer."

"In that case I will assemble the troops and you can brief them. Come on sergeant we've got things to organize."

"Take your time, we will meet you at the shed in a little while," Norman said as they left the mess hall.

WHEN I arrived at the shed there were a large group of soldiers lined up in ranks and the captain was talking to them. He was saying something about how important this operation was. When I walked up he said to the men.

"Here is, Mr Freeman, now he will brief you on your duties."

"Thank you captain, we are looking for some containers, one is as large as a 200-liter drum. The other ones are smaller, about like a 20-liter container; they should be painted army green. The large one is harmless but the two smaller ones are very dangerous and should not be handled. When you find them report to Sargent Jones and he will organize their removal. Also there is a large trailer missing. It is rectangular in shape and hollow in the center with large balloon tires. It is painted bright yellow, you can't miss it. Thank you for your attention. Over to you, captain."

"Thank you Mr Freeman. Now men we will form into groups of five and spread out to search everywhere including all the buildings. One group will remain here and clean up the shed, the rest of you move out."

As the men left, an army truck pulled up near the shed. I gathered the working party around me and explained about the static line and being quiet and staying away from the weapon. The men were picking up the pieces and loading them on the truck. I was separating the parts from the junk in the shed. As we were working a solider came up to the door and said.

"Excuse me Mr Freeman but Captain Slattery asked for you to come to the house immediately."

"Take over sergeant," I said and followed the solider to the house.

Inside the house were the colonel, his crew and the two captains were in a heated discussion with an enlisted man. They stopped when I entered.

"You were 100% right again Dave," Allen said. "Soldier tell Mr Freeman what you just told us."

"Yes sir, we were on patrol at first light when we found some fresh tire tracks leading from a hole cut in the fence and leading toward the house. We came upon a sort of a camp area about 500 meters south of the house. It looked like they were there for a while because they left a lot of garbage strewn around the area."

"Did you disturb anything?" I asked.

"No sir, we just circled around and found their tracks where they left."

"Good job, soldier," I said. "What is your name so we can call you to show us where the site is."

"Trooper Antonio Larmarra, sir."

"What, you don't look Italian to me."

"No sir, my grandfather came to Queensland to cut cane and met my grandmother there."

"OK, hang around so we can find you later."

"Are you thinking the same thing I am?" Allen said.

"Yes," I said. "If the troops had not arrived last night, you would have arrived here today and found us dead and the weapon gone. What are we going to do about it?" I said.

"We are going to get these guys," Allen said. "Jim get the police officer that arrested Fowler on the phone, I want to talk to him. We may find something out there that will lead us to them."

Jim handed Allen the phone.

"Good morning, Sargent Harris, we had some unwanted visitors here yesterday and I want you to come out here with your detectives and investigate the site. When? Right now of course, before something disturbs it. What do you mean you cannot do it today? If you are not here in one hour, I will call in the federal police and you will never live it down that the job was too big for you and the feds had to be called in. One hour Sargent. The nerve of that guy," Allen said as he put the phone down.

"I figure those guys were out there all afternoon waiting for dark to come in but were scared off when the troops arrived," Captain Slattery said.

There was a knock at the door and a trooper came in, "Excuse me sir but Sargent Jones wants to know if this is important, we found it in the shed," he said as he handed it to Captain Slattery.

"It looks like a plastic ticket, is it important?" he said as he handed it to me. As I looked at it,. the room began to spin around and I fell back on the chair.

The next thing I knew was someone saying, "Dave, are you all right? He has had a stroke call a doctor. Get some water!"

They were all talking at once. I regained my senses in a couple of minutes and just sat there staring at the wall.

"Dave are you all right? What is wrong?" Allen said.

After a couple of sips of water I said, "I am OK just a little shocked, that's all."

"How could looking at a little piece of plastic do that?" asked Allen.

"This little piece of plastic has just thrust us down into the deepest bowels of hell," I said with a quivering voice. "Everything has changed. Forget all we said yesterday. Gentlemen, that is not a *Mark Six Atomic Weapon* out there."

"What are you saying," Allen said.

"That thing out there is the most diabolical evil thing that mankind has ever made. That is a *Plutonium Bomb*."

"What the hell is a *Plutonium Bomb*?" said a voice from the group.

"It is a radiation bomb," I said. "If that thing went off everything in a three-hundred-mile radius would be dead and the land would be contaminated for hundreds of years. The dust cloud would contaminate everything from here to the sea and on to New Zealand. We would have a Chernobyl just like Russia. There is no hope of destroying it now, we will have to dismantle it."

They were standing there silent, shaking their bowed heads.

"One more thing, that tag came off the end of a long thick aluminum chain that was inside the core of the weapon. There is enough plutonium in the sphere to start an atomic reaction without the nuclear core. We have to find that chain and replace it in the sphere to prevent an atomic fission. Captain Slattery get the men out of the shed and close the doors and put a sentry there. No one goes in there without my permission."

"Right away," he said as he left the room.

They were all talking at once when two police cars pulled up in front of the house.

Captain Williamson went out to meet them. The Sargent got out of the car and said, "Where is this so-called crime scene?"

"Somebody find Trooper Larmarra," the captain ordered. Then he said to the policeman, "He will escort you to the scene. We hope you can find some evidence as to who these people are. If not, we want you to seal all the evidence because there is a new system now called DNA and we will use this evidence to place them here if we catch them some time in the future. This is a lot more important than you think it is, so please do your duty and do it well. Here comes Trooper Larmarra, he will give all the help he can.

Trooper escort these men to the camp site and give them all the assistance they need. If you are here for a while you can lunch at the mess. Please report to me before you leave. On your way, Trooper."

Then the captain returned to the house.

Inside Allen was talking to the group.

"This is a lot more serious than I could ever imagine, what are we going to do?"

"All we can do is dismantle the weapon, and do it as quickly as possible," I said.

"We won't do anything until I talk to the top brass." he said.

"All right," I said. "But right now we have to find that chain and secure the weapon."

There was a knock at the door and a solider entered.

"Excuse me sir but sergeant asked if you and Mr Freeman could come at once."

"What in God's name can be wrong now?" the colonel said. "You go Dave, I have to report all of this to headquarters."

The solider and I walked along the path past the shed with a sentry at the door. Pass the barn to a smaller shed the last one there. Sargent Jones and his crew were waiting at the doorway.

"It was locked so we had to break it open," 'he said.

"You found the missing containers?" I said.

"No such luck, this is your worst nightmare."

"Can't be any worse than what we just found out," I said.

"Want to bet?" he said as one of the men opened the door.

Inside was a bright yellow trailer with a thick curtain around it.

"Oh God not another one, the colonel won't like this," I said. "Take the curtain off and let's have a look."

There was not a lot of room but a couple of the men were able to get the curtain off. There in all its shining glory was another *Plutonium Bomb*.

"Nothing we can do right but to close the door and put a guard here. Will you see to it, Ian? I will inform the colonel. He will have another fit."

Meanwhile out at the so-called crime scene, the detectives were searching through and bagging all the items spread around the site.

"Looks like they were here for a while," one of them said.

"Yes for about four hours," Trooper Larmarra said.

"How would you know?"

"It is obvious, count the cigarette butts. One of them smoked a lot, another a few, and the other one only five," Larmarra said.

"You mean there were three of them?" one of them said.

"Not three, four."

"How do you know that? Are you a tracker?"

"No but my father is, I was never initiated. He worked on a cattle station out west; we use to track wild dogs and pigs to keep them away from the young cattle."

"How do you know that there were four of them?" asked the Sargent.

"That's easy, just look at the tracks. One was a large fellow, one was small and light, and the other two were about average size about, like you. Also one of the average ones wore cowboy boots, the other ordinary shoes, the big fellow had heavy boots with deep cleats and the little one soft smooth shoes. He was hard to track."

"Are you taking all this down, Pete?" said Sargent Harris.

"As fast as I can, sir."

Trooper Larmarra continued,

"It was a four-door car, the big guy sat in the back on the passenger side. You can see his boot cleats here on the ground.

He was a light smoker but ate a lot look at all the food wrappers and bottles around here. The little fellow sat in front of him. Not much from him, he didn't smoke and only ate one candy bar."

They followed Trooper Larmarra to the other side of the car.

"The driver was the moderate smoker probably ex-army, he field stripped his butts. The cowboy boots guy was a chain smoker and very nervous, he stubbed his butts also, you can see all the heel prints around here where he walked. He also walked off in that direction towards the house, probably to those bushes to get a closer look."

"We will go over there when you finish here."

"Amazing," said one of the detectives. "There is enough information to keep us busy for days."

"Anything else?" asked Sargent Harris.

"Only it was a large car. You can see the deep tire marks that also tell me it was here for a while."

"I'll make a cast of them and it will tell us what type of car it was," said one of the detectives. "While I am doing this you guys can check out those bushes over there then we can go back to the base, I'm getting hungry."

WHEN I got back to the house Allen was on the phone so I told the boys what Sargent Jones had found. They were all amazed and dismayed at the same time.

"Who is going to break the news to the colonel?"

"Not me," each said in turn he will go off the deep end.

"Don't worry I will do it," I said.

"What are you going to do now?" asked Allen as he came into the room.

"I am going to take you for a cup of coffee," I said.

"Good idea, I really need one after the argument with headquarters. They will not believe we have a Plutonium Bomb."

"Come on you can tell me about it over coffee. The cook promised me a treat of scones and jam."

"Scones and jam: how come you get treated royally? I'm supposed to be the big cheese around here," Allen said with a smile.

We arrived at the mess and poured ourselves a coffee and sat down. A couple minutes later the cook came over with a tray with scones, jam and cream.

"Good morning Mr Freeman, Colonel, here are your scones just as I promised. I hope they are satisfactory."

Allen's eyes were popping out of his head.

"In all my years in the service I have never experienced anything like this. I have never had a pleasant word from a cook, never mind a plate of scones too."

"And a smile," I added as a little dig.

While we were enjoying the coffee and scones Allen briefed me on his discussion with headquarters.

"They refuse to believe that we have a Plutonium Bomb. But they did agree to let us dismantle it. They thought blowing it up was too risky. Also they hinted that the Americans refuse to acknowledge the fact that there are atomic weapons in Australia."

"I could have told you that," I said. "They will never admit to anything. Right now the most important thing is to find that chain. We have to make the weapon safe. I will check with Sargent Jones in case it has been found."

"I am sure you would have been told if it had," said Allen. "What will you do if they cannot find it?"

"I have an idea," I said. "There are a lot of troops here and I am sure they are drinking a lot of soft drinks. I will gather the aluminum cans and place them in the core."

"Good idea," Allen said. "By the way what did Sargent Jones want earlier this morning?"

"Did you enjoy your coffee and scones?"

"Yes I did, why?"

"Are you calm and peaceful?"

"Of course I am, what is going on?"

"No one else has the courage to tell you this, so they put it on me."

"You are not making any sense," Allen said.

"Colonel sit back and hold on to your chair. Sargent Jones found another weapon."

Allen stood up, "That isn't funny Dave, I've have enough on my mind, I don't appreciate your silly jokes."

"Sit down Allen," I said. "This is no joke there is an intact weapon sitting out there in the last shed. If you don't believe me, come on I will show it to you."

Allen slumped into the chair and said, "This is awful, what are we going to do now?"

"I think we should forget about it for now and concentrate on the problems we have now," I said.

"I suppose you are right," Allen said. "Where do we go from here?"

"Now that we are going to dismantle the weapon, we have a lot of preparation to do. We have to prepare the sandpit so we can detonate the charges. There will also have to have a smooth road from the shed to the sandpit so we can move the explosive charges safely."

"Looks like we will need the engineers," Allen said. "I will get on to Captain Williamson, he can handle that."

"The sooner we get started the better," I said.

"Let's get going then," Allen said. "I will find Williamson."

"And I will look for Sargent Jones."

We left the mess and went our separate ways.

I found the Sargent returning from the army campsite.

"I was just coming to find you," he said. "We looked everywhere but could not find anything, except the weapon. What else can we do?"

"Instead of the chain we will use aluminum cans, there should be plenty of them around the camp. Get someone to gather them and wash and crush them. Then we will fill the sphere with them."

"If you say so. I will get some on it right away. By the way, what is a Plutonium Bomb anyway?"

"I don't have time to explain it right now."

"How about over lunch?"

"OK, see you then."

I was heading towards the house when I met Captain Williamson.

"What do you need the Engineers for?" he asked as we walked along.

I explained to him that we had to detonate the explosives in a suitable place and that the sandpit was the ideal spot. Also the charges had to be moved very carefully over a smooth road to the pit. When it was explained to him, he agreed and said.

"You will need some bomb disposal boys too. Leave with me."

"Thank you. By the way have you heard the latest?" I said.

"No what is it?"

"Sargent Jones found another weapon," I said as we were going up the steps to the house.

The captain stumbled and nearly fell.

"Another weapon, no that cannot be possible. We cannot handle the situation now, how are going to handle this too? What else can go wrong?"

"It could all go boom," I said with a smile.

Inside the captain went into the other room looking for the Colonel and the crew all started talking at once. The situation is out of control, was what I got out of them.

"What are we going to do?"

"Sit tight and everything will ease off," I said. "The main concern right now is to make the weapon safe. I have Sargent Jones rounding up some drink cans to take the place of the chain."

"Good idea," they agreed.

"Once that is done, I will begin to dismantle the rest of the frame so I can get to the sphere. Keep the truck here to put the pieces in. Once that is done we can take it easy until the engineers finish their work."

"What about the other weapon?" one of them said.

"That can stay where it is for now. We have enough to do with this one. When we dismantle the core we will know how stable the charges are and then we can decide on what to do with it."

"What do you mean?"

"Well if the explosive is fairly stable we can give it to the army and it's their problem then."

There were smiles and nodding heads all round.

"That is great and then we can all go home."

I did not want to spoil their glee, so I did not say any more. The chances of the explosives being stable were very slim, practically nonexistent.

While they were talking among themselves and I was pondering the situation the door opened and the Police Sergeant and his crew came in. One of the men went to get the Colonel, the room was rather crowded, so the sergeant said, "We won't stay long we will send you a report. You did have some unwanted visitors and with the help of your trooper we have a good chance of finding them. Now we are hungry and would like to take up your kind offer of lunch."

"Right this way gentlemen, you can tell me all about it while we are eating," said Captain Williamson as he led them out of the crowded room.

I turned to Allen and said, "Things may be a little chaotic but in their own way they are moving along."

"I hope you are right," he said, as he returned to the other room.

I was getting hungry so I decided to head to the mess tent. While I was walking along, I thought to myself, *Why are they all turning to me to solve their problems. Let them solve their own, you have enough to do dismantling the weapon. Tell them you have enough to do. A good idea,* I thought, *I'll do it. Fat chance,* said the little man on my other shoulder.

As I arrived at the mess I met Sargent Jones.

"I have two hundred cans for you. The men will wash and crush them after they eat."

"That's great, let's get some lunch."

We entered the mess tent and Ian headed to the serving line.

"This way Dave. Haven't you been here before?"

"It's OK," I said. "I will find us a seat."

A few minutes Ian arrived with his tray.

"Aren't you eating? I thought you were hungry."

"I am, don't worry I am being taken care of."

"You are kidding me? Not in an army mess, it is every man for himself."

Just then the cook appeared with a tray.

"Good day Mr Freeman, here is your lunch just as you ordered," the cook said.

Ian's jaw dropped on to the table, he just sat there staring at the sandwiches and glass of milk.

"I baked the bread myself," the cook said as he walked off.

"I don't believe it, in all my years in the army I have never seen anything like that," said Ian.

"I know, the Colonel said the same thing this morning."

"How come I have to eat this gaol house food and you get gourmet sandwiches?"

"Come on the food isn't that bad and don't fret, I will give you half a sandwich."

On the other side of the mess tent Captain Williamson was talking with the policemen. The Sergeant was telling how Trooper Larmarra had tracked the visitors.

"He gave us everything except their names and addresses. We radioed their description to headquarters, if they are still in this area we will find them. We could really use him around here, there is a lot of cattle duffing going on and he could help us find the culprits."

"Maybe we can loan him to you," said the captain. "Thank you for the update I am looking forward to reading your report."

"Right away," the Sargent said, as they got up to leave.

"One more thing sergeant we are looking for a long aluminum thick chain and a funny looking yellow trailer with balloon tires. Give us a yell if you find them, it's important."

"Things are getting weirder all the time," said the sergeant as they left the mess.

While we were having our coffee, I was explaining to Ian what a Plutonium Bomb was.

"During the early days of the cold war they realized that it was nearly impossible to stop a large fleet of aircraft from bombing America, some would get through. So they invented a ground to air missile that would get high altitude planes. But some would still get through. So someone came up with the idea of a radiation bomb, set it off in the middle of a group of planes and the bomb would kill all the crews for miles around. A great idea for a little while until intercontinental missiles came along.

Of course they didn't stop there, why not use it on an army? One shot and the whole army is wiped out. Then why not on a city, wipe out all the inhabitants and take over the city.

Of course with every great idea comes a downside, of which they did not realize until much later and that is. Setting it off at high altitudes has no long-lasting effects, but at ground level the radiation lasts for hundreds of years. So the great advantage is lost so the weapon has no real use. But they did not realize that when they manufactured them."

"That is madness, how could a country make something as horrible as that?"

"That was over thirty years ago," I said. "What do you think they have now? That is enough history for now, let's get those cans ready."

"OK, I will meet you at the shed."

When I arrived at the shed, I dismissed the sentry.

"Tell your sergeant to have a man here after chow," I said as he left. I opened the doors, slapped the static line and went in. The weapon looked like a half-eaten whale with its ribs sticking out. *I will be glad when this is over,* I thought.

WHILE I was getting things ready, Ian arrived with a group of men carrying plastic bags full of aluminum cans.

"Put them down out there and all but two of you can return to camp."

The two that stayed were told how to use the static wire and I explained to Ian what we were going to do with the cans.

"I will see how many will fit through the opening in a bag and the boys can put that many in each bag and hand them to me."

I tried various amounts of cans and found ten cans fit the best.

While the men were preparing the bags I said to Ian.

"With all the vehicles here, they must have a mechanic."

"Of course, they do."

"Would you find him and bring him here, I have some work for him."

"I will be back soon."

While we were loading cans into the sphere Captain Slattery and another officer appeared in the doorway. I went out to meet them.

"This is Lieutenant Fitzroy of the Engineer Company. He would like to survey the area and decide what equipment he will need."

"That is good," I said. "But I cannot stop right now. Take the Lieutenant for coffee and I will meet up with you soon. I have to finish this first."

"Can we look around?" asked the captain.

"Later," I said. "There are too many in here now. I'll meet you at the mess."

We were just finishing when Sargent Jones arrived with the mechanic.

"I have brought you the best mechanic in the army, meet Corporal Donald Kelly."

As we went inside Ian explained the static line to him.

Well, someone is listening to me, I thought.

They went over to the weapon and looked at it. After a couple of minutes, I said to the corporal.

"I hope you are not too nervous about working here?"

"It is mind blowing but I guess I can handle it," he said.

"I hope so because I have a couple of things for you to do."

"First the frame has to be removed so we can get to the sphere. And then all of those large bolts have to be loosened so we can dismantle it. And all this has to be done gently so as not to disturb the weapon it is very unstable. Think you can handle it?"

"When my nerves settle down, I will be all right. May I look it over so I can get an idea of how to do the job?"

While he was examining the weapon, I said to Sergeant Jones.

"Would you go to the mess and bring back Captain Slattery and the lieutenant, they are waiting for me."

Corporal Kelly said, "I have an air saw that will easily cut through the aluminum frame with no sparks and also a ratchets spanner for the small bolts. The large bolts will have to be done by hand the ratchet would vibrate too much."

"I know I have the right man," I said. "I agree with you except the compressor will have to be kept as far away as possible because of the noise and exhaust. We think the explosives are giving off fumes, so no smoking or exhaust heat nearby."

"Explosives, what explosives," the corporal said.

"Didn't anyone tell you? There is a ton and a half inside that silver sphere." The corporal's eyes widened as he backed away from the sphere and headed towards the door.

"There is nothing to worry about, it is safe as long as you do not upset it," I said smiling.

"Let me think about it overnight," he said

"See you in the morning," I said as the corporal left.

The two officers arrived soon afterwards and I gave them a tour of the shed. Afterwards Captain Slattery went back to his troops and Lieutenant Fitzroy began discussing the work I wanted him to do.

"Let's look at the sandpit first," he said.

After the tour and some discussion, the lieutenant explained that the job would need some heavy equipment and when it arrived it would take about a week to complete.

"I'll get on it right away," he said.

"There is one more thing," I said.

"We have had intruders here already. They got within 200 meters of the house without being seen. Would you clear away this scrub so I will feel more at ease?"

"That is easy," he said. "We have some tractors and slashers at the base. They will be here tomorrow. Anything else? 'No', Then I will get started. A couple of engineers will be here tomorrow to survey the road. The heavy equipment should be here by the time they finish and we can get on with the job. Goodbye for now."

It had been a long day. I waited for the sentry and closed the doors and headed for the house. When I got there the cars were gone and there was no one there, the crew had already left for town and the colonel was not in his office. So I headed for the mess tent. My cook did not work the evening shift so I had to eat the same as everyone else. I always liked army food when I was in the service and this was good.

Back at the house I found a book and sat down to read for a while. Later on a car arrived; it was Captain Williamson and Sergeant Jones.

"We didn't mean to leave you behind but you were busy with the engineer," Norman said. "We all went into town to interview the Fowler feller. The feds are taking him to a more secure location.

We grilled him for at least an hour, but he would not talk. Even when we told him that he would never be released unless he confessed. It is hard to believe that a moron like him could be involved with this gang."

"I have been thinking the same thing," I said. "Because we have not found any tools used to dismantle the weapon, I figure the gang was working on the weapon and left and took their tools with them."

"And while they were gone they left Fowler on guard but he went into town instead and got drunk." Norman added.

"I bet he took the trailer with him and sold it," said Ian.

"That's where he got the money," I said.

"We were talking about that with that policeman," the captain said. "So, they are going to check the bigger farmers around here because they are the only ones who could afford to buy it. Also the police want to fingerprint the weapon in case they left any prints."

"The only part we haven't touched is the nose," I said. "It is worth a try. I will tell Corporal Kelly not to start until the police have finished. You guys had an interesting time in town."

"Also, a good meal at the hotel," Ian said.

We discussed the event of the past two days and I told them of my discussion with the engineer.

"Looks like we will be busy for the next few days," said Norman.

"Well, I am going to hit the sack," Ian said.

"Good idea," said Norman. "By the way the colonel will not be back. He and two of the crew are going to Canberra. He is really spooked about the Yanks having a hidden depot over here, so they are going to look up all the old records to see if they can find any clues as to its whereabouts."

"They will be there forever," I said. "Tell him they would have come into Pine Gap and then gone out by road. Look for old mines, the Yanks like to store things underground."

THE next morning, I was up early and headed to the mess tent. My cook greeted me with a cheery.

"Good morning, your breakfast will be here shortly."

"Sit down for a moment," I said. "I don't even know your name."

"I am Corporal Walinski, Ivan Walinski."

"Glad to know you, Ivan. You know I am a cook too, a pastry cook."

We sat there talking about baking bread when one of the men came with my breakfast tray.

"This is Private Stavinski, he is my apprentice. Nice talking to you but I have troops to feed."

The tray contained a mug of coffee a bowl of fruit and three thick slices of whole meal toast and jam.

AFTER breakfast I walked around into the compound. The trucks were lined along one side and the tents on the other. The mess tent and the shower tent were at this end and the other end was open, a rather large area. I spotted a Sergeant near the trucks and went towards him.

"Good morning Sergeant," I said.

"Yes Mr Freeman, how can I help you?"

"I am looking for Trooper Larmarra, could I borrow him for about an hour?"

"You can have him for the day, I think he is in the shower. There he is now, just coming out. Trooper Larmarra, front and center."

The Sergeant introduced me and left.

"Have you had breakfast?" I asked.

"Yes sir."

"Good, I have a little job for you."

"Let me store my gear in my tent and I will be ready."

"I was told about your tracking abilities. I would like you to look at something for me?"

We walked towards the shed.

"In a little while there will be people stomping all over here, so I want you to look it over first."

"Have you seen our little toy?" I said as we walked up to the small shed.

I spoke to the sentry and opened the door. After a few minutes I said to Larmarra, "You see how large that is, and there is another one in the other shed over there. Well, I believe they were brought here by a large truck and I would like you to look around and see if you can find any evidence of that vehicle."

"I will try," he said. "Don't expect too much."

I walked along with him for a bit when I heard some loud talking coming from the other side of the large shed. Coming around the corner I saw Sergeant Jones standing nose to nose with the sentry and they were both shouting at each other. There were two policemen standing nearby trying not to get involved.

"What is going on?" I said in a loud voice.

"This man will not stand aside and let us into the building. I am the senior rank here and he is disobeying me." Shouted Sergeant Jones.

"Calm down Ian. He is not disobeying you, he is following my specific orders."

"What do you mean by your orders?"

I smiled at the sergeant and spoke to the sentry.

"Sentry, what are your orders?"

"Sir, I am not to allow anyone, no exceptions, into this building without your permission, sir."

"There sergeant, he was only following orders, and doing a dam good job at it."

"All right, I didn't know that. I am sorry soldier. Good job son. You look a bit upset, take a break and go to the mess and have a coffee, tell the cook to give you a couple of my scones," I said as he walked away.

"Well, I am glad we cleared that up. You guys must be the fingerprint crew. Sergeant Jones will take care of you I have to talk to this man over here. Don't forget the safety drill, Ian."

While we were talking Corporal Kelly had arrived and was unhitching an air compressor from a truck.

"We cannot start until the police finish in there. But we can set it up and go and have a coffee."

When we arrived at the mess we saw a group of soldiers standing around the sentry, he was slowly and deliberately spreading jam on a scone while the rest of them watched. We had just sat down when Sergeant Jones came in.

"That didn't take long," I said.

"They are still there, I came looking for you, Trooper Larmarra sent me to find you."

"Looks like he found something," I said. "Let's go. Finish your coffee Kelly, take your time."

As we went to find Trooper Larmarra, I told Ian what he was doing.

"Do you think he has found something?"

"He must have, that is why he sent for me."

"Let's hope so." Ian said.

Larmarra was talking to the sentry at the small shed when we found him.

"You were right sir; there was a large vehicle here."

"Go get the policemen," I said to Ian. "I want them to hear this."

"It was at least a month ago because that is when it rained last, or two weeks ago because that is how long it takes for the grass to straighten up, since the vehicle was here. Come, I will show you."

"Let's wait for the police," I said.

A couple of minutes later, Sergeant Jones and the policemen arrived and with them was Captain Williamson.

"Good morning, Norman."

"Glad you are here, I think you will find this very interesting."

"Gentlemen, this is Trooper Larmarra. He is our resident tracker," I said.

"We have heard about you, you're the fellow who started the manhunt," said one of the policemen.

"I asked Trooper Larmarra here because I believe a large truck brought the weapons here and I asked him to look around. Let's hear what he has to say, over to you trooper."

"Would you please follow me and stay close together. A large vehicle was here but it did not come down the driveway. Maybe because it was too large. But I think the driver was inexperienced and did not want to drive between the trees and the house. So, he came around this side of the house, the long way around.

He turned here and backed up near the small shed. He stopped here, and let down a ramp, you can see the grove it made here. Here are the tire prints of a large dual wheeled vehicle. It had eight rear wheels and four front ones. A large heavy truck. Also, there are some good tire tracks over there in the sand if you want a cast of them."

"You mean to say you could see all that here on this empty ground?" asked the captain.

"Yes sir, and there is more. The driver was your friend who wears cowboy boots and smokes a lot. There are heel prints near the front wheel marks where he jumped from the truck and cigarette butts everywhere."

"That is amazing, all I can see is grass," said the captain.

"While we are here, we will make a cast of the tires and pick up a few butts," one of the policemen said. "Trooper, show us where the tire tracks are."

"Well, you are right again," Norman said. "That trooper is amazing, he is wasted driving a truck, I am going to make a couple of phone calls when I go back to the house."

"I agree," I said. "It looks like they unloaded the weapons here and towed one around to the other shed and pushed the other one in this shed."

"Are you trying to be a tracker too?" said Norman with a smile.

"Oh no not me, but I will make a little bet with you."

"Like what?"

"I bet I know where the missing hardware is. I bet you a dinner in town that the missing drums are right next to us in this shed."

By then the others had joined us and were listening to our conversation.

"Come on tell us," they said.

I pretended to look around the ground for a minute and then said.

"It is simple those drums are heavy so when they unloaded them they did not take them very far, so they put them in this shed then pushed the trailer in afterwards."

"Could be but how are you going to prove it?" someone said. "There is no room to squeeze in there to look."

"Come on," I said. "Let's go have some coffee and scones and talk about it."

We left the sentry standing there and headed to the mess tent.

"I forgot about Corporal Kelly, I will meet you at the mess."

The corporal was sitting in his truck waiting for me.

"Sorry I left you I have to go to the mess. Can you find something to do for about a half hour?"

"No problem I have to return the truck so I will do that."

"Take your time," I said.

They were all sitting around a table when I came in and sat down. They were still talking about the truck. Soon Ivan came over with a tray, on it was a large mug of coffee, a plate of scones and jam and cream.

"Good day Mr Freeman. Captain, gentlemen. I Hope there are enough to go round, they are fresh out of the oven, enjoy."

Needless to say that brought the conversation to a halt; all eyes were on the scones. For a little while we forgot about our troubles and enjoyed a nice coffee break.

After coffee the policemen went off to make a cast of the tires. The sergeant and I headed for the shed. Captain Williamson said to Trooper Larmarra as he was leaving

"Report to my office in the house at 1500 hours."

"Yes Sir," said the trooper.

Corporal Kelly was waiting for us when we arrived at the shed.

"I could not get the equipment ready because the sentry would not let me in."

He got a big smile from the sergeant.

"Let's get started," I said. "Ian the engineers should be arriving soon. Would you take care of them? I want all the brush cleared and the grass mowed.

"I'm on my way."

Kelly and I laid out the air line and set up the tools. He walked around the frame for a couple of minutes and said.

"We can easily remove the tail section with the air saw. I think we can dismantle the nose with the ratchet."

While we were working, I could hear the tractors mowing the paddock.

TROOPER Larmarra knocked on the door of the house not knowing what to expect. As he entered one of the men said.

"The captain is expecting you, go right in."

"Trooper Larmarra reporting, sir."

"Sit down trooper."

"I'm sure you are wondering why you are here. I heard about your investigation of the visitor's camp and I saw your work today and it gave me an idea. Our department has three outstanding cases that must be solved before the evidence is destroyed. We would like you to help us solve these cases."

"I don't understand, sir."

"I am asking you to transfer to the intelligence corps."

"I would be honored sir, but how? I understand that only officers are in the corps."

"That is true, don't worry it is all arraigned, the paperwork is being drawn up now. You will be promoted to sergeant and you will have two years to complete your studies to qualify as a lieutenant."

"What can I say, sir. I am honored, thank you."

"Good, go pack your gear. You and Lieutenant Rogers will leave right away for Queensland. You have a half an hour."

Corporal Kelly was finishing the last of the tail section, so I said, "Let's call it a day."

"Fine by me," Kelly said. "I have a tripod hoist that we pull motors with, I will bring it over tomorrow and hang the sphere on it because we will have to remove the sandbags to take off the nose."

"I agree, we can lift up the nose, remove it then set the sphere on some sandbags that will make it easier to work on."

We packed up the gear and shut the doors, that was it for today.

AFTER a shower and a change of clothes I headed towards the mess. The tractors had been busy, all the brush had been cleared and the grass was cut. There was a large pile of brush in the middle of the paddock ready for burning.

I went through the line and got my meal and headed to where the captain was seated, Lieutenant Dickson and Sergeant Jones were with him.

While we were eating Norman said.

"There is a lot of news for you. Firstly, you must have noticed Lieutenant Dickson; he will be bunking with us. There is a spare bed in Ian's room. He does not want to stay in town alone now that Lieutenant Rogers has gone."

"Where did he go?" I asked.

"He and Trooper Larmarra are headed to Queensland. The Trooper's skills are needed to solve a difficult case up there."

"The police have a lead on the car," Ian said. "A patrolman was at a roadhouse on the border when a Statesman pulled in with four men in it.

They bought petrol, candy and cigarettes. They headed onto Queensland. When he read the notice, he reported it."

"That's great," I said. "At least they will leave us alone for a few days."

"Also, by talking to all the service stations in the area there was a sighting of a large truck about two weeks ago," Lieutenant Dickson said. "He was just closing when the truck pulled up for fuel. It had a sign on it, *Refrigerator Rentals*. There were two men in the truck but only the driver got out. He was wearing cowboy boots. They also headed North."

"The police are checking all truck rental agencies to find the truck. They also think the car maybe rented too. If it has, they will find it," Norman said. "The police are doing a great job."

"Do you think it is because the colonel threatened to bring in the feds?" I said jokingly.

We finished eating and sat and talked a bit then headed towards the house, there were lights in the paddock near the brush pile.

"Looks like they are going to burn it," Ian said. "I'll go and watch."

"I'll come along," said the Lieutenant. As we were walking Norman said.

"By the way headquarters wants those parts as soon as possible. They also want all the drums, and anything else that has to do with the weapon."

"We will have the nose off before noon," I said. "I will get some men and remove the iron off the rear wall of the shed and get the drums out that way. They will have to screw the iron back on because it will be too dangerous to nail it."

"I am sure you can handle all that," Norman said. "We will ship it out as soon as it is loaded."

EARLY the next morning as I headed towards the mess the smell of smoke hung in the still air. At the mess I sat at my regular table and waited for Ivan to bring me my breakfast. He soon arrived with a smile and said, "After our talk yesterday I am attempting to make Danish Pastries today. They are in the oven and will be ready by morning break."

He laid out my breakfast and sat down for a chat while I ate.

"You know Dave, my coming here and being assigned to you is the best thing that has happened to me in years."

"That is a pretty profound statement," I said.

"Seriously, making breakfast and sandwiches for you has given me a new interest in life."

"That is an even more profound statement."

"Seriously, I was thinking of leaving the army, but the look on the colonels' face when I served you those scones was worth all the beer in Queensland. Usually a cook's life is rather dull but having you here has livened things up. The whole kitchen is laughing and joking, it is a nice place to work now."

"That is great," I said. "But remember I won't be here for long so enjoy it while you can."

After breakfast I walked to the compound looking for Captain Slattery. Instead, I found the same sergeant again.

"Good morning Mr Freeman, how can I help you?"

"I was looking for Captain Slattery."

"He has been called away and won't be back until tomorrow. I am in charge now."

"I need a detail to help load the material from the shed."

"That will be Corporal Simpson, it is his truck you are using."

"I will need a few men; some parts are fairly heavy."

"I will take care of it. The men will be at the shed in twenty minutes."

When I arrived at the shed Corporal Kelly was waiting. He had two men with him and a tripod hoist lying on the ground.

"We will erect the hoist and lift the nose so we can remove it.

There are only a few bolts holding it so it shouldn't take long."

"All right, show the guys how to slap the wire."

"I told the sentry to have some breakfast and return.

Tell the cook to give you a piece of my toast."

While we were erecting the hoist Sergeant Jones arrived.

"Good morning Ian, glad you are here, I have a job for you. Come with me to the other shed."

As we walked along Ian told me that the phone hasn't stopped ringing all morning.

"The lieutenant has a couple of clerks helping him. The typewriters are humming."

"We will find out during coffee break," I said.

When we arrived at the shed, I explained to Ian that I wanted to remove some sheets of iron from the rear of the shed so we could get to the drums. It has to be done with care and the sheets will have to be screwed back on, no pounding.

"Why not pull the weapon out and take the drums out the front?" asked Ian.

"We do not move that thing until we know the condition of the explosive in the sphere.

They are sending some men and I want you to take charge of this. I will load the truck at the shed and send it over here to load the drums, then it will be on its way.

We walked back to the large shed and found Corporal Kelly there alone.

"Where are you two helpers?" I asked

"They got nervous and left, sir, I explained about the static wire and sparks and to be quiet while they worked. Everything was fine until Pete dropped a bolt on the nose. It made a loud noise and he nearly fainted. They were out of here in a flash."

"How about you, were you scared too?"

"Sir, I been scared since I first saw that thing but I have a job to do and I will do it."

"Good on you son, with any luck we will be finished here today."

"I hope so sir, my nerves are about shot."

While we were talking, Corporal Simpson and the sergeant arrived with ten men. I explained to the corporal what to do. The two sergeants were talking together. Then Ian came and asked me if they could have a look at the weapon.

"Of course, you take the first group in and then take them to the other shed and start on that. I will keep the others here to load the truck."

As the groups came in, I gave them a brief explanation of the weapon. Ian took his group away and the others started loading the truck. The sergeant thanked me and said, "There were a lot of rumors going around the camp, this will smooth things over," he said goodbye and left.

I turned to Corporal Kelly and said, "Let's get this nose off and out of here."

We gently lifted the sphere and removed the nose with the help of the other men. Then we rearranged the sandbags and gently placed the sphere on them.

"We can remove the hoist; the sphere will not fall off the bags."

"What if it rolled out the door across the paddock and into the camp?" Kelly said.

"Don't even think about that, you will have nightmares."

"I already do," Kelly said.

We put the hoist and the tools outside and closed the doors.

"I will leave you to pack up, I am going to the other shed. Don't forget to come back here after lunch. Remember I told you we have to loosen the bolts on the sphere. It will not take long."

Kelly did not look very happy.

The men and I walked to the other shed. We arrived at the same time as the truck. Ian and the men were standing there telling army jokes.

"I was just about to send for you. We got the iron off. You were right the drums are there."

"Good," I said. "We will start with the large ones, they are the fusses. They are heavy it will take a few men to move them."

"What about these two?" Ian said.

"Don't touch them they are the explosive charges that go in the sphere."

"Now you tell me, I was going to toss them on the truck."

"We will just take those small ones, they are the most important," I said. "You guard them; I want to look in the shed before we close it up. In case there is anything else in there."

I came back in a couple of minutes.

"Nothing there, you take one can and I will take the other."

"They are heavy. What is in them?" asked Ian.

"I'll tell you later, they are going in the cab, not the back. Will you get the iron back on the wall? I want to talk to Corporal Simpson."

The corporal was in the back securing the drums.

"I want to talk to you corporal, are you driving this vehicle?"

"Yes sir, Private Ryan and I are taking it out. He is sleeping now so we can change drivers along the way. We will leave as soon as our escort arrives."

"Do you understand the importance of your cargo?"

"Yes sir. Just a pile of junk."

"Son that junk could cause another cold war between the USA and Russia."

"Wow."

"And it is not all junk. I put two small drums in the locker behind the seats, a lot of people would kill to get them so don't tell anyone they are there, not even Private Ryan. They are that important that I want you and Private Ryan armed. So, check out a pistol each before you leave."

"Is that really necessary, sir?"

"If the bad guys find out what you have in the cab you will need a machine gun. If anyone tries to get in your vehicle you are to shoot them. Understood?"

Simpson just stood there speechless.

"Another thing, can you seal the back of the truck?'

"Yes sir, there straps to hold down the back cover."

"I want the straps sealed by your sergeant, Understood?"

"I think so, sir."

Just then Ian walked up.

"I am giving Corporal Simpson his instructions. By the way has an inventory been taken of the cargo?"

"Lieutenant Dickson was here and wrote it all down. It is being typed up right now."

"Then we are all done, let's have lunch."

"Good idea."

Ian dismissed the men and we started for the mess.

"One more thing corporal, are you able to lock your vehicle?"

"Yes sir, this is a domestic not a combat vehicle I can lock the ignition and the doors."

"That is good. While you are eating lock the doors and put a sentry to guard it."

"Is that necessary, sir?"

"Do as Mr Freeman says, solider," said Ian.

"Yes sir."

At the mess we met Captain Williamson and Lieutenant Dixon, the captain asked.

"Everything loaded?"

"Loaded and ready to roll."

"Good the escort will be here soon," Dixon said.

"I have ordered the truck to be sealed and the drivers to be armed," I said.

"Isn't that a little drastic?" the captain said.

"Well, what would you do? There is enough uranium on board to make four or five modern bombs."

"Well, when you put it that way, you are right."

"I would like to check the truck before it leaves," I said.

"I think we all will," said the captain.

"Now for some interesting news," Norman said

"Yes, a lot has happened this morning." Dixon added.

"Firstly, they traced the car and the truck. Both were rented, the car in Sydney three weeks ago and the truck in Gladstone about the same time. From the descriptions the big guy rented the car and we think the cowboy rented the truck. About two months ago the big guy walked into a bank in Darwin and opened an account with $20,000 under the name of Desert Explorations. They gave him a cheque book and a bank card. He vanished until he rented a car in Sydney six weeks later. There is a large investigation to trace the movements of these men."

"The car was left at a rental yard in Toowoomba yesterday by three men fitting the descriptions we have. It was moved on to Brisbane by the company and rented again. The agent in Toowoomba said it was filthy, full of bottles and food scraps. But the best news is they found the chain."

"When the car was cleaned the aluminum chain was found in the boot along with some tools in a canvas bag. There was also some clothing in the boot, a hat a jumper and a pair of soft soled shoes."

"Sounds like the small guy's clothes," I said. "What happened to him?"

"They found a body in a creek near Toowoomba yesterday afternoon," Dixon said. "We think it is our man, Sergeant Larmarra will be there by now to investigate."

"He is a busy man," I said.

"We have their description and their names but we cannot find them," Norman said. "They walked out of the rental agency and disappeared. No one knows where they are."

Ian who had been quiet all this time said, "I bet they are leaving the country. It is getting too hot for them here."

"Maybe," said Dixon. "Or they could be coming back here for the weapon."

"I doubt it," I said. "There is only three of them. I think they will reorganize themselves and then go back to the depot for another weapon."

"That is a terrible thing to say," the captain said.

While we were discussing this there was the sound of trucks moving outside.

"Sounds like the convoy is about to leave," Ian said.

"Let's get out there before they get away," said the captain.

As we started to leave the Sergeant came in.

"Sir, we are about to head out and we need the manifest."

"We are coming, Sergeant," said the captain. "We want to inspect the vehicles before they leave."

"Is that necessary sir? Everything is in order."

"I'll be the judge of that Sergeant."

There were two land rovers parked near the truck and some solders standing in a group. They all came to attention when the captain walked up.

"As you were, who is in charge here?"

"Sir, Lieutenant Hargrave, Duty Officer Local Command Headquarters."

"Do you know what your mission is?"

"We are to escort this vehicle to command headquarters, I understand it is carrying some special equipment."

"Do you know what that equipment is?"

"No sir."

"Do you know where the command headquarters is located?"

"Yes sir, I just came from there."

The lieutenant could see that the captain was not pleased with his answers.

"Sir, this morning I was called into the C.O's office and was told to come and escort this vehicle back to headquarters."

"Did you receive any written orders?"

"No sir, just a routine job. So I rounded up these vehicles and men and came here."

"Lieutenant Dickson, do you have a copy of the orders?"

"Yes sir, right here in my briefcase."

"Give a copy to the Lieutenant. I suggest you read it very carefully and then we will discuss it in detail."

While the captain was busy I walked over to the escort vehicles and talked to the drivers and then I looked over the truck.

"Corporal Simpson."

"Yes, Mr Freeman."

"Corporal, why aren't these straps locked and sealed like I told you to? And where is your weapon?"

"Sir, the sergeant decided that all that was not necessary."

"You mean, Private."

"No sir, Sergeant."

"He will be a Private when I am through with him. You and your driver get to the supply room and arm yourselves right now. Get two clips of ammo. You can handle a pistol, I assume."

"Yes sir, we are all combat ready."

"Don't forget to lock the truck."

I walked back to the others and said to the captain.

"Norman, these vehicles are not suitable for a long trip. The driver said that they are only used around the base and have not been serviced for months. Also, one has only a half a tank of fuel and the other only a third. And to top it off the men are not armed and one of them cannot drive."

I could see Norman getting red around the collar and I haven't told him about the Sergeant's insubordination yet. Heads will roll over this."

"Sergeant Jones, take over the servicing of the vehicles, I want them ready in a half hour. Fuel, oil, water and tires."

"Right away, sir."

"Ian. Get Corporal Kelly, he will be waiting for me at the shed."

We took Lieutenant Hargraves with us and returned to the mess and sat down with a coffee when a clerk from the office came in and talked to Lieutenant Dickson.

"Excuse me gentlemen I have to go, I will explain the delay to headquarters."

The captain said to the lieutenant, "You have read your orders?"

"Yes sir, but I don't understand them."

"All right I will explain them to you. You are to supply an armed escort for that vehicle out there from here to regional command headquarters. You are to drive non-stop from here to there. Stopping every four hours to change drivers and have a leak. The cooks have prepared food and drinks for the trip."

"Excuse me sir but where is regional command headquarters? And what is in that truck that is so important to go through all this trouble?"

"The headquarters are in central Victoria."

"What, that is at least twenty hours away, and it is all back roads from here to the Newell Highway."

"That is correct, at least you know the way. You are only to stop at rest areas along the way and only in vacant ones you are to keep clear of all people and vehicles. If anyone approaches you, you are to warn them off. If they ignore your warning you are to arrest them and call the local police. If they resist you may shoot them."

"Captain, what is in that vehicle that is so important that we have to take such drastic action?"

"It is better that you do not know. I will say this, it is so important that there are some nasties out there that will gladly kill all of you to get their hands on it. That is why we are moving it from here. If you are not willing to take on the job, I will understand and we will find someone else."

"No sir, I will do it. Just that I thought I would only be away for the day, this will take a whole week. May I call my wife?"

"Of course, as long as you do not tell her where you are going."

"By the way, Captain, I have not been introduced to this gentleman, who is he?"

"This is Mr Freeman, he is the organizer of this expedition. You had better see to your men and vehicles. I will find you another driver. We are already four hours overdue. Let's get going."

We walked back to the vehicles I went around to the back of the truck and the sergeant was putting seals on the strap buckles.

"Sergeant," I said. "I did not report your insubordination to the captain, but from now on when I ask for something I expect it to be carried out without question."

"Yes Mr Freeman, I am sorry, it won't happen again."

Captain Williamson gathered the men and gave them their final instructions and they headed for their vehicles. I approached Corporal Simpson and said, "Have a good trip and remember tell no one what is behind the seats."

They got in their trucks and headed out.

"Well, that is one less worry," the captain said. "Let's go and find out what Lieutenant Dickson is up to."

We sat in the captain's office and Lieutenant Dickson told us the latest news.

"The man in the creek is our man. He was taken from the car and walked to the creek. They took off his clothes and shot him in the heart then in the side of the head as he laid on the ground. Then they rolled him into the creek and threw his shirt and pants in also. They were found a little further downstream. Sergeant Larmarra discovered all of this, plus he found shoe prints of the big guy and the cowboy. He also found some tire tracks that matched the ones found here. The local police were very impressed with his work."

"Speaking of police, the local boys found the trailer. A local farmer took it to the registry to get a number plate for it. They knocked him back because it had no lights or brakes. Then they called in the police who went to his farm and confiscated it. The trailer is now in the police lock up beside Fowler's ute. The army will pick it up and ship it to Victoria.

The police think that the night Fowler was arrested he hooked up the trailer and drove along the back road to the farmers place and sold him the trailer. That is where he got the money he had on him. Then he went into town and got drunk and arrested."

"Just think," Ian said. "If Fowler had returned the same way, we would have never found out about this place and those murderers would have completed their mission."

"Let's not dwell on what might have been," Norman said.

"Things are moving along nicely. All we need now is to capture those murderers, any news from the colonel?"

"He has narrowed the possible sites to twenty-two and is arranging to have aerial photographs taken of all of them. There is a bit more interesting news from the colonel."

"Yes, yes what is it."

"It concerns Sargent Larmarra again. When he left here with Lieutenant Rogers apparently they stopped at the gate to talk to the sentry and Larmarra got out of the car to check the mailbox. He found a pile of mail there. While they were driving he looked through it and found a personal letter to Fowler. He opened it and when he read it, they stopped at the nearest phone and called the colonel."

"Come on man what was in the letter?" said Ian, who was sitting on the edge of his seat.

"The letter is from a mate of Fowler by the name of Bluey. No other name. But he gave Fowler a phone number. It appears from the letter that last year they were prospecting out in the never country and Bluey wants to know if Fowler would be interested in going out again soon — He said he was staying in Rockhampton with a woman named Hazel. The colonel has dispatched a team to find them."

"This is great news," said Norman. "I bet he will know where the depot is located."

"What are we going to do when we find the depot? We cannot handle what we have here." Asked Ian.

"Let's just stick to the matter at hand, that is enough for now." said Norman. "Is that all Lieutenant?"

"Yes sir."

"Good, I am hungry let's eat."

THE next morning, I was up early as usual. As I walked towards the mess tent the sun was just rising. The days were getting shorter and the weather was changing. It was getting colder. I made a mental note to ask Sergeant Jones for some warm clothes. Then the realization hit me that I was a long way from home and when would I get back there? I had nearly forgotten about my old life. I had adapted to army life so easily it seemed like I had always been in the army. I was homesick.

"What is wrong?" Ivan said. "You look sad."

"I just realized that I am homesick and I am wondering if I will ever get back there."

"Well at least you have a home to go to, all I have is the army. By the way where were you yesterday? You missed your Danish pastry. I couldn't keep them. When you did not show for coffee, the men devoured them. But not to worry there are more in the oven but be on time or you will miss out."

I apologized and thanked him and smiled.

"What is the smile for?" asked Ivan.

"I would have liked to have seen the men eating those pastries."

We talked while I ate my breakfast and my homesickness faded away.

It was too early to start anything so I headed back to the house. I began thinking, this is my little world house, mess tent, and shed with an occasional forage into the compound, No Harley rides sailing or shopping trips. There I go getting homesick again.

When I reached the house, Lieutenant Dickson was on the phone and I found Ian in the kitchen.

"I am not hungry this morning, just going to have a cup of coffee and a piece of toast."

"Looks like we will have an easy day," I said.

"I hope so, I need a rest. I would like a few days leave, but that is not possible."

"Before you go on leave, I need some warm clothes and maybe another blanket. The days are cooling down."

"I was thinking the same thing, I will order in some winter gear. That will give me something to do."

While we were talking Captain Williamson came in. I am going into town, a truck is coming to pick up the trailer and I want to be there. Also,

I want to thank the police for their good work. You never know we may need them again. What are you doing today, Dave?"

"I am going to find my mechanic and prepare the sphere for dismantling, that is about all until the engineers finish the road."

We walked into the other room and the captain asked.

"Any news from the colonel?"

"Yes sir, he and the crew are headed to Rockhampton to take over the search for Bluey. It seems they cannot find him or his girlfriend."

"It won't take the colonel long," Norman said.

The phone started ringing and we left. The captain for town, the Sergeant for the supply tent and me to look for Corporal Kelly. He was also looking for me. We met halfway and walked toward the shed.

"Will this take long?"

"Not more than an hour."

"Good. And then I am all finished here?"

"You don't like this job?"

"I am a nervous wreck being around explosives, I am a motor mechanic not a bomb disposal technician."

"Well, it is almost over and you have done a remarkable job and I will make sure your superiors know about it."

"As long as they don't transfer me to bomb disposal duties."

We arrived at the shed, I dismissed the sentry and we went inside.

"All we have to do is loosen the bolts holding the sphere together so it will be easy to dismantle later on. It shouldn't take long."

"Let's get it over with then."

The corporal had two long handle socket wrenches and he turned the nut while I held the other end. Most of them came loose easily but a few were stubborn and hard to free up. It took longer than expected. We packed the tools and I said to Kelly,

"Take your tools back and send the sentry back and I will meet you in the mess and treat you to a Danish pastry."

A few minutes later the sentry arrived in a Land Rover. When he got out I beckoned to the others to come too. There were four of them.

"Would you like to know what you are guarding in this shed?"

We stood inside the door and I said, "If someone got in here and put a block of plastic explosives in that ball and blew it up, there wouldn't be anything left here except a large crater and that includes your camp. If they took it away it would destroy an average sized city. So don't think you are wasting your time standing outside the door all night. What you are doing is very important. So always remember when these doors are shut no one opens them except me."

They all assured me they understood and thanked me for explaining the situation to them. I shut the doors and headed to the mess.

Sergeant Jones and Lieutenant Dickson were already there and I sat with them. When Corporal Kelly came in, he did not want to sit at the same table with an officer.

"You are my guest, come sit here. Lieutenant Dickson this is Corporal Kelly. He has been working with me on the weapon under very hazardous conditions and I would like you to write an accommodation for him and get the captain and the colonel to sign it —"

"No problem you can tell me all about, Corporal."

While we were talking Ivan the cook arrived with a tray of Danish pastries.

"You arrived just in time, Mr Freeman and the crew in the kitchen were about to devour them. I hope you like them, I think they are an improvement on yesterdays."

While we were talking and enjoying the pastries and then we heard the sound of trucks in the compound.

"That will be Captain Slattery," Kelly said. "He is due to return today."

A few minutes later Captain Slattery walked into the mess.

"Good day gentlemen," he said. "I am looking for Captain Williamson."

"He is in town," said Lieutenant Dickson. "And will not be back until late this afternoon. Anything I can do to help?"

"Are you in charge now?"

"Yes sir, while the captain is away."

"Corporal Kelly what are you doing here?"

"He is my guest, Captain," I said.
"He has been a great help to me and we just sat down for a coffee."

"Are you finished with him? If you are I need him."

"Yes, I think so. For now, anyway."

"Good Corporal, those vehicles need your attention, they must be ready to leave in the morning."

"Yes sir, I am on my way. Good day to you all and thanks for the coffee."

As Corporal Kelly left, we were all looking at Captain Slattery. It was Lieutenant Dickson who spoke first.

"What do you mean when you said, 'the vehicles are leaving in the morning?'"

"That is what I was going to tell Captain Williamson. The outfit is leaving for Sydney tomorrow. We are a transport company and our services are needed down there."

"What is going to happen here? To us?" we all said at once.

"Don't worry only the large trucks are involved. The security and general duties personnel will still be here. In fact, there will be another detachment arriving in the next day or two. We are only taking the drivers, mechanics, and cooks. All the tents and other structures will stay. Actually, you do not need the trucks, they have been idling since they arrived. They are needed elsewhere."

"Sit down Captain and have a coffee," I said.

"Thank you but I have a lot to do so if there are no more questions, I will say goodbye."

The captain left and we sat there for a few minutes and then walked back to the house discussing the events along the way.

"We really do not need those vehicles," Dickson said.

"True," I said." "There isn't much to do until the engineers build the road and the demolition boys get here." As we walked into the house a clerk handed the lieutenant a piece of paper.

"A dispatch hot off the teletype, it is from the colonel, sir."

Dickson read the message and just stood there for a couple of minutes.

"Well, what is it sir?" said Ian. "Something important?"

"Yes, it is. The colonel is on his way to Townsville. It seems the man we called *the solider* just walked into the Townsville Barracks and surrendered. The colonel is going there to take charge of the interrogation. It is more important than looking for Bluey."

"That is good news," said Ian. "Now we will learn what this is all about."

We stood there discussing the breakthrough when Dickson was called to the phone and Ian said, "I am going to the supply tent to check on our winter gear."

Having nothing to do, I decided to go to my room and stretch out on the bed. It was the first time I had any rest other than sleep since I arrived.

I must have dosed off because I was woken by the sound of trucks in the compound. When I walked into the office one of the clerks said, "The engineers have arrived."

About then Lieutenant Fitzroy walked in.

"Good day Mr Freeman, we will unload after lunch and start first thing in the morning."

Then he turned and talked to Lieutenant Dickson. Looking at the clock I realized that I had a good sleep and lunch was nearly over, so I headed for the mess hall.

There was a lot of activity in the mess. The engineers were there and the others were in groups discussing their departure. I found a vacant table in the NCO's area and Ivan came over with my sandwiches.

"I don't have time to talk right now but I want to speak to you, could you wait until I finish so we can talk?"

So, I ate slowly and waited for Ivan to finish in the kitchen.

A little while later he came and sat down.

"I suppose you have heard the news?" he said. "About the outfit pulling out?"

"Yes, I have."

"Well, it is not good for me. I am being sent to the main depot."

"What is so bad about that?"

"The head cook is still there. The one that had me demoted, he doesn't like me and it will be hell there for me."

"Have you talked to the captain?"

"He doesn't think it is important. Could you have a word to him?"

"Me, what can I do?"

"He will listen to you because you have a lot of influence around here."

I laughed at that and said, "I don't know about that but on the other hand I will miss my personal cook so I will give it a try."

"I knew you would help," Ivan said as he left.

Outside I met Lieutenant Fitzroy.

"The first thing in the morning we will go over the route to make sure it is what you want and then we will get started. I figure it should take about a week. That is what we have planned for."

"A week, I thought it would only take a couple of days."

"That is enough for a track but you want it to be smooth and a track will soon be full of ruts as the vehicles travel over it, so we will do it right."

"That is good to know," I said.

"See you in the morning," he said as he walked away.

I had a look around for Captain Slattery but could not find him, so I walked to the shed and spoke to the sentry and opened the doors and had a look inside. I liked to open the shed to ventilate the area in case the old explosive is giving off any fumes. It would be a disaster if they accumulated in the room. Also, it gave me something to do.

"**BLOODY** damn cooks," Captain Slattery said when I caught up with him. "All they are is trouble. Whining, auguring, and complaining all the time. Most of my personal problems are with those damn cooks. The replacement does not want to come here and your cook does not want to leave, bunch of bloody women. But to keep the peace and would it make you happy if the other cook took your cooks place at the depot I will send him there and you can keep your cook. Take him to Whoop -Whoop with you when you leave for all care."

"Thank you, Captain, you are a good man."

"Send someone for me when Captain Williamson returns, I want to talk to him," Slattery said as he walked away.

BACK at the house things were quiet for a change. The clerks were getting ready to leave and Lieutenant Dickson was doing his paperwork.

"The captain is on his way back and will be here shortly," he said as I came in.

Ian came out of the other room.

"You will find a pile of winter gear on your bed. I got there just in time they were packing it to take with them, so you will sleep warm tonight."

It wasn't long before the captain arrived. He was pleased to hear the news about the surrender of the solider and the arrival of the Engineers. Then he told us of his day in town.

"I spent the day with the police and it appears that all the transport vehicles are on their way to Sydney. So, the police tracked down a car transporter on its way to Melbourne and it stopped by and loaded the trailer. I went to the hardware store and purchased a tarpaulin and some elastic straps and we wrapped up the trailer. You never know someone might know what that is and start asking questions. That took most of the day I had a nice long lunch with Sergeant Harris and thanked him for his cooperation. I told him I would write a letter of appreciation to his superiors. That made him very happy because he is going for a promotion and the letter will put him on top of the list."

"I told the captain that Captain Slattery would like to talk to him and if he was ready I would send him along. The clerks had left and it was near supper time so I would look for the captain on the way to the mess.

When I arrived at the mess Ivan was there waiting for me.

"What are you doing here at this time?"

"I am working the evening meal because of all the extra men, and I wanted to ask you what the captain said."

"Well, I won't use his exact words but he said if the other cook will exchange places with you, it is fine with him."

"That's great, I know that guy and his wife get awfully cranky if he is away from her for more than a few days. I am sure that he will agree. I will make you something extra special tomorrow. Thank you again."

The weather was changing; it was cold and dark as I walked to the mess for breakfast. The weatherman was right a storm was coming our way. The mess tent was crowded the troops were preparing to leave. They were happy and joking with each other. At last they were leaving here and it meant some leave time in the big city. Looked around and found Corporal Kelly.

"Goodbye Corporal and thank you for all your help."

"Glad to have met you and working with you but I am very pleased to be leaving here. That thing in the shed makes me very nervous."

"You can rest easy now; have a safe trip and thanks again."

We shook hands and parted. I found a quiet corner and sat down. One of the kitchen crew came over with a tray.

"Good morning Mr Freeman, Ivan worked late last night and he left instructions for your breakfast. I hope it is satisfactory."

While I was enjoying my coffee Lieutenant Fitzroy Came over and said, "When you are ready, we will examine the route for the road."

"Have you had your breakfast?"

"Yes sir, I just finished."

"Let's go then."

We drove across the paddock towards the sandpit.

"No great problems here, the land is fairly flat but it is soft so we will have to work it over so you will have a firm surface."

The sandpit was a lot larger than I thought it was. We drove around a bit and picked out a route and a spot to detonate the charges. The whole thing took about an hour. The lieutenant dropped me at the house and went off to organize his men. As I climbed the steps to the house, I suddenly realized that I had nothing to do for the next few days.

Inside, the clerks were busy at their typewriters. Norman came out of the other room.

"Things are quiet, so we are catching up on the paperwork. There is no word from the colonel but we heard from headquarters, the material arrived safely. They were followed along the highway for a while, so they called the highway patrol and they stopped and questioned them. They were lost tourist."

"I hope the patrolmen took their names," I said.

"Why?"

"Because when the colonel interrogates the prisoner we may find out that they are part of the gang."

"That is a thought, I will put Dickson on it when he comes in."

"The best part of the episode is when the driver handed over the two Uranium cores. They had no idea of what to do with them. It caused quite a stir. The big brass are going to meet to decide the issue."

"Well, if that stirs them up, what are they going to do when we send them fifty kilos of plutonium? And speaking of plutonium, we will have to contact someone in the Atomic Energy Commission to find out how to handle and ship it. Inside the core it is shielded but I do not know the correct procedure when it is exposed. We may need protective clothing and a special container to ship it."

"There goes my easy day," Norman said. "I knew it could not last."

"Don't worry about it right now, let's have a cup of coffee and think about it later."

"A good idea, let's go."

As we walked towards the mess tent the transport vehicles were leaving.

"It will be quiet around here now," Norman said.

"We still have the engineers," I said. "They are out there in the paddock now starting on the road."

"I forgot about that," Norman said. "How long will it take?"

"They said a week but there is a storm coming and that will slow them down."

"There will not be much for us to do, we should go over to the coast for a few days' rest."

"I am sure the colonel would approve," I said.

We sat at a table in the near empty mess and Ivan came over with a tray with coffee and Danish pastries.

"Good morning, Captain and Dave. I hope you like these they just came out of the oven."

We sat there enjoying the treat when Norman said, "I just realized why the army serves its soldiers such unappetizing food, if we had good things like this, we would soon be fat and lazy and unable to fight. I am sure going to miss this when you are gone."

"Why don't you get the colonel to assign Ivan to your group and take him wherever you go."

The captain had a good laugh. One of the clerks came in and the captain left with him.

I was about to leave when Ian came in.

"Things are a bit slow, I was out with the engineers just for something to do."

"Have a coffee and Danish," I said signaling Ivan. "It is going to get a lot slower when the storm arrives, I hope we have a couple of decks of cards."

When we finished, I said, "Walk over to the sheds with me and we will check on the guards."

We walked to the shed and I opened the doors and went in for a look around while Ian talked to the guard. When I came out Ian said.

"The guards are complaining about the cold and the storm that is coming, it is going to get tough for them."

"What can we do?" I said. "We have to keep a guard here."

"We would like to sit in the truck," the guard said.

"Well maybe that could be arraigned but you cannot keep the motor running, it is too dangerous."

Just then a vehicle polled up and the sergeant walked over to us.

"Hello Ian, Mr Freemen, what is wrong?"

"Nothing John, we were discussing how the guards could keep warm especially with the bad weather on the way."

"That is what I came here for, to discuss with Mr Freeman the security arraignments. We are short staffed since the transport troops left. They were filling in gaps in the roster I want to discuss the idea of sealing this building like we have the other one."

"What do you mean by sealing the building?"

"We put a special wide tape around the shed so no one can get in unless they break the tape and the mobile patrol will see it when they drive by on each of its rounds."

"This is the first I have heard of this."

"It was done last night after you had retired; we were short staffed and had no other choice."

"I will have a look, but we cannot do that here this is too sensitive to leave unguarded. Also, I have to open the doors a couple of times a day to allow the fumes to escape. Let's go look at the other shed."

There were two rows of blue and white tape going all-around the building.

"This is special tape, it is stretched and glued and when it is broken it shrinks and cannot be pulled together again and tape will not stick to it. We use it all the time, it is standard procedure."

"I suppose that will have to do," I said as we walked back to the other shed. We stopped near the doors and I said, "The best I can do is allow a vehicle to park here but no closer and the motor must be off and no smoking because it is inside the safety zone."

"In my younger days when I stood guard," Ian said. "We would sit in the trucks and the windows would fog up. The mobile patrol would pull up and the stationary one would go mobile, that way the vehicle would heat up and the windows would clear."

"That is a good suggestion, do you agree John?"

"I will go along with that."

"I better get going and make the arraignments."

I closed the shed doors and we walked off.

"What do we do now?" I said.

"I don't know; let's go to lunch maybe something will turn up."

MEANWHILE in Rockhampton, Colonel Martin and his crew were organizing the search for Bluey. He had called in the men who picked me up and any other available personnel that could be found. He even brought in Lieutenant Rodgers and Sargent Larmarra to help in the search. All they have is a phone number and a woman's name, Hazel. They soon found the address but no one was there and the neighbors had not seen them for days. The colonel was arraigning a large manhunt with the Queensland police when the report came in of the solder's surrender. He quickly arraigned transport to Townsville and left Lieutenant Rodgers in charge of the manhunt.

On arrival at the Townsville barracks headquarters, Colonel Martin was briefed by the base commander.

"This fellow, Robert Muller, a former Lance Corporal from this barracks, walked in here yesterday and asked for protection. He said he was being pursued by a gang of international gangsters and he had vital information concerning our national security.

Now and then we get a Vietnam veteran who is suffering from delusions so we did not take too much notice of what he was saying until he said he witnessed a murder near Toowoomba and he was afraid he would be next. So I rang the police and they said that the army was investigating that case and I should contact them. When I did all hell exploded. I was told that this man was an important witness in a national security matter and I was to keep him securely confined, even if I had to lock down the base until you arrived. We were not too sure of what to do with him because he was very distressed and sometime if you put these fellows in a cell they go berserk. A former mate recognized him, so we assigned him to watch him. When we told him that you were coming to interview him, he calmed down and accepted the situation. He is confined in the NCO barracks with his mate and there is a guard at the door."

"You have handled the situation very well, Major. Inform the fellow that I am here and because it is late I will start the interrogation at eight-thirty in the morning. Make sure that he is comfortable and has everything he needs. Above all make sure that nothing happens and he is ready for me in the morning. This man is involved in probably the most serious security situation that has ever happened in this country and his information is vital to the safety of the country."

"Excuse me Colonel, if this such a serious situation why wait until morning, why not start now?"

"Major, I have a lot of preparation to do before I interview this man and I have been travelling most of the day and I am tired. I want to be fresh and ready for him tomorrow. I cannot make any mistakes this is too important."

"I understand Colonel, if that is all I will show you to your quarters."

"You are Lance Corporal Robert Muller, Vietnam veteran and formerly attached to this barracks?"

"Yes sir."

"I understand you witnessed a murder that happened near Toowoomba recently."

"Yes sir."

"Did you take any part in the killing?"

"No sir, I only witnessed it."

"Do you know a man named Norman Fowler?"

"Yes sir."

"Were you with the group that was spying on us at Fowlers Farm?"

"Yes sir, I was there."

"Right, now that we have established that would you please tell us from the beginning your involvement in all of this."

"Yes sir, that is why I am here.

Many years ago, my father worked at one of the large homesteads near Fowlers farm and I went to school with him. We played rugby on the school team. About six months ago I was driving a taxi in Brisbane and Fowler got in my cab. I had not seen him since school days. We met that evening at a pub to talk over old times. It was then he told me that he had made a great discovery that would make him rich but he did not know how to pursue it and would I help him.

He had been prospecting in the far West on restricted Aboriginal Land and had discovered a cave with large bombs stored in it. He said they were large on trailers and covered under a canvas canopy He said they had American markings on them. From his description I thought they were daisy cutters left over from Vietnam and nobody would want them but he kept on insisting that I had connections and knew people who would be interested in buying them. During our talk I told him I spent three years in the Burmese army and he thought I would know someone there to contact. I suggested that he have his sister do that because she was already over there."

"You were in the Burmese army, and Fowler has a sister who lives in Burma?"

"Yes sir. Fowlers brother-in-law works for a large international company and he runs the Burma division. His sister and husband and two teen age children live in a high-class suburb in Rangoon. The eldest daughter lives in Brisbane, she just graduated from college that is why Fowler was in Brisbane. He was there for her graduation."

"When I came back from Vietnam, I had a hard time trying to settle into normal army life. After a couple of years the army discharged me as unfit. I wandered around trying to keep out of trouble. I finally ended up in Bali on the beach. The only thing I enjoyed was surfing so I rented a room near the beach and the couple that owned the house cooked my meals and washed my clothes and I surfed all day. One day I met an Aussie who had been offered a job in the Burmese army. They were looking for experienced solders to train their new army. I was getting bored with surfing, so I went for an interview. They wanted someone to teach the men how to march and general army discipline. Well, I got the job and shipped to a large army camp in Burma. They made me a Captain and gave me a fancy uniform. I made it plain before I joined that I would not take part in any fighting of any kind.

I started with a group of 160 new recruits and soon had them marching like old veterans. The first eighteen months were good, I liked the work and the generals were pleased with what I had done but oriental jalousies began to surface and I realized that some of the other officers did not like the attention the generals gave me so I decided it was time to leave. I went into town with a couple of other officers and told them I had met a lovely lady and would like to spend some time with her and would get a taxi back in the morning, I went straight to the airport and on the first plane out of the country."

"Is that where you met the men who were with you at Fowlers farm?"

"Yes sir, General Hon Dow and Mr Van Sing the former minister of the interior. They were both members of the original coup and were rewarded with government jobs. The minister also has a large Import export company and that is how I contacted him over here."

"Which one is which?"

"What do you mean, sir?"

"One is a large man and the other one wears cowboy boots."

"Ah yes the cowboy boots, that would be the minister and the general has put on a lot of weight."

"Let's stop for now and have some refreshments. We will start again in a half hour, by the way you do realize that you are not to say anything to anyone about what you are telling me."

During the break the major spent most of it at the teletype sending information to headquarters about Fowler's sister and the general and the minister. Then he sent a message to Captain Williamson telling him that Fowler had a sister in Burma and that is why Fowler would not talk because the men they were looking for were from Burma.

"I have instructed the foreign office to get them out of the country as quickly as they can. They are in terrible danger if the Burmese officials found out who they are. We are also going to contact Fowler's niece and explain the situation to her and offer her protection until this is over."

"Before we get started again do you know a friend of Fowlers who goes by the name of Bluey?"

"There are a lot of people named Bluey. Let me think, that was a long time ago. There was a kid with red hair in the school about that time but I did not know him very well because he did not play football.

"What was his name?"

"Dawson, that's right I remember now, Fredrick Dawson. He hated the name Fredrick and even hated Freddie even more, so everyone called him Bluey because he had red hair."

"Did you get that Rodgers, get on it right away. Now where were we?"

"Do you know where the cave with the bombs is?"

"No sir, I stayed in Darwin when they went out there."

"All right let's get back to your story."

"Yes sir. I knew the minister had a shipping office in Brisbane, so I went there and told them who I was and said I had a business proposition that their boss maybe interested in. I gave them my phone number and waited for a reply. I received a call a couple of days later to come to the office that afternoon. I talked to him on his overseas telephone in the office. At first, he was not interested but then asked me to describe the bombs. So, I told him what Fowler told me. He was very interested in the trailer and seemed to know a lot about it. When I told him, it had large balloon tires he got excited and wanted to see them and said he would make arraignment to come to Australia and for Fowler and I to prepare to meet him in Darwin in a week or so. Fowler was overjoyed when I told him but I was wondering what got the minister so excited.

About two weeks later I was called to the office and picked up a package from Mr Van Sing. Inside there was a satellite phone and some envelopes. One contained a map of the Darwin area with an x marked on a beach. Another contained one thousand Australian dollars and the third the instructions.

We were to go to Darwin and wait for a call from him. We had a week to get there. We decided to go in Fowlers ute to save money. When we arrived, we booked into a reasonable hotel and waited for the call. The instructions were that when he called we were to book them into a suite in a nice hotel. They gave us the names of a couple and one not to book in because they were known there. Then were to go to the beach and wait for them to arrive. I was getting worried because they were sneaking into the country and using fictious names.

It all went according to the plan. The call came we booked the rooms and went to the beach and waited. They arrived about two hours after dark, there were three of them and we took them to the hotel. The next couple of days they spent talking with Fowler and planning the trip to the cave. They hired a land rover and bought some camping gear. The little guy and I stayed in Darwin while they were gone. A week later they returned and they were all excited. Fowler said we had hit the jackpot and would be very rich very soon. The next couple of days there was a lot of running around and phone calls. Then one night I was told to drive Fowler's ute back to his farm in the morning. I was to get the place ready for them for about a week's stay. They would be arriving in about a week. When I went to leave in the morning there was a large white van in the hotel parking lot.

Fowler told me later that they loaded a bobcat and lots of water and fuel into the van. They needed the bobcat to clear the entrance to the cave and to tow the bombs out to the van. They left the bobcat and the rest of the fuel and water there. When they were finished, they closed the entrance and hid the bobcat and returned to Darwin. The general and the little guy left them in Darwin and the cowboy and Fowler drove the van to Fowler's farm.

The little guy was the general's aide, he had been with him for many years He was a sly sneaky sort of a fellow. When we were spying on you at Fowlers place, he wanted to sneak up and kill all of you."

"Tell me why did you get involved in this anyway? As a soldier you should have reported this as soon as Fowler told you about it."

"Yes sir, I thought about doing that but I was broke. Because I left without saying goodbye, I lost all the money promised to me in Burma and driving someone else's taxi didn't pay very well. This was a chance to make some good money, and at the time I didn't think that daisy cutter bombs were not much good to the Burmese because they did not have any planes large enough to carry them. The thought of the money overrode my sense of duty."

"I suppose you realize now that you made a very bad decision."

"Yes sir, I realized that when I saw the weapon when they uncovered it at the farm."

"All right let's have a break, I have to make some calls. We will meet again after lunch."

"The name, Fredrick Dawson, hit the jack pot," Captain Williamson said to the colonel. They haven't found him yet but they know where to look. He is a jackeroo and is well known around the Rockhampton area. Right now, he is pig shooting somewhere near Emerald and will soon have to come in for supplies."

"That is good to know, how are things at the farm?"

"It is raining and cold here and everything has stopped. The engineers have left their equipment and gone back to their base until things clear up."

"Any news of the other manhunt?"

"No, it looks like they have vanished."

"Well, I have a feeling that they are heading back to the bomb depot. They will need a four-wheel drive so do a sweep of all the rentals from Darwin to Alice Springs."

"How are you doing with your interrogation?"

"So far, we knew everything except Bluey's name and Fowler's sister. But he may come up with something else we can use. He does not know where the depot is except that is a couple of days from Darwin and accessible to a large van."

"We knew that already, Freeman told us the same thing. Anything else? Call me as soon as they find the Dawson fellow, we have to get to that depot before they do."

"When I arrived at the farm the place was a mess because we left in a hurry to go to Darwin. I cleaned up and bought some beds and other things we would need and stocked up on food. The van arrived first and we unloaded the bombs. Fowler and the cowboy headed off with the van the same night, I had to stay to cook for the general. The next afternoon the general and his aide arrived in a large car. They had been in Sydney but I didn't know why, they never told me. The next morning they left again and returned in the evening with Fowler and the cowboy.

It took most of the next day to get the bomb off the trailer and hanging in the shed. Then they started taking it apart. They really did not know what they were doing and there were many arguments, the little guy did most of the work. The cowboy helped a little and Fowler just got in the way, he was not much good with tools. I spent most of the time cooking and cleaning.

They were getting frustrated because it was taking them a lot longer than they had planned. Their plan was to take the bomb apart and crate the sphere and ship it to Burma as farming equipment. The thing was larger than expected and they were working long hours and getting nowhere. There was a lot of swearing and arguments. It all came to a head when the little guy got sick.

It seems that he had malaria and had run out of medicine. He got so sick he could not work so they had to take him to a doctor. They did not want to do that because they did not want anyone to know they were here. But the little guy was really bad, so I suggested that I take him to the hospital and say he was a friend of mine here on a holiday. That's what we did. We left Fowler to watch the place and we drove to the city and the hospital. We had only expected to be gone for the day but the little guy was so sick that he was admitted and stayed for four days. That really made the general mad. He kept trying to call Fowler to make sure nothing went wrong but the phone was not working. After four days he could not wait any longer, so I took the little guy out of the hospital and we headed back to the farm. That is when we saw the helicopter landing at the farm. What happened to Fowler, how did you find him?"

The colonel told Muller how Fowler sold the trailer and went into town and got drunk and arrested.

"I can understand that because Fowler was broke and he liked to drink and he was getting very nervous with all the arguments taking place."

"It is very fortunate for all of us that he did get drunk and arrested," the colonel said. "Let's call it a day and we will carry on tomorrow."

THAT afternoon it started to rain. I found a book and spent the afternoon reading. By evening the rain had settled in and it was cold, windy and wet. The engineers had stopped work and left. They did not want to stay in the tents in the rain.

"We will be back as soon as it clears up," Lieutenant Fitzroy said as they left.

The next day was spent in the house playing cards and drinking coffee. On our way to lunch, Ian and I walked around the sheds and checked on the guards. A very slow boring day.

The next morning the rain had eased and the wind was gone. I had a slow breakfast and sat talking with Ivan. He had this dream to start a chain of bakeries and sell bread and pastries and he wanted me to join him.

"In a couple of years, we will have a whole chain of stores and all we will have to do is watch over the," he said.

"I'll think about it," I said but I was not very enthusiastic about it.

By noon it was still cloudy but the rain had gone. We were about to go to lunch when we heard some vehicles pull up. I thought the engineers had returned and went outside to look. Four new shiny Land Rovers were parked in the drive and some men in new shiny uniforms got out.

"Where is this explosive device?" one of them said.

"And who are you?" I asked.

"I am Sergeant Sampson from the Northern area bomb disposal group and these are my crew. We have come to disarm an explosive device. If you show us where it is, we will get on with the job."

"Glad to meet you Sergeant, I am David Freeman the civilian coordinator of this post. I am afraid that you are a few days too early; we are not ready for you. The engineers have not finished the road yet."

"What road? We don't need a road, we have a special explosive proof canister on one of the Jeeps, we will load the device and take away and dispose of it. So, show us where it is and we will take it from there."

By now all the guys had come out of the office and Captain Williamson came up and asked the Sergeant.

"Have you been briefed on this mission, Sergeant?"

"Sir, I was told to come here and dispose of an explosive device. We do it all the time."

"Were you told what type of device it is?"

"No sir, they are usually an old hand grenade or a couple of sticks of dynamite. We had a live howitzer shell once."

"Well, I think you had better examine this device before you do anything else. Mr Freeman will show you where it is and what is involved, he is the expert."

"Yes sir. Thank you, sir."

"Over to you, Mr Freeman."

"Thank you, Captain. Come with me men."

We walked around to the shed and I dismissed the sentry.

"What is the guard for?"

"This whole area is guarded. We have a whole company of them to guard this device. You should have been stopped by them at the gate when you arrived."

"Yes, we were, we were told that they were having some kind of maneuvers here, so we thought someone had misused a hand grenade or something."

"I think you will find that is a little more than that," I said as I opened the shed doors.

They just stood there staring at the large sphere shining as the light shone on it.

"As you can see it is too large to fit on your Jeep, and it is also too heavy. It weighs nearly two tons, go have a closer look."

They started towards the sphere moving very carefully.

"Don't forget to slap the static wire, one spark could set it off."

One could tell by the way they acted that they were way out of their depth. They had no idea of what they were looking at. They slowly walked around the sphere looking at it very closely but not touching it. Then one of them said, "Hey sarg, look at this it is full of old drink cans." The sergeant looked into the sphere for a moment and said.

"What kind of a joke is this? It is just a dummy full of junk."

"No Sergeant, it isn't a joke. They are aluminum cans and they are in there to prevent the plutonium from starting a nuclear reaction in case of an accidental explosion."

"Plutonium, nuclear reaction. What in the hell is that thing?"

"That, Sergeant, is a genuine real atomic bomb. It doesn't look like much because it has been stripped down to the bare core, but it is still lethal and if it went off it would devastate this whole area."

They were backing out of the shed while I was talking and when they cleared the door they quickly vanished around the corner. By the time I had closed the doors I could hear the engines revving up. I had to wait a few minutes for the sentry before I returned to the house. The men were still laughing when I went inside.

"You missed all the fun. You should have seen them scrambling into their vehicles. It was just like the *Keystone Cops*," they said while still laughing.

"They were just a bunch of cowboys and they deserved what they got. We had a bit of fun but what do we do now?"

"What do you mean?" Norman said.

"Well, there goes our demolition crew. Where are we going to get another one? If we have to do it ourselves, we will be here all winter."

"Don't worry, I will get on to it right away. Headquarters will find us another team."

"Make sure they are qualified this time. I'm hungry after all of that; I hope the mess is still open."

"Are you ready to continue?" Colonel Martin asked Corporal Muller.

"Yes sir, I slept well and worked out in the gym this morning. I'm sorry I messed up my army career, army life agrees with me."

"To late for that now, son. Let's start with when you saw the helicopter."

"I was driving and the general and the cowboy were in the back planning how they could speed up the shipment and return home. They stopped at a hardware store to see what kind of material they could get to make a crate. They were going to buy an electric grinder to speed things up but decided that was too dangerous because of sparks.

We were driving along the main road about to turn into the farm when we spotted the helicopter flying low heading towards the farm. Then we saw a police car in the road leading to the farm so we kept on going. We drove to the main intersection and stopped at the service station and had some lunch. The general was upset, mad and nervous all at once. He did not know what to do.

After a while he settled down and he decided to find out what had happened, so we drove back passed the road and the police car was still there. We then drove along the dirt road that ran along the back of the farm. There was no one around and we found a level spot to take the car in so we cut the fence and drove as close as we could to the house without being seen." We must have been there for a couple of hours and only saw a couple of people. It was then they decided to wait until dark and go in and kill everyone and take the nuclear cores and leave. The little guy was all excited; he couldn't wait to cut their throats."

"What about you?" the colonel said. "Were you going to go with them and cut my throat?"

"No, no sir. I told them I would not take part in killing my fellow Australians and if they did that every police and army person would be looking for them and they would never get away. I said we should wait till dark and go to the rear of the shed where the cores were and take off a couple of sheets of iron and leave. No one would know we were there. After a bit of a heated discussion, they agreed but if anyone disturbed us they would kill them. We settled down to wait till dark then the army trucks arrived. We hid in the trees until about an hour after dark then we left. I had to walk in front of the car to guide it across the paddock because we could not use the headlights. We drove along the dirt road to the main road and then headed North.

When we got on to the highway, we stopped at a service center and filled the tank and had something to eat. The general made a couple of phone calls and we headed North. While we were at the farm the little guy was very nervous and kept taking the pills given to him at the hospital. Well either he overdosed or the pills did not agree with him, he was sick and as we travelled he got worse. After a while we stopped at a rest area. The cowboy and I stretched out on picnic tables for a little nap. The general and the little guy stayed in the car. Well, the general didn't get much sleep with the little fellow moaning all the time. Before we left, he got out of the car and threw up and was pleading to go back to the hospital."

"The general was already pretty pissed off about losing the weapons so he told him to shut up and get in the car. It was daylight now and we had driven for about an hour when the little guy started screaming that he was going to be sick again and to stop the car. I was driving and found a spot in a clearing near a river. The fellow was so sick I though his insides were going to come out. He started screaming and swearing and pleading to be taken to a doctor. He and the general were screaming and swearing at each other. Finally, the general ordered him to shut up and get in the car. He said no, he would wait here and get a ride to a doctor and after a lot more shouting and swearing the general took out his pistol and shot him.

He fell on the ground and was kicking and screaming so the general walked up to him and shot him in the head. The cowboy took off his shoes and jacket because they were made in Burma and would help identifies him. Then they rolled him into the river and we drove off. In about half an hour we arrived in Toowoomba and drove to the car rental yard and left the car. All the way I was thinking that I would be next and had to get away from them.

We walked out of the rental yard and through the office on to the street the shop was next to the entrance to a shopping center. There was a car at the curb and the general motioned for us to get in. The cowboy walked around to the street side and I opened the rear door for the general. He took his time getting in and I closed his door and opened the front door and said to the driver 'let's go' then I shut the door and ran into the shopping center. I looked back and saw the car driving away. I wondered how long it would be before they realized I was not in it.

I hurried through the shopping center and out another exit hailed a cab and went to the train station and was on a train that was just leaving for Brisbane. While I was on the train, I changed my clothes and tried to disguise myself as best I could. I got off the train at Ipswich and took a bus north. I moved around for a few days and realized that I was running out of money and couldn't think of anything else to do so I came here and surrendered."

"Well, that is quite a story. Do you have any more to add to it?"

"No sir, except the cowboy has a large company here and every one of his people will be looking for me for a long time."

"I don't think you will have to worry about that. We will quit for lunch and I will make some calls and we will decide what to do with you."

WHEN I came out of the mess the sky had cleared and the sun was shining. The storm had not been as bad as expected. I walked to the sheds and checked on the sentry then went back to my room and the book I was reading. A quiet afternoon. Later on, Norman came and told me he had arraigned for a new demolition team.

"These guys are experts; they handle large items like bombs and torpedoes. They are Navy, flying up from Melbourne, and will be here in a couple of days."

"That is good news and the engineers should be back at work by then. Maybe we will get out of here before winter.

NEXT morning it was a clear cool day and I enjoyed the walk to the mess. Ivan was there with a smile.

"This is the best job I have ever had. Only have to cook for about fifty people, and I have a good happy crew." We chatted for a bit then Ian came in.

"The boys have set up a rifle range in the sand pit and we are all going to catch up on our weapons training. Would you like to come along?"

"It has been a long time since I have fired a weapon but I would like that."

"The best score buys the other a beer."

"You are on."

We hitched a ride to the sandpit. There were a few vehicles there already the men had set up a row of targets against the wall inside the pit and had established a firing line about fifty meters away. They were already firing. We signed up and got our targets and waited our turn. When a group finished, they brought their rifles to a truck and then walked down and retrieved their targets. A new group walked with them and set up their targets, then came back and were issued a rifle. That way there were no accidents we stood around talking until our turn came.

On the way back from hanging our targets Ian was boasting about how good the beer I would buy him would taste. Although I never liked guns, I was a good shooter and rarely missed. So when we finished and I beat Ian he was not so cheerful.

That afternoon Lieutenant Fitzroy returned and after examining the road he declared that it was dry enough to work. As he left, he said the boys could play in the sandpit until noon tomorrow.

Things don't always go as planned and nothing happened for the next couple of days. The engineers did not show and the navy guys were still in Melbourne. Since the engineers did not arrive the troops continued to practice shooting in the pit. Ian challenged me to another contest.

"This time I will beat you," he said.

"I bet you have been practicing."

"I will admit I did pop off a few rounds yesterday afternoon."

He came close but I still beat him with more hits near the center.

IT was late in the afternoon when the colonel sat down with Corporal Muller.

"I would like to thank you for your cooperation, you have been a great help. We have not located the Burmese gentlemen as yet but we are sure it will be soon. I have been talking with headquarters about you and as yet they have not decided what to do with you."

"Excuse me, sir. What do you mean by that?"

"Headquarters are deciding whether to trial you as a traitor or a common criminal."

"Sir, I am no traitor. All I did was try to make some money."

"What would you call a person who joins a foreign army without permission. Helps three illegal foreigners into the country and makes a deal to sell illegal arms to them. Then does not report it to the authorities until he thinks they are going to kill him."

"You are right, sir. When you look at it that way, I really messed up."

"Well as I said they haven't made up their minds as yet and it depends on how you cooperate with them will determine their decision."

"Yes sir. What do I have to do?"

"A.I.S.I.O. wants' to be briefed on your Burmese friends and the foreign office would like to have an insight as to what the Burmese government is up to. So, you will stay here until they can transport you to Canberra where they will interview you. Remember your cooperation is vital to the outcome. If you are lucky, they will pass you off as a poor mixed up Vietnam veteran who made a stupid mistake, all I can do is wish you luck and say goodbye."

COLONEL Martin and his aide finished their work at the Townsville barracks and prepared to return to Rockhampton. It is a long drive so they planned to stop somewhere for the night. They arrived late the next morning and were briefed about the search for Bluey.

"We set up a command center at Emerald and are searching a wide area from there but so far, we have not found him. We have a watch on Hazel's house in case they go back there. We also have his vehicle registration, an old Toyota four-wheel drive, but we have not found it yet. All the local police and highway patrols have their descriptions and they have alerted all the service stations in the area to be on the lookout for them."

"Good work men. It appears you have done everything possible so now all we can do is wait for a result. I will be in the other office catching up on paperwork. Inform me as soon as something breaks. He cannot hide forever."

I was barely awake when I heard the vehicles coming down the driveway. I went into the kitchen and Ian said, "The engineers have arrived, looks like we are back in business."

"I met Lieutenant Fitzroy in the mess and he said they would work in shifts to get the road finished as fast as possible."

"Two, maybe three days at the most," he said. I had my usual breakfast and chat with Ivan and then went back to the house. Lieutenant Dickson and Sergeant Jones were just leaving.

"Where are you going?"

"We just received a call from the navy. The crews are on their way and will be at the airport by the time we get there. We are taking two cars because there are five of them and they have a lot of baggage. We will be back early this afternoon."

I went inside and met Captain Williamson.

"Looks like our little holiday is over, we could be out of here in a week or so if all goes well."

"A week. I doubt it. Maybe for the sphere but not the second weapon, that will take a couple of weeks on its own."

"Maybe not," Norman said.

"The navy boys have a plan and if it works, they are going to ship the second weapon to Victoria."

"That is a wild idea," I said. "Don't count on it."

"Let's wait and see what they have in mind."

I decided to go to the shed and have everything ready for the team when they arrived. I had been there for about an hour when Captain Williamson and lieutenant Fitzroy came in.

The captain said, "I just received a bulletin from headquarters. When we finish here, they want this site completely cleared. Nothing is to remain here except grass. Even the driveway is to be removed. In the end there will only be the side gate to the back road left."

"It is going to be a big job," Fitzroy said. "We don't want to be here any longer than we have to so we want to know what we can do now that will not interfere with your operation."

"As long as you keep away from the road and this shed you can do anything you want. Why don't you start with the barn? Get a scrap dealer to clean out the junk and the machinery in the other shed and the lean to, then you can take them down. That will not interfere with our work here. All that will be left is the house and the two sheds and when we leave you can burn them down."

"That is a good idea except we do not want a bunch of civilians going back to town and telling everyone what is going on out here," said Norman.

"Tell them that we are testing a new type of cannon. And get them swear to the secrecy act. If they are paid to take the junk away and the sell it, they will sign anything. All they will see is a couple of trucks going up and down the road occasionally."

We walked to the barn and looked inside.

"What a load of junk," Fitzroy said. "The only way to get rid of this stuff is to have someone haul it away I don't have the men or equipment to do a job like this."

"This is only half of it," I said. "The other shed and the lean to are full of tractors and machinery."

"That settles it," Fitzroy said. "Someone else will have to do it."

"I will call the police, Sergeant, he will know who can do a job like this," said Norman.

We were just finishing when the two cars pulled up in the driveway and a group of men got out.

"The demolition team has arrived," Norman said.

We all went over to meet them. There were introductions and hand shaking all round. Three of them were older than the average service man and you could tell by their mannerisms that they were very experienced. The other two were a lot younger, and I guessed they were trainees.

"We brought along a couple of apprentices," said one of them. "This will be their baptism of fire."

Then Ian said, "We will unload your gear and then go to lunch."

We sat around the mess table laughing and joking and getting to know each other. They were especially interested in my stories about my exploits in the air force. After lunch we went to the shed, they were anxious to see what they were up against. After a good long look at the sphere one of them said.

"It is a lot larger than I thought it would be. All we have seen is drawings."

"There is a ton and a half of super high explosive in there," I said and one of the young ones gave a long low whistle.

"This is only the inner workings of the weapon. We have a complete one in the other shed. I will show it to you later."

I explained what we had done so far and the plan to dismantle the sphere and dispose of the explosive in the sand pit.

"You have done an excellent job, very professional. You have made out job a lot easier. We will get our gear organized and then set down and draw up a battle plan."

As we were talking one of the young ones said.

"Excuse me sir, but what are these drink cans inside here for?"

"Oh, I forgot to tell you this is not an ordinary atomic weapon, it is a plutonium bomb."

"You mean a Neutron bomb?"

"Yes, you can call it that. If that thing was to go off it would kill everything within a hundred-kilometer radius from here to the sea and then a lot of people and animals in New Zealand and make a lot of people sick in South America. If it had its nuclear core, it would do a hundred times that much destruction and a great chunk of this country would be uninhabitable for hundreds of years."

"Holy hell," the leader said. "No one told us about a Neutron bomb, let's go somewhere and discuss this."

"A long way," one of the young ones said.

"You guys go back to the house, I will lock up and wait for the sentry then catch up with you."

BACK the house they were setting around the table and all talking at once. The leader was pacing back and forth and talking to himself and when I came in, he turned on me.

"Why were we not told about this Neutron bomb? What if something goes wrong who will they blame? Not you, they will blame me. I have never handled anything like this before and you are loading it on my back."

"Settle down, Sam. First of all, this is the most secret operation going on in the country and the less said about it the better. Also, don't worry about taking the blame, if something goes wrong you will be vaporized along with the rest of us.

You were sent here because you are the most experienced person in the country and we need you to complete this operation so we can all go home. We will sit down and go through this exercise step by step and nothing will go wrong. I am sure that I do not want to be vaporized."

Well that brought a laugh and broke the tension and we all relaxed.

"The captain said you have a plan to ship the other weapon to Victoria. Would you mind explaining that to us?"

Sam had settled down after the little joke and was eager to take charge of the meeting.

"That is why it took us so long to get here," he said.

"A few years ago, a team went to the U.S. to learn how to salvage an atomic weapon in case a plane came down near us. We went to the Sandia corp. at Albuquerque to train. While there I made friends with one of the instructors. He was a retired Sandia engineer and had worked on the weapons like the one here. He didn't like the new ones because they were sealed and all one did was hang them in a plane. Anyway, when I found out about this job I contacted him and he sent over some old manuals from the archives at the museum one is a construction manual and the other is on the explosives. It explains how to test the material for sensitivity. If the explosive passed the test, we could move the weapon to our workshop and train others how to dismantle it. I understand that you believe that there are more of them."

"Yes," Norman said. "Dave believes that there could be at least twenty or more planted somewhere in the desert."

"That many, wow!"

"Well, he hasn't been wrong yet. By the way, how do you plan to transport the weapon to Victoria? I am sure the authorities will not let you move by road through any populated area."

"A few years ago, the navy found some old WWII torpedoes stored in a forgotten bunker. They were so fragile that we did not dare to move them, so the boys invented a vehicle to move them. It is a specially built truck with a vibration free bed. It worked and we disposed of the torpedoes without an accident. The bed is being adapted to carry the weapon and when it is ready they will drive up here. It should be here by the time we are through with the one out there."

"There is no way you will be allowed to transport the weapon on the road," said the captain.

"We do not plan to transport it by road. There is a minesweeper coming from North Queensland. We will move the weapon from here to the nearest port with a dock for us to use. The weapon will be transported by sea to our workshop in Victoria."

"Well, you have planned that out well," said Norman. "Where will you find a dock large and deep enough to handle this?"

"The only one that fits our needs and is not near a large population is Iluka. It has a deep port to service the island trading ships."

"Iluka, that is a long way from here."

"We will only do it if we find the weapon is safe. If it is not, we will dispose of it here just like the other one."

"We will have to wait and see how the tests come out, but I hope your idea works. We have been here to long already," said Norman. "Is there anything else?"

"Only one more thing. We flew here and do not have any vehicles to work with. Are there any available?"

"I have already looked into that," said Lieutenant Dickson. "All we have here are the security and engineer's vehicles. The security has three vehicles being repaired and the engineers have only one vehicle, the rest are their working plant. So the answer is no, we do not have any spare vehicles."

"We need at least two or three vehicles," Sam said. "What about the vehicles we came here in?"

"No way," Captain Williamson said. "We need them and one of them needs some repairs."

"Do not despair, I have a solution. That is if Captain Williamson approves of it."

"And what is that?" the captain said.

"We go into town and buy some utility trucks."

"You know the army lieutenant; it will take months of paperwork to do that."

"Maybe not, sir. I had a talk with Lieutenant Fitzroy and he has a requisition in for months for five four-wheel drive utility trucks. We just use our national security clearance and fast forward the requisition and go into town and buy the vehicles, we can have them here by noon tomorrow.”

“Brilliant,” said Norman. “Make up the paperwork and I will sign it.”

“It has already been done, sir.”

“You are not going over my head, are you?”

“No sir, just speeding things up, sir.”

“All right. Get Fitzroy in here and we will decide what type of vehicles to get.”

“Beg your pardon, sir. But we have already done that.”

“You are stretching your luck, soldier.”

“Sorry sir, but when I talked over the plan with Lieutenant Fitzroy, he got all excited and went into town to find out what was available. When he came back, he gave me a list of the vehicles available and their locations. All we have to do is decide what type is best for our needs.”

“What about Fitzroy? Will our needs comply with his?”

“The lieutenant saw two Land Rover utility’s and that is his first preference, but he will take anything as long as it is four-wheel drive.”

“What does the navy need? They come first.”

“Sir, we will need at least two vehicles to transport the charges to the sandpit and we could use another one for our own use. The Land Rovers are not suitable for moving the charges, they are too heavily spring. Regular utilities will do for that. The other vehicle could be one of your station wagons.”

“No, you cannot have one of our vehicles, we use them constantly and one of them is playing up and needs a service before it breaks down. Therefore the best solution is to go into town tomorrow and buy five vehicles, three for the navy and two for the engineers. When we are through with ours, we will return them to the engineers, after all they are officially theirs anyway. Lieutenant you will take care of that, and I expect to see them here by noon tomorrow.”

“Yes sir, I will take care of it.”

“Anything else? No, then Sergeant Jones will help our navy guests to get settled and we will start again in the morning. Good evening, gentlemen.”

I did not contribute to any of this conversation. Also, I did not consider that the navy team would need any vehicles to do their work. I was beginning to feel left out and wondering if there was anything for me to do here. The rest of the team was functioning well without me. Maybe I could go home. No, I wanted to finish this and was sure there was still something I could contribute to the cause.

Everyone had left and I was thinking of heading to the mess when Norman came out of his office.

"Good work Dave, you saved the day again.'

"What? I didn't do anything, I just sat here listening to the rest of you."

"Don't be so modest you stepped in at just the right time and saved Sam from freaking out. I was getting worried because I have seen a lot of Vietnam veterans go that way and I thought Sam was about to crack. When they do crack sometimes it takes months for them to recover. I was afraid if he did it would set us back again and we would never get out of here."

"I didn't think I did anything. Anyway, it is over now. Come on let's go get a bowl of good old army stew."

THE next morning I was up early, it was still dark but cold as I walked to the mess the air was still and crisp. I knew it would be a nice day.

"You are here early," Ivan said.

"I thought I would get here before the rush."

"You mean the navy boys. The evening crew told me about them, they didn't like our army chow."

"That's why I came early to ask you to give them the same VIP treatment you give me."

"What, why should I?" After the performance they put on last night."

"Come on now Ivan, you would do the same thing if you had to chow down at a navy base."

"Yah, I suppose you are right. I will try."

"Those fellows are going to do a very dangerous and strenuous job and a good meal will help boost their morale."

"When you put it that way it makes me feel important."

"Of course, you are important. I would have gone over the hill long ago if it wasn't for your Danish pastries."

He had a good laugh and we talked while I ate my breakfast.

"I will get started on their breakfast," Ivan said, as I left.

When I got back to the house the rest of the gang were just getting up. Lieutenant Dickson was excited.

"I am meeting Fitzroy at the mess and we are going into town right after chow. Fitzroy is taking one of his men and Ian has lined up two of the off-duty guards to drive a couple of the lutes. He and I are going to flip to see who drives the other one. I called the dealers late yesterday and they are excited as I am over the sale."

"How come you did not ask me to go? I would have liked to drive one of those new utes."

"I was going to but the navy boys want you here to organize their work."

"Oh, well thank you for thinking of me. By the way why don't you pull rank and have one of the guards drive your car back."

"I had thought of that but I will probably have to stay behind and do a lot of paperwork anyway."

It was not long before the station wagon, with six men in it shot down the driveway. Norman had just come in and he said, "They seem to be in a hurry."

"Yes, they are all excited and want to get their hands on the new trucks. But if they don't slow down the sentry at the gate, I will shoot them for trying to escape."

Norman chuckled and said, "You sure have a weird sense of humor. I understand that you will be working with the navy crew today."

"It looks that way. Why don't you come along to supervise?"

"I would like to but I have to catch up on what is going on with the rest of the team so I will be here most of the morning."

I met the navy crew coming out of the mess.

"How are we going to spend the day?" I said.

"We want to start by doing some test on the charges. Fred, who will be doing most of the detonations, wants to check out the sandpit and I understand you have a couple of charges available for him to start with."

"Yes, they are the nose cones; they are in canisters in the other shed."

"OK, how do we get Fred and one of the apprentices out to the sandpit?"

"That is easy, just stop a guard vehicle and they will take them there and return them."

As we walked to the shed, I said to Sam.

"You will need some sort of a cushion in the tray of the utes to protect the charges. Do you have anything in mind?"

"No, I had not even thought about it. You are right, do you have any ideas?"

"The only thing I can think of is a foam mattress, cut them up and make a pad in the tray of the ute."

"That is a good idea, we can form it to fit the charge so it will not move. Where do we get the mattresses?"

"The boys are in town right now, we can contact them and they can bring them back. Send someone to the house and the clerk will call the lieutenant and he will take care of it."

"Harry, go up to the house and make sure the lieutenant understands what we want."

"How many mattresses do we need for two utes?"

"Not too many, we can pack sandbags around the outside and foam in the center. Say two double beds per ute."

"OK Fred, four double bed mattresses and make sure they are foam and not springs."

BY then we were at the shed. I told the sentry that we would be breaking the seal and opening the other shed. Also tell the sergeant that I wanted to talk to him when he comes by on his rounds. As we walked to the other shed, I asked Sam if he had seen a *Mark Six*.

"Yes," he said. "We had a tour of the museum at Sandia base, it was part of the course."

"Well, we have a nice shiny one here in this shed," I said as I opened the door.

"It looks a lot larger sitting on a trailer than on a stand in the museum."

"Where are the canisters?"

"They are in the back behind the weapon."

"Can we pull this out?"

"No, we will not move it until you declare that it is safe. We will go round the back and pull off a couple of sheets of tin and get the canisters that way."

The three of us easily removed the tin sheets and we went inside.

"There they are. We sent the nuclear cores and the fuses to the divisional headquarters in Victoria."

"Can we move the chargers?"

"Yes, as long as you do not drop them. They are not very heavy."

By then Harry had returned and told us he talked to Dickson and he would bring the mattresses back with him. The two Land Rovers were already on their way. We propped the sheets against the wall and took turns carrying the canisters to the other shed.

Sam said, "We will not open these until we are ready to test them. The seals have not been broken, they will be our standard and we will compare these charges against the ones in the sphere and that will tell us the condition of the explosive."

"What sort of test are these?" I asked.

"We have the graphs from Sandia. One is for shock and the other is a gas emissions test. The more gas the poorer the condition. There are also some lab tests we can do but I don't think we will have to do them. We only want to know if the weapon is stable enough to move and seeing they got it here, I think it will pass the tests."

They had a good look around the shed and the sphere. I told them I had loosened the bolts on the sphere so it would be easy to disassemble. Sam said when we open it, we will have to quickly disassemble it and seal the chargers because the air would cause the explosive to disintegrate faster. I told them we had a pack of plastic bags leftover from making sandbags.

"They will do. We will put the charge in them and seal it with tape until we are ready to dispose of it."

"There is only one problem," I said. "What will happen when we expose the plutonium? I am sure that we will have to take precautions. We asked for a manual from the atomic energy commission but so far we have not heard from them."

"Don't worry I know someone who can give us all the information we need," Sam said. "Anyway, it will be a couple of days before we start on the sphere."

Sam looked around and said, "I guess that is all we can do here for now."

"OK," I said. "Let's have some coffee."

"Coffee, what do you mean by coffee?"

"Come with me, we will wait for Fred at the mess and enjoy some good coffee and Danish pastries."

"You are joking, good coffee in the army and Danish pastries, no way."

We walked into the mess and sat down at a table.

"Well, where is the coffee?"

"Be patient it is on its way."

"You are having a good joke at our expense,' said Harry.

Just then Ivan and another cook came up with trays of cups etc. And laid out the table and another one brought a large thermos of coffee. Then Ivan returned with a tray of Danish pastries.

"Good morning Mr Freeman, these are just out of the oven, I hope they are satisfactory."

"I don't believe it," they all said.

"Gentlemen, this is Ivan Walinski. My own personal cook assigned to me by command headquarters, and I have instructed him to give you the same VIP treatment as I receive. Of course, he was a little reluctant to do so until I threatened to transfer him. So, sit back and enjoy."

Ivan had a large grim as he returned to the kitchen.

A few minutes later Fred and the apprentice came in. They were all talking at once, telling him about their morning coffee. About then one of the clerks came in and told me Captain Williamson wanted me at the house. I grabbed a pastry and a cup of coffee for him and followed the clerk back to the house.

"There are some civilians here with a large truck and the captain does not know what to do with them."

The men were sitting in their truck when I went inside to talk to Norman.

"Fitzroy is not back yet and I do not know what to do with these men."

"Have they signed the security form yet?"

"I don't think so."

"I will bring them in and you can explain the situation to them and have them sign up and then I will take them over to the barn and show them what to do."

I took them around to the barn and told them about the restricted area.

"If you wander into the restricted area, you will be arrested and will have to do some fast talking to stay out of jail. Just come and do your job and no one will bother you but remember they will be watching you all the time."

They were a little nervous but when they saw the barn full of scrap metal their attitude changed and they started loading the truck.

"It will take a couple of days to empty the barn," the leader said.

"That's all right," I said. "Just tell the sentry at the gate and sign in and out. Make sure that you stay together all the time."

Then I took them to the other shed and the lean to and when they saw all the old machinery, the leader said, "Can we have all of this too; it is worth a fortune if it was restored."

"Well, you can take and restore it, and we will pay you to take it away. When you are in this area there will be a guard with you because you are close to the restricted zone, so tell the guard at the gate when you are ready to start here."

"What are you doing here that is so guarded?"

"Please don't ask questions about this place or tell anyone what you see here, you have a good thing here don't spoil it. One mistake and you will be in so much trouble you will never get over it. I will tell you this much, the army is going to use this area as a training area and the buildings are in the way.”

“You are going to knock them down?”

“Yes, that is why you are cleaning them out.”

“That old barn has a lot of good old timber in it. If you give me the wood, I will take it down for free.”

“I will ask the superiors about that but for now clean up this mess and keep out of trouble.”

As I was walking towards the house Lieutenant Fitzroy drove up in his new Land Rover. And the other one pulled up behind him.

“This is like Christmas. We have been waiting a long time for these. Come on, I will take you for a ride.”

“I am looking for the navy crew; you can help me find them.”

He drove around showing me what a great machine it was. We found the navy boys at the sphere shed talking to the sentry.

“All our gear is in there and the guard will not let us in,” said Fred.

“He is only doing his duty. He has strict orders not to let anyone in without my permission. That is why I want to talk to his sergeant to make arrangements so you can work here.”

“I called the sergeant sir, he will be here shortly.”

“Thank you, soldier. Wait here until he arrives.”

“All we want is some of our gear,” said Sam. “We are going out to the sandpit and get it ready, we want to start the tests tomorrow morning. The engineers are out there now building a barrier for us.”

The sergeant arrived and I explained what had happened and introduced him to the navy crew.

“I want these men to have access to this and the other shed at all times. Also, we pulled a couple of sheets off the rear of the small shed.”

“I know, it caused a bit of excitement and the patrol was going to sound the alarm but they talked to the guard first and he told them what was going on. Are you going in there again today?”

“No, we will not go in there again until we finish here.”

“Fine, I will have it sealed before dark.”

“There is one more thing Sergeant, I am sure you have seen the civilians and their truck at the barn.”

“Yes sir, I understand they are cleaning out the junk.”

"That's right, I want you to watch them closely, when they finish the barn they are going to clean out the lean too and the shed next to it. When they are there, I want a guard with them. They are not to wander away from their work area and they are not to talk to the guards. They have been asking too many questions already."

"I understand sir, we will take care of it. By the way the patrol found some fresh tire tracks in the Northwest corner of the paddock. Looks like someone came along the back road and came in the gate then turned around and left. probably sometime late yesterday after noon."

"You sound like Sergeant Larmarra."

"Well sir, we learned a lot from him."

"Come with me, I bet I know whose tire tracks they are.'

We walked to the barn and I introduced the sergeant to the cleanup crew. He told them what he expected of them and he would cooperate with them. We chatted for a few minutes then I casually said, "By the way the patrol found some fresh tire tracks by the old road would you know anything about them by chance?"

"Well yes, after we were told about the job, we decided to have a quick look. We drove by the main entrance but saw the guard so we drove on then Charlie told me of the back road so we decided to have a look. We drove through the gate and stopped in the paddock for a minute. Then we saw a Land Rover heading our way, so we left. We only wanted to have a look."

"Mister, you are dangling on the end of a very thin thread," I said. "One more incident and the sergeant and his boys will use you for target practice. You were lucky you were not shot at yesterday."

"I am sorry sir, we will obey your rules, this is too good of a job to mess up."

As we walked back to the sergeant's car, he said.

"I think I will have the boys keep a close watch on those guys."

"A good idea, they are a pretty slippery outfit."

I went into the shed where the navy crew was just finishing their chores.

"All we need now is some transport to the sandpit and we can get started," said Fred.

"That is easily fixed," I said. "All I have to do is wave my hands like this and your transport will magically appear."

I stepped out into the lane and waved my hands and Sargant Jones pulled up in one of the new utes.

"I thought you guys would be here, here is your new truck. It is a real honey to drive. There are a couple of mattresses on the back. What are they for?"

"Thank you for going to town for us Sergeant," Sam said. "We are going to use the mattresses as packing to transport the charges."

"I thought you guys wanted some soft beds to sleep on," Jones said with a smile.

As we started towards the house the navy boys were attacking the mattresses.

"I think there will be trouble over the other two trucks," Ian said as we walked along. "The guards are short on vehicles and I think they will pull rank and take the two utes until their vehicles are repaired or replaced."

"That is a problem for the captain; we don't want to get involved."

The captain was not too pleased with the idea of the guards taking the utes from the navy.

"The demolition of the explosives comes first; the guards may use the trucks at night if they need them.

Corporal, ask around and try to commandeer a few more vehicles. By the way, Dave, thank you for the coffee. I have not left this room all morning."

"Speaking of coffee," I said. "Looks like we have missed lunch. Let's go to the mess and see what is left over."

"Before we go there has been a lot of information come over the line. First someone thought they had spotted the cowboy, so customs did a routine check on his warehouse in Brisbane but did not find anything. Also, the foreign office has successfully transported the Fowler family out of Burma. They are on their way home to be reunited with their daughter. Because of this the colonel is planning a trip down this way, unless they find Bluey, to interview Fowler. He thinks he will talk once he knows his sister is safe."

"One other thing the Sergeant of the guard asked me to check up on those junk yard men so I called the police sergeant because he is the one who recommended them. I understand one of them is his brother-in-law. He is not a bad fellow just an opportunist, always looking to make a quid. The Sergeant is coming out this afternoon to talk to them and I want you and the guard NCO to be there. I guess that is all, let's get something to eat. Lieutenant Dickson is not back yet. I think he is having lunch in town."

ATLAS Ambani is the third son of a large Indian family business of importers.

Atlas is constantly competing with his brothers for more recognition and a better position in the family business.

His older brothers were the favorites of their father. They had been educated in England but is father decided that he wanted a more aggressive person to improve the company, so he sent Atlas to Melbourne to a modern business college.

Atlas could not adjust or cope with the different attitude there, so he transferred to A modern sophisticated college in Brisbane. Much to his father's displeasure.

He did well there and graduated with honors. That is where he met and fell in love with Henrietta Fowler.

His father banned him from the company when they married so they lived and worked in Australia for many years. During that time the family grew with two girls and a boy.

Atlas was called back into the family business after the coup in Burma because the company there was failing and no one else wanted to go there.

The new government soon realized that the company was making a lot of money for them. Atlas became one of the top company executives in the country.

The British Embassy was the only western government still operating in the country and all the businesspeople working there relied on them for their news and contacts with their home countries.

The official who looked after them was Alisha Burns-Jones. She had lived in Burma since a child and knew the mood of the government. Everyone relied on her for advice.

The new government was erratic and unstable, so the expats had to walk a skinny high tightrope. Occasionally one of them would get in trouble. They had devised a plan among themselves to help each other.

Once a week was the regular cocktail party and every month a semi formal dinner party so they could keep in close contact.

They had codes like if Alisha heard rumors about someone, she would invite them for coffee. If someone was in trouble, they would be invited to a birthday party. If they were about to be arrested, it would be a special birthday party.

Out of the blue one morning Henrietta got a special birthday party invitation.

Every family had an evacuation plan. Henrietta did not hesitate she packed her and the children's bags and said goodbye to Atlas.

Someone in the group picked them up then drove towards the embassy.

All this secrecy was necessary because they lived in the best area of Rangoon. Their houses were large compounds with many buildings and a group of servants. They could not trust anyone but each other.

In the heavy traffic in the center of the city the car pulled up at a stop light.

Henrietta quickly opened her door then she and the children got out and into the car beside them. The light changed and the other car went straight ahead and their car turned the corner then dove straight to the airport and in a side gate then stopped beside a large shed.

The three of them walked around the corner of the shed then down to where a plane was loading. They joined those boarding and were quickly safely seated. A couple of minutes later the plane departed. They were on their way back to Australia but did not know why.

I left the others at lunch and went looking for the navy crew. They were not at the shed so I knew they were at the sandpit. I was thinking of how to get out there when the guard sergeant pulled up.

"The navy wants you at the sandpit," he said.

"I was just trying to find a way out there."

On the way I told him about the police sergeant and the junk yard boys.

"When he arrives, I will send someone out there for you."

Then I told him about the captain's plan for the vehicles.

"I guess it is the best plan. I just thought I could pull a fast one and get a couple more vehicles. I don't think they will find any spare ones, we already tried that."

At the pit Sam said, "I am glad they found you, we are ready to test the cores in the canisters and I want you to witness the tests."

He showed me a frame with pullies and ropes attached to it.

"This is a shock test. The charge is attached to the pulley and dropped on that flat rock."

"How high, and how many times can you drop it?" I asked.

"It depends on a lot of variables, its age, exposure to the elements and if it has been dropper before. Fred is our math wizard and if it can take a meter drop it will pass the test."

"What do you do if it passes the test?"

"We can take it up as high as two meters, it should go off then, if not we have some explosive bullets. They do the trick every time."

"Everyone ready? Let's go."

They opened the canister and removed the charge and placed it into a plastic bag and taped it to the pulley. The rest of us stood behind the large mound of sand the engineers had made. The charge is about the size of a four-liter water jug except it is slightly rounded at the top and bottom. Also, it is not square but tapered, smaller at the bottom. They are molded to fit together into a sphere. There are two layers in the sphere. There is the inner hollow core then the inner layer of explosive around that and the outer layer of explosive and the outer shell of thick cast aluminum sections bolted together. That is why the sphere is so large and heavy.

We all gathered behind the mound and the obligatory 'Fire in the hole' was called, the cord was pulled but nothing happened. Sam peered over the mound and looked for a moment and said, "The test was a success, the charge dropped. Let's pull it to the top and drop it again."

It took two more drops before the charge went off with a loud sharp 'Crack'.

"Oh man," Fred said. "That is the most powerful explosion I have ever heard. That is very powerful stuff."

We walked to the site and had a look. The rock was still there but that was all. There was a large hole around the rock and the end of the cord was ten meters away.

"We are dealing with some very powerful forces here," Sam said.

"All right let's get on with the next test, this test is to tell how badly the charge has deteriorated. The charge is placed in a large plastic bag and a spark ignitor is fixed into the top of the bag and we wait for the gas to form and time how long it takes to go off. Depending on the age, exposure, and temperature the chart will tell us the condition of the material. Then we will compare these tests with the ones we will do on the core and then we will have a fairly definite condition of the other weapon."

Fred and one of the apprentices were setting up the test when a patrol vehicle drove up.

"Looks like I will have to go," I said.

"We will give you the results later," Sam said and I went off with the patrol.

AS we arrived at the barn there was a police car, a fancy looking Land Rover with blue lights on it and the Sargent's new ute. They were all standing there and an army officer in full dress and a beret and MP band on his arm was talking. He was saying that this area was too sensitive to have these civilians here.

The lieutenant and his aide had arrived from the local command headquarters to check on the security and had come upon the junk yard boys. They had arrived unannounced as these inspectors like to do. I stood by the vehicle listening when someone said

"Here is Mr Freeman, he will explain everything to you."

As I walked towards the group I said to the driver.

"Get the captain here right now."

"What is this? Another civilian? Who in the hell are you, and what are you doing here?"

"Good afternoon, Lieutenant, I am David Freeman and I am in charge of this operation, and I want to know how you got in here without my permission."

The lieutenant just stood there.

"You may be here to check on the efficiency of your men, but you should have asked for permission first."

"Sorry sir, if I had asked for permission I would not get a true account of my men."

While the lieutenant was speaking two vehicles pulled up. The captain and Lieutenant Fitzroy in his new Land Rover.

"I will agree on that, Lieutenant, but why are you ordering these men off the base?"

"Sir, I am in charge of security and the base is not secure if there civilians here."

"Does that include me? Lieutenant, you may be responsible for the actions of your men. But you do not have anything to say or do about anything else here including the security. That is my responsibility and mine alone. So, I suggest that you get on with your inspection and if you find any faults, I will be glad to discuss them with you."

There was complete silence among the group standing there. The lieutenant looked around and then said, "If that is all sir I will get along with my inspection. Come along Sergeant, we will inspect the mess."

He turned and walked to his vehicle and drove off. Norman came up and said, "You handled that very well. I am glad that you did not go overboard because I would have had to step in and protect a fellow officer from being embarrassed in front of regular soldiers."

"I think he was embarrassed," I said. "I am sorry I called you here but I needed you in case it got out of control."

"You did the right thing. Now let's straighten out this other mess once and for all, by the way we could argue about who is in charge here."

We both smiled at each other.

Before the lieutenant arrived the police Sergeant was explaining the consequences of any shady actions to the junk yard boys.

"Boy that lieutenant really shook these guys up, I don't think you will have any more trouble with them," the policeman said. "There was one thing though, they told me that they had been approached in town by a couple of men who said they were news reporters and would pay them $500.00 dollars to sneak them on and off the base."

"That is serious, Sergeant. If it is all right with you, I will get my men on it. All you can do is tell them to stay away but we can put them away until this is over."

"That is fine by me, Captain, I have enough to do anyway."

Lieutenant Fitzroy came up and said, "Is it true these men have to leave the base? Who will clean up the junk?"

"Everything has been straightened out, they will be back tomorrow," the captain said. "Sergeant, I would like to invite you and your fellow officer to a cup of the best coffee in the army, gentlemen let us retire to the mess hall." Then he said to the leader of the scrap boys, "When you leave, I want to talk to you. Wait for me at the house."

Then we all headed to the mess.

As we walked along Lieutenant Fitzroy came up to me and said, "Lieutenant Hartley was a year ahead of me at the academy and he bullied me so badly I nearly quit the army. What you did to him today was a pleasure to witness. Dave, you made my day. I wish I could thank you in some way."

"Just making you happy is thanks enough. We will really enjoy the coffee."

While we were sitting there the navy boys came in and joined us and we sat around the table having a good old gabfest. I thought to myself, *Would it have been like this if I had stayed in the service?*

IT was late in the afternoon as we walked towards the house the scrap truck was parked in the drive loaded to the top.

"You two come with me and listen to what I have to say to these men."

The clerks had gone for the day and there was Captain Williamson, Sergeant Jones, myself and the three junk yard men in the office. We all sat down except the captain. He stood there facing the men.

"You men have only been here one day and you have caused enough trouble to get the whole camp in an uproar. You are only keeping your job because we have a tight schedule to keep and we cannot look for another company to do the job. So, don't give us any more trouble.

I was greatly disturbed when the police informed me that some newsmen want you to sneak them in here to snoop around. You do realize that you would have been caught and would face up to twenty years in jail."

The men looked at each other and were upset and frightened.

"If they had written a story about this base, it would be one of the worse breaches of our national security in the history of our country and you would have been tried as traitors. Now, I am going to give you a chance to redeem yourselves."

"Yes sir, anything, sir."

"Now listen carefully. Two of my men will visit you early in the morning before you come here. I want you to follow their instructions exactly as they tell you. They want you to identify the reporters to them. No one will know what you have done and it will be a great help to us."

"You are not going to shoot them, are you?" one of them said.

"That all depends, they may not be reporters but foreign spies and if they are we will shoot them."

The men were really scared now and wanted to leave.

"May we go now, sir?"

"I guess so as long as you understand what you have to do and I will remind you again not to talk about this place to anyone for any reason and that includes your family."

As the men were about to leave, I said, "Excuse me sir, may I ask the men a question?"

"Yes Mr Freeman, go ahead."

"You only found out about this job a couple of days ago and have only been here one day, how did the reporters know how to contact you and ask you to get them in here?"

"I think you had better sit down and explain this and it better be good," the captain said.

Now the men were really scared. They were all denying they told anyone.

"Well, someone must have talked," said the captain. "We will sit here until we have the facts."

They talked among themselves then one of them said, "I didn't mean any harm I only told my wife that we were going to come out here to do a big job. She works at the diner at the service center near the highway. She must have talked to a costumer. Please sir, she didn't know that she did anything wrong."

"All right give me your name and address and my men will interview her, probably this evening."

The men were really upset now.

"You are not going to arrest her, are you?"

"Nothing like that they will just want her to identify the costumer she talked to, that's all."

"May we go now, sir?"

"Yes, go on and do what my men tell you."

As they left Norman said, "After that episode I doubt if they will come back here."

"They will be back," I said. "There is too much money involved and I think they will behave themselves from now on."

Then Lieutenant Dickson arrived, he had been in town all day.

"Well, I finally finished all the paper work. Had a nice lunch at the golf club and no I didn't play, but I was tempted. I saw two of our men in town, what are they doing here?"

"Thanks for reminding me," Norman said. "I almost forgot to give them their instructions. I will meet you at the mess later."

"We talked to Dickson for a while, he wanted to know what the mattresses were for and we told him about the episode with Lieutenant Hartley," he said. "I am glad someone put him in his place, but I know him he will not stop until he has his revenge. You have not heard the last of him."

Norman came out of his office and we all walked to the mess tent

The navy crew was there so we all sat together and swapped war stories. As we left Sam said that they would start on the sphere tomorrow after breakfast, the gas test was better than expected and they hoped the test tomorrow would be the same.

Back at the house Norman told us that Lance Corporal Muller had been transferred to Canberra and was cooperating with the officials there.

We sat around and played cards for a while but it had been a long day and we all retired early.

The navy crew was already at the mess when I arrived for breakfast. They began by telling me how good the food was when Ivan came along to say good morning.

"Here is the reason for the good food, I said, why not take him back to Melbourne when you leave here?"

They had a good laugh and thanked Ivan for looking after them so well.

"Let's go we have work to do," Sam said.

Sam the two apprentices and I walked to the shed and Fred and Harry came in the ute. I opened the doors and dismissed the sentry and told him to come back after lunch. We went inside and looked around and while the men unloaded their equipment Sam said,

"You set this up like an expert, I have seen a lot of foolish things done with explosives because the people handling in did not know what they were doing but this is done by the book."

"Thank you, I was well trained and have a great respect for explosives."

"We can take the top outside layer of explosives off without any problem but when we expose the plutonium we will have to wear protective clothing, including breathing gear and we have to seal the plutonium from the atmosphere because anything that comes in contact with it becomes contaminated."

"How do you know all this?" I asked.

"The manual came yesterday by courier and I read it last night, so now I am an expert."

"I guessed as much but I never had anything to do with plutonium, so it is good to know we are doing it right."

"There is a special container coming to ship it in, we will have it all ready and ship it as soon as the container arrives."

"That is a good idea, get it out of here, half the world would kill us all to get their hands on it," I said.

"Let's get started," Sam said. "We will take the sections out and wrap them in plastic and cover the exposed ones with plastic sheet and sandbags to keep it sealed. How many segments are there?"

"I don't know, I never opened a sphere."

"Anyway, we will bag them and store them here until we transport them to the sandpit."

"How about the road, is it ready?" I asked.

"The engineer fellow said it would be ready by noon today. Also, we will need another ute to move these things."

"No problem I will see to it right away."

"Well not right now we need you here to open the sphere."

It did not take very long to open the sphere. The first segment was hard to get out because they were so close together but when we got the first one out the rest were easy. We soon had a dozen of them laid out on the floor wrapped in plastic bags.

"That will do for today," Sam said. "It will take us the rest of the day to dispose of these. You can get us a truck now while we finish up here."

I went to the compound and found a ute and a guard. On the way back the guard said, "I was just coming to get you, they want you at the house."

"Drop me off on the way."

The sergeant was talking to Dickson and the captain when I came in. The captain was reassuring the sergeant that everything would be all right. The sergeant thanked him and left.

"What is that all about?" I asked.

"Your shakedown of Lieutenant Hartley has backfired," said Dickson. "He cannot get back at you so he is taking it out on the sergeant. He has charged him with insubordination, clamming he has turned the men against him. He has also charged the two guards at the front gate for trying to prevent him from entering the base. Every outfit has one of these guys, they are former school yard bullies."

"Do you want me to testify on behalf of the sergeant?"

"No, you cannot do that," Norman said. "You are not even here officially and we do not want anyone to know who you are. I will call the colonel and by the time the inquiry comes around he will be guarding kangaroos in Arnhem Land. Leave with me."

"I called you here to tell you that our lads have the reporters in custody and are going to transport them to Sydney. They caught them this morning at the junk yard waiting for the men to leave with the truck.

They are a couple of freelance guys looking for something to sell. They will keep them for a couple of days and read the security act to them, I am sure they will not bother us again. Would you please go to the mess and bring me back a large coffee. I am becoming addicted to it.”

“With pleasure I will bring back a pot for both of you.”

On the way I met Lieutenant Fitzroy.

“I was just coming to find you. The road is finished and we want to start tearing down the buildings.”

“You are ahead of schedule, I said. Come with me and we will tell the junk men to start cleaning out the small shed and the lean to and you can start on them.”

“We are nearly finished here. One of them said we will dump this load and start on the shed as soon as we return.”

“Tell the lieutenant when you are ready to work on the barn and his men will help you take it down,” I said.

In the distance there was a sound like a thunderclap and the ground vibrated slightly. The junk men all stopped and looked around.

“You didn’t hear anything,” I said with a smile.
“Just ignore it. It is a long way from here.”

I said to Fitzroy, “I am going to take some coffee to the captain and then I will meet you at the mess and we will have a cup.”

“Good idea.”

Fitzroy was waiting for me at the mess.

“We are going to start on the barn as soon as the men leave. The heavy equipment will move out soon and the rest will work till the weekend taking down the buildings. Then we will have a few days off and then come back and finish the job. You guys should be nearly finished by them.”

“Yes, we should. These navy men know their business and it will only take them a few days to finish up.”

We sat there drinking our coffee and I told him what Hartley had done.

“I am not surprised. I hope the colonel has enough pull to take care of him. It will make a lot of guys very happy.”

After we finished, I asked Fitzroy if he would give me a lift to the sandpit to check on the navy crew.

"That is a good idea I would like to see them in action."

"Good, I will grab a flask of coffee and take it out to them."

"Thanks for the coffee it hit the spot," said Sam. "We are just about to detonate another one."

The younger apprentice was walking back from setting up a charge. We watched as he prepared to blow the charge, it went off with a mighty roar.

"Wow," said Fitzroy. "That is an all-mighty blast."

Just then a ute came up with another charge.

SAM said to Fitzroy, "I will explain the procedure to you and you can help because it is my turn."

They got into the truck and drove into the pit, unloaded the charge and placed on the rock.

Sam said, "Before we got in the truck, I disconnected the leads from the firing mechanism and earthed them. That way we will not have an accident. Now we attach the detonator to the leads and go back to the barrier and set it off." Sam attached the leads to the control and handed it to Fitzroy.

"All you do is flip the safety cover and press the button. Wait, you have to call ';Fire in the hole' first."

Another loud blast and Fitzroy had a big grin on his face.

"That was super; I always wanted to do that. Thanks a lot."

"Glad to make your day," Sam said. "That's all for today. We will go back and have an early chow and get back to work."

"What is the rush?" I said. "Can it wait until tomorrow?"

"The transporter will arrive sometime tomorrow and it will have a container to carry he plutonium and I want to have it all ready to loan and get out of here."

"You will have to work all night," I said.

"Probably but I will have you to help."

"Thanks a lot, we will talk it over during chow. Come on let's go."

ON the way in Fitzroy said to me.

"You know I wanted to be in the demolition corps and even applied but there were no vacancies, so I went into construction instead. It was a lot of fun out there but I have got it out of my system now. Did you see that apprentice when he came up to hook up the wires? He was shaking and sweating that job is not for me."

"I know what you are saying. I always had that fear in the back of my mind so I did everything by the book so nothing would go wrong. Let's drive by the barn and see how things are going."

We pulled up at the barn but no one was there, so we went to where the junk men were working.

"We will be finished late this afternoon and it looks like we will not be coming back to take away the barn."

"Why not?" I asked.

"I don't know all the officer said was that they changed their minds and the barn was not coming down."

"Come on we will go talk to the captain."

We walked into the house and one of the clerks said, "The lieutenant is in the office, sir."

"Where is the captain?" I said.

"He is not here, sir."

We went into the office and Lieutenant Dickson and Sergeant Jones were there.

"I suppose you have heard the news," Dickson said.

"Yes, what has happened with the barn?"

"Oh that, I thought you had heard about Captain Williamson."

"No, we haven't," I said.

"Well, he has been called to Sydney to interview Fowler. The colonel was going to go but they have sited Bluey so he is staying in Rockhampton to organize his capture."

"We go off for an hour and all hell breaks loose," I said. "We came here to ask about the barn."

"OK, we will start with the barn. We received a memo from local area command not to remove any of the buildings here on the base. They have decided to turn this place into a training camp."

"What do you mean by a training camp?"

"It is Lieutenant Hartley's idea. He believes this is an ideal site for a military police anti-terrorist training camp. Headquarters have been looking for a location for a while and when we finish here they will come and appraise the site. I understand it has a good chance because of the location and it has a good water source and is rather isolated.'

"It looks like I am out of a job," Lieutenant Fitzroy said.

"Now tell us about Captain Williamson," I said.

"As you know Fowler's sister has been rescued from Burma. She and her family are in Perth and the colonel thinks that Fowler will talk once he knows his sister is safe. When the captain interviews him he will arrange a phone call to his sister to prove that she is safe in this country. The colonel is afraid that the general will get to the depot before we can find it and is hoping that Fowler will give us the location."

"Let's hope so," I said. "And what about Bluey?"

"He was spotted on the Capricorn Highway at a service station near Emerald with a woman presumably Hazel. They filled up wilt petrol, had something to eat and headed East towards Rockhampton. That was a couple of hours ago, so I suppose they have them by now. We should hear about it soon."

Sergeant Jones said, "The way things are moving we should be finished here in a few days."

"It looks like I am finished here now," Lieutenant Fitzroy said. "I will have to make a few phone calls to find out what I am going to do; I won't leave before morning so I will see you all in the mess then."

"Speaking of the mess I am supposed to be helping the Navy Crew with the sphere so I will have to leave too. Keep me informed of any developments."

On the way out one of the clerks said, "Mr Freeman, there is a package here for the director of operations from the atomic energy commission."

I opened it and there was a pamphlet on plutonium and a note asking if they could have a few grams for experiments. Enclosed was a small safety capsule for radioactive samples. I put it in my room and headed to the mess.

Norman Fowler was sitting in a small room at a small table on a hard chair.

He was worn out from all the interviews and questions.

He was thinking of the mess he had made but was determined not to get his sister involved. I maybe in a lot of trouble but I am going to make sure Henrietta and the kids are kept out of it.

His reverie was broken when the door opened.

"Mr Herbert, Fowler, I am Captain Williamson of the intelligence corps. I have some interesting information for you."

"I do not care who you are or what you have to say. Go away I have nothing more to say."

"Mr Fowler, you have important information that concerns the wellbeing of our country I suggest that you cooperate with us."

"This is the last time I will say it or anything else, go Away."

"Mr Fowler we need this information and we need it now, please cooperate."

"Are you going to torture me to get it?"

"No sir, if you tell us when and where you found the weapon, we will let you talk to your sister."

Fowler jumped out of the chair and shouted.

"You are fiends if they find out about my sister, they will kill her and her family. If they are harmed I will hold the government responsible."

Fowler was sweating and shaking and talking loudly, nearly crying.

"Calm down sir and listen to what I have to say. We have your sister on the phone she is safe. If you tell us where the depot is, you can talk to her."

Fowler glared at the captain then said.

"You are a low dirty scum they listen to every overseas phone call and read every letter that is why I do not correspond with them. You have murdered them."

"I assure you sir, they are safe back here in Australia. Now tell me what we need to know then you can talk to them."

"I do not believe you it is a trick."

"Come with me, sir."

They walked into another larger room. There were two guards there.

"I will let you listen to your sister's voice but you cannot speak to her until you tell us where the depot is.

The Captain picked up the phone and spoke,

"Mrs Ambani, I have your brother here please tell him that you are save here in Australia."

"Norman is that you? We were rushed out of Burma. We are in a Perth hotel. Say hi to Raffi and Sharon."

At the sound of their voices Norman broke down. He quickly gave the location of the depot then took the phone from the captain.

Bluey and Hazel had been fossicking in the digs at Ruby Vale near Emerald. They were sitting on a friends claim while he went to the hospital after a fall with a suspected broken ankle. They had only thought they would be there for a few days but that turned out to be nearly three weeks. They were glad to be on their way back to Rockhampton. They left in the morning and drove through Emerald and stopped at the service station on the highway.

They took their time and enjoyed their lunch because it would only take a couple of hours to reach home. Hazel was in the ladies and Bluey went out to fill the ute with petrol. When he went to pay the attendant said to him

"Did those two guys find you?"

"What guys?"

"These two guys were here about a week ago looking for you. They came back a couple of days later."

"What did they want?"

"I don't know, maybe they have a job for you."

"Well, if they come back tell them I will be at Hazel's place for a while until I find another job."

"I'll do that. Have a good trip."

As he left the manager came up and asked the attendant.

"Was that the Bluey bloke they are looking for?"

"Yes sir, that is him."

"I have to make a phone call. I am to call as soon as I spot him."

ABOUT a half hour later on a quiet stretch of the road Hazel said, "What is that noise?"

"I don't know, maybe we have blown a tire."

As they were talking an army helicopter flew low over them. It flew ahead of them and turned and a man appeared in the open door and signaled them to pull off the road. They pulled up and stopped and the chopper landed nearby. While they sat there wondering what was going on two soldiers jumped out and hurried over to them.

"Are you Fredrick Dawson, sir?"

"Yes I am, what is this about?"

"I must insist that you come with us, immediately."

"What in the helicopter?"

"Yes sir. Please follow me."

Dumbfounded Bluey got out of the ute and walked to the chopper with the soldier. The other one spoke to Hazel.

"Miss Clark, we are going to interview Mr Dawson. No harm will come to him as long as he cooperates and he should be home in a couple of days. Please wait here, a highway patrol officer is on the way and they will escort you home. Thank you for your cooperation."

The soldier hurried back to the helicopter and it immediately took off.

The helicopter caused a traffic jam on the highway as the motorist slowed down the look. Hazel sat dazed in the ute trying to understand what had just happened. She did not notice the patrolman until he spoke.

"Are you all right, miss?"

"Sorry officer, I did not see you standing there."

"I am to escort you to your home in Rockhampton. Give me a few minutes to get the traffic moving and we will be on our way."

A few minutes later he returned and said, "All clear we can leave now."

"I am all right and can get home by myself."

"Yes miss, but my orders are to see you safely home and that is what I will do. Please follow me and I will take you to your door."

Hazel followed the police car along the highway. She was confused and mixed up. She could not understand what had happened, a little while ago she and Bluey were driving along happy and talking and now she was all alone and confused. The police car drove up her street and slowed down then drove off. How did he know where I lived? She thought.

Bluey sat between the two soldiers. It was rather noisy so no one spoke. The flight was not very long and they landed at the helicopter area at the airport. A car was waiting for them and they moved quickly to it and drove away heading towards the city. The car turned into a large motel and stopped in a section that was that was closed off with no parking signs. The driver got out and went up to one of the doors and knocked. Then the other two got out and escorted Bluey from the car and into the room.

The room did not look like a motel room, the regular furniture had been removed and tables and chairs were in their place. Soldiers were sitting at the tables either talking on telephones or typing. One of the men walked across the room and knocked on the door. An officer Came out and walked up to Bluey.

"Good afternoon, sir, I am Lieutenant Rodgers, would you please come with me."

They went into the next room. There was a large table in the middle of the room with a few chairs scattered around the room. The Lieutenant pointed to a chair and Bluey sat down.

A few minutes later another officer came out of another room which appeared to be the kitchen.

"Good afternoon, sir. I am Colonel Martin the officer in charge of this operation. I understand that you are Fredrick Henry Dawson, a jackeroo of no fixed address, currently residing with a Hazel Clark of Rockhampton."

"Yes sir, that is right."

"Good. Before we begin, I would like to emprises the importance of this operation. All of these plus nearly fifty personnel in all have been looking for you for two weeks. You have some very important information that we need. I must warn you that we know most of the answers to the questions that I will ask you. If you fully cooperate with us, you could be out of here this evening or tomorrow. If you do not cooperate you may never see the real world again. Do you understand?"

"No sir, I do not understand. I do not know why I am here and I do not have any information that anyone would be interested in."

"Let me clear this up for you in a few words. I understand that you know a Norman Fowler, is that right?"

"Yes sir, I know Norman Fowler, so what?"

"Now this is important, tell me the exact time and place you last saw Mr Fowler."

"That is easy, it was just over a year ago at the Top Springs Roadhouse on the Buntline Highway. We had been fossicking in the desert in the dry creek beds and had pulled in there for supplies."

"Do you know where Fowler went when you parted at the roadhouse?"

"Not really but I have a good idea. We had to go through the aboriginal reserve along the highway and Fowler wanted to come back there and look around he was sure it was a good spot. You could go on some reserves but I knew that they were very strict there and it wasn't worth while getting caught."

While they were talking Lieutenant Rodgers left the room.

"Let's stop now and have some lunch. I am sure you are hungry."

Lieutenant Rodgers went into the next room and found the appropriate map and studied it for a few minutes and then called headquarters. He gave them the coordinates from the map and said, "That is in the general area that we thought. I am sure we will find it now."

He went back into the room and an orderly brought in some food and they ate their lunch.

Later the colonel said, "Start from the beginning and tell us all you know about Norman Fowler."

"Our fathers worked on the same station. We went to school together. We did not hang around together because he was older than I was and he played football. His father was a good cattleman and he raised high quality cattle on his farm. We met off and on over the years and we met again last year. We decided to go prospecting together. We headed West and fossicked around for about three months. In all we did fairly well but only little bits here and there. Fowler was looking for the big lode that would make him rich. When he saw the area in the reserve, he knew that would be a good place to explore. I did not want to go into the reserve and when we stopped at the roadhouse, I saw a chance to leave."

"While he was having a shower and I was loading up the ute I met a mate who was going to work in one of the mines and he asked me to go along with him. I made a deal with Fowler, I gave him half of my poke and the ute and we parted friends. That is the last I saw of him."

"That is one of the reasons why we could not find you. We were looking for your old ute. What happened after you left Fowler at the roadhouse?"

"I went to work in the mine. You only stay for three or four months but the work was easy and the pay was good so I stayed for nearly a year. I bought the new ute from a fellow who lost all his money gambling and on the way back East I did some fencing and roof shooting on a station for a couple of months. When I returned here, I met up with Hazel and we went pig shooting with her brother near Emerald. On the way back I met an old friend who had to go to the hospital and he asked us to watch his ruby diggings while he was away. He was away a lot longer than expected and when he returned we headed home and them that is when your men found us."

"Now that I have told you everything, I would like to know what has Fowler done to cause so much trouble?"

"I cannot tell you the whole story, all I can say is when Fowler left you, he went back into the desert and stumbled on an old forgotten army storage depot full of explosives. Instead of informing the proper authorities about it he tried to sell some of the material to some foreign criminals. He was soon found out and is now in custody. While we were checking his background, we found your letter and that is how you became involved. Give us a little time to check out your story and if you are not involved in his illegal deal, we will let you go."

"I have told you the truth and all I know. I have no knowledge of this army depot thing."

"If that is so you will soon be out of here. That will be all for now, you will find some refreshments in the kitchen. Please confine yourself to these two rooms and do not try to leave. We will get back to you shortly."

The colonel and the lieutenant got up and left Bluey on his own.

When they entered the next room one of the clerks said, "Excuse me sir, here is an urgent telex from Captain Williamson."

Lieutenant Rodgers read the message and said to the Colonel.

"Fowler has told the captain where the depot is and the army are on their way there now. He also says that he has not seen Dawson since they parted at the roadhouse over a year ago."

"That is all good news. Call a cab for Dawson and inform the boys at the farm to meet us in Darwin as soon as possible, then shut this operation down and send everybody home."

After a quick bite, I joined the boys at the shed and apologized for being late.

"We are about to take down the inner core," Fred said. "The first group is getting into their contamination gear. They will be the only ones allowed in the shed while the plutonium is exposed."

"What are we going to do?"

"You and I are going to pull the other weapon out of the shed and get it ready to be transported. Then we will take a turn at the sphere because it is hot and trying in those suits. We will move the weapon near the barn there is plenty of room there."

It seemed strange to be taking orders instead of giving them but these guys know what they are doing. We walked to the smaller shed and opened the door. The apprentice came up with the ute and we attached the trailer yoke to it.

"Take it very slowly," I said.

We slowly moved along the lane way to the front of the barn.

"What do we have for tools?" I asked.

"There is a toolbox in the tray of the ute, and a couple of containers to put the detonators in.

I suppose I will find a couple of rolls of sealing tape too."

"Of course, I was waiting for you to ask."

IT was late in the afternoon and getting near dark and turning cold.

"If all goes well, we should finish within the hour," I said.

We took off the canvas cover and removed the struts. The weapon looked bran new just like it just came off the assembly line.

"How can something so horrible look so good?" Fred said.

"Find a large hex spanner and take off the rear hatch; I want to make sure there is no fuse."

"How will I know?"

"You cannot miss it is as large as a fuel drum and takes up the whole rear cavity. I will check the nose and then we can remove the detonators."

The fuse was out and the front cavity was sealed and the safety plugs were in the nose.

"We can take off the side panels and remove the detonators."

It did not take long Fred knew what he was doing.

"All that is left is to disconnect the capacitors in case they have any residual charge in them."

While I did that Fred and the apprentice taped over the detonator holes and any other opening they could find. By now it was nearly dark and we used the lights on the ute to finish putting the cover back on.

"We cannot leave it here all night let's put it near the big shed so the sentry can guard it," I said.

We hooked it to the ute and walked it to the shed.

"I will be glad to see the last of that monster," I said.

We called into the shed and Harry answered.

"We have exposed the plutonium core. We will remove it and pack it and you can come in and finish the job."

"Can you cut a little chip off? I want to send it to the scientist at the atomic energy lab. I will go get the container."

I went back to the house to get the container. Ian was there.

"They have Bluey, he is in custody in Rockhampton and Fowler told the captain where the depot is and the army is there now. They were searching near there."

"You know what that means?" I said. "Tomorrow will be our last day here."

"That would be great but I think you are stretching it a little."

"Have I been wrong yet?" I said as I left with the container.

I went back to the shed and tossed the container to Sam.

"Is that all you want?"

"If we give them any more, they will make their own bomb," I said jokingly.

Soon Sam, Harry and the apprentice came out. They went around to the side of the shed to a hose and washed their suits.

"Do you have any instructions for us?" I asked.

"No, just finish the job and get everything ready for shipment tomorrow. We will see you in the morning; we are finished for the night."

Harry, the apprentice and I put on aprons, long gloves and respirator masks just in case. In the shed was a large plastic container that looked like an oversized esky. The plutonium core was in there and sitting on top of it was the container with the small piece for the lab boys.

It took us about an hour to finish removing the explosive charges and sealing them in plastic bags. We placed the pieces of the aluminum core next to the esky and Harry said, "Looks like we can call it a night."

I looked around the shed and there were large plastic bags of explosive everywhere.

"You will be here for days getting rid of that lot," I said.

"Piece of cake," Harry said. "We will do them three at a time and be done by tomorrow afternoon."

"Three at a time, that will be one enormous explosion. Someone is bound to complain."

"Let them by the time someone comes around we will be long gone from here. I want to catch up with the transporter and sail back to Melbourne on the minesweeper. A nice sea voyage will do me a lot of good, why don't you come along?"

"I would love to but I am sure the colonel has other plans for me. I bet we will all meet again in the middle of the desert in a few days. So, enjoy your holiday while you can."

"Lieutenant Dickson told me you were full of doomsday scenarios, now I understand what he meant. Thanks for spoiling my holiday."

"That is not the worst of it, once you are out there in the hot dry sand hills you will not be able to leave until the dastardly job is finished and that could take years."

"Shut up, I don't want to hear any more of your doomsday predictions."

"I don't mean to upset you but you have to remember I have been one hundred percent accurate so far."

"Now I won't sleep at all tonight."

It was warm while we were working but it was cold when we closed the doors of the shed.

"I will see you in the morning, sleep well," I said with a smile.

I spoke to the sentry as I left.

"Looks like we will finish here tomorrow and you guys will move on."

"Well sir, it seems some of us will stay on here. This is going to be a permanent base and someone has to guard it. At least we will have new trucks, some of the guys left this morning to drive them back. We hope to get ten new Land Rovers with heaters in them."

There was no one in the house when I got there and the fire was almost out, so I stoked up the fire and put in a couple of large pieces of wood. I was not tired so I decided to go to the mess and have a late snack. There were a few guards in the mess sitting at a table talking and then I spotted one of the clerks sitting alone reading a magazine and drinking a beer.

"Good evening Mr Freeman, would you like a beer?"

"That's a good idea; I will get it because I would like a sandwich and some potato chips to go with it."

I came back in a few minutes and sat down with him.

"Where are the lieutenant and the sergeant?"

"They were invited to town for a meal with the police Sergeant. I think he has heard rumors about this place and he wants to know what is going on."

"That is his job. What is the news with the colonel?"

"It looks like we will be moving out very soon either tomorrow or the next day for sure. The captain is not coming back. He is going to Sydney to take charge of Fowlers sister and her family. The other clerk and I will return to headquarters as soon as we shut down the teletypes. You and the Lieutenant and the Sargent will probably leave soon to meet up with the colonel, probably in Darwin."

While we were talking Ivan came up to the table and we both said, "What are you doing here?"

The clerk excused himself and left and Ivan sat down.

"Looks like our holiday is over," Ivan said.

"Yes, after tomorrow there will only be a few military police here. Will you stay here?"

"I have been asked to take charge of the new kitchen when the new base is operating. Things will be slow for a while so I can have some leave time before I start."

"There you go, boss of your own kitchen. You are moving up in the army. Next you will be head of catering for the whole command."

"A couple of years ago I would have jumped at a chance like this but now I don't know. After being here and cooking for you and the boys I think my talents are waisted cooking army food. I wrote to my rich uncle in Melbourne a couple of weeks ago and he thinks that a chain of boutique bakeries is a great idea and he will help me get started. So, I have decided to resign and go into business and I want you to come with me and be an equal partner. What do you say?"

"I am really flattered that you would consider asking me, but my life is in turmoil right now and I do not know what I am doing. I may be sent home tomorrow or I maybe still on this project next year. So, I cannot give you an answer."

"You are the one who inspired me to do some real cooking and you gave me all those recopies. I need you to inspire me in the new business."

"I understand what you are saying but the best I can do is have you give me an address and I will look you up when this is all over."

"You promise you will?"

"Yes, I promise."

We talked for a little while then Ivan said.

"I have to get back to the kitchen I am planning a big party for tomorrow before you all leave, Thanks for the promise."

It was late now and as I was leaving the mess Sam walked in.

"Thought you were tired and was going to bed."

"I had a shower and it woke me up. Then I went to the clerk's office to see if there were any messages. I have been in there for an hour. Come and have a beer with me and I will tell you all about it."

"The minesweeper has arrived. It sailed up the Clarence River to Grafton for a good will visit. It will come back down and visit Yamba and Iluka and wait for the cargo. The transporter is on its way. It is coming by the back roads and will be here before noon tomorrow. We will load it and it will leave late in the afternoon."

"I suppose you will leave with it."

"I hope so but we have to dispose of all those segments first."

"Do not worry about them, Fred has a plan."

"He has, we will talk about that in the morning."

"I think his plan will wake you up."

"While we are disposing of the explosives, I would like you to supervise the loading of the weapon."

We sat there talking and sipping our beer then Sam told me about the convoy.

"There are twelve vehicles in this convoy. It is causing a traffic jam everywhere it goes. That is why they are taking the back roads. Even some news reporters are following it. Can you imagine this monster of a truck and its support truck plus an assortment of vehicles full of soldiers with weapons? It must be quite a sight."

We were finding it too hard to talk any more and headed towards our beds. On the way out I said, "By the way Ivan is planning a party for tomorrow. I suppose it will during morning coffee time. So set your schedule for a break about then."

When I got to the house Ian and Dickson were there.

"We just came it," Ian said. "Those policemen can really throw a party."

"How did you get back? Surly you did not drive."

"One of the sober policemen drove us," Dickson said.

On my way to bed I said, "Ivan the cook is throwing a party during morning coffee. Hope you are sober enough by then to enjoy it."

Even though it had been a long hard day and I was tired I could not sleep. I was thinking about where we were going and what Ivan had said. When morning came I was tempted to roll over and sleep in but I remembered that Lieutenant Fitzroy would be waiting at the mess, so I reluctantly got out of bed.

DAWN was cold and brisk and by the time I reached the mess I was wide awake I found Fitzroy in the chow line getting his breakfast.

"I will get a table," and went and sat down.

"That's right, Sir Lord Fauntleroy does not have to get his own food like ordinary people do," he said as he sat down.

"Maybe someday you will work your way up the pecking ladder and have a batman like the colonel," I said.

One of the cooks came over with a tray and said, "Good morning Mr. Freeman Sargent Dorvick is busy in the kitchen so he sent me with your breakfast. I hope you like it." I just smiled at Fitzroy.

I had barely taken a bite when there was an almighty boom. The ground shook and the tent flapped from the pressure wave. Everybody in the tent looked around to see if there was any damage.

"That will be Harry and his quick way of getting rid of the explosive," I said. "I don't think he will try that again."

"They came around early to pick up the trucks and I insisted that my men drive them because I did not want to lose them. We will be leaving today and the trucks are going with us."

"You are playing right into their hands. They can move three cores at once, and I bet that is what that explosion was."

Just then Sam came into the mess.

"What was that? Where are my men? Did you authorize a big blow like that?"

"Relax Sam, that is just Harry trying out his idea to get rid of all the cores before noon. Sit down and have some breakfast."

"I have to get out there, will one of you take me?"

"Relax he won't try that one again. I bet his ears are still ringing."

I signaled one of the cooks to bring Sam some coffee.

"Sit here and wait for the transporter, it will be here soon. Harry knows what he is doing."

Sam agreed and settled down and the cook brought a tray with the same breakfast as I had,

"We will have some more coffee," I said

While Sam was eating, I asked Fitzroy what his plans were for the day and where he would be transferred to.

"I have all day so I am in no hurry to leave and I would like have a look at this transporter that will be here today."

"That is good," I said. "Because Ivan has been cooking all-night to give us a farewell party and I would not want you to miss it."

Just then there was a loud succession of booms.

"I told you that Harry would not blow three at once again. That time he shot off six. It won't take him long to finish at that rate."

Sam did not like but he had to agree.

"If I go out there I will have to put a stop to that, so I think I will take your advice and wait for the transporter."

"That is good thinking, have some more coffee."

"You were going to tell us where you will be posted when you leave here," I said to Fitzroy.

"I am going back to university to continue my degree. When I finish I will have a masters in structural and design engineering. I usually only get in one or two semesters because I get sent somewhere like I did here. But in a few years I will be a master engineer. Once I have my degree I will be assigned to a project and have a desk. Then I can settle down in one spot."

Just then another series of explosions echoed through the camp. Also, Lieutenant Dickson and Sergeant Jones came into the mess.

"What is going on?" Dickson said. "That first explosion knocked me out of bed."

"They want to finish up today so they can leave with the convoy," Sam said.

"How long before they finish?" said Ian. "Those explosions make my headache."

"What do you expect when you party all night?"

We all sat and talked for a while and then I said to Sam.

"Let's go and check on the cargo and make sure that everything is ready."

"Good idea, it will give us something to do, anyone else want to join us?"

"Before you go," Dickson said. "Our orders came through this morning, we are going to meet the colonel in Darwin."

"How soon do we leave?" I asked.

"As soon as I can arrange your transportation."

"Make it late this afternoon. We have a farewell party and we need time to pack."

Sam, Ian and I walked towards the shed. There was another series of explosions.

"They cannot have many left," Sam said.

As we arrived at the shed Fred and the apprentice were standing in the doorway.

"We have two shots left," Fred said. "Won't be long now."

The three utes pulled up and Fred and the apprentice began loading them.

"How many cores are you putting on?" asked Sam

"Two to a truck. They are well packed."

"I think you had better relieve Harry, so you two go back with the trucks and send them back here. We don't want anyone getting overconfident."

We looked around in the shed.

"There isn't much left,' said Ian.

In the middle of the room were the large container with the plutonium core and two smaller containers with the detonators in them. The last six chargers were in plastic bags lined along the wall and other than the aluminum castings all that was there were a lot of sandbags lying in piles around the floor.

"A big difference than when we first arrived," said Ian.

"Looks like everything is ready," Harry said.

My mind flashed back to the first time I looked into this shed. All the surprises drama and decisions that were made are all in the past and this place just looks like an ordinary old shed with a few objects lying around in it. We are all done here but what is in store for us tomorrow?

There was a noise outside and the first truck of the convoy had arrived. Harry went out to greet the men. Soon there was a row of trucks parked in the compound.

The transporter was a very impressive vehicle. It was the largest ridged truck I had ever seen. The wheels were large and heavy two front wheels on each side and double dual rear wheels. A large cab over the front wheels then a folded crane behind the cab, then what looked like a large steel bathtub on wheels.

"It was designed to move old torpedoes," Harry said. "If they went off they would only make a lot of noise, all the force would go upward."

"It looks like it has never been used," I said.

"It has been modified and painted just for this mission. It has had a few rough cargos."

There was another series of explosions and the new crew looked around.

"What are you doing here?" one of them asked

"We are playing war games with live ammo," Harry said.

The utes arrived with Sam and he said, "This is the last shot so we will be able to leave with the convoy." They all stood around talking for a while, and then Sam said.

"We all want to witness the last shot, so we will get organized here and then go out to see the fireworks. Hold things up Harry, until we get there."

"After the fireworks we will have our party," I said. "That will be a great way to finish up here."

They all stood around while the cover was removed from the weapon so they could all have a look at it.

"When I was in the service I would have had to shoot all of you to prevent you from looking at that. It was classified top secret."

After a few minutes one of them operated the crane and lifted the weapon. I showed them how to disconnect the yoke from the trailer and they put the whole thing into the tub. There were all kinds of anchor points inside the tub and in no time the weapon was secure. Then in went the container with the plutonium core. The rest went into the support vehicle. When everything was loaded they brought out some large canvas bags.

"They are spacers," Sam said. "They will fit them between the cargo and blow them up to separate them."

"While they are doing that, I will inform Ivan of our plans and Ian can inform the lieutenant and we all can go out to the pit to watch the fireworks."

"Everything is ready," Ivan said.

"Not quite, we are all going to the pit to watch the last explosion. Want to come along?"

"I might as well if the party isn't going to start until the fireworks are over."

"We will have to find a lift," I said.

We went outside and Lieutenant Fitzroy was driving by.

"Where are you going?"

"I am looking for my men."

"I know where they are." give us a lift and I will take you to them."

"Where are we going?"

"To the sandpit."

As we drew near the sandpit it looked like the whole base was there and half of the local town. There must have been forty to fifty vehicles including a couple of police cars. We parked and had to walk a way to the edge of the crowd.

"I hope someone is guarding the gate," I said.

We found a place to view the scene and someone said.

"We can start now the big boss is here."

There were three loud toots on a whistle then they started counting, five, four, three, two, one. Then as one the crowd shouted, "Fire in the hole!"

There was a slight pause and then boom, boom, boom, boom, and then a slight pause and then a terrific *boom*. A large column of sand shot up in the air and everyone felt the shock wave as it passed by. There was a few seconds of silence and them a great roar of applause from the crowd. The talk amongst them was, great, wonderful, never seen anything like that. As we walked back to the truck.

Ivan said, "What am I going to do? I figured that there would be about fifty for the party, I cannot cater to this mob."

"Don't worry, most of them have to get back to their duties. Just wait until things settle down and then we will start the party."

Later, when we entered the mess the talk was still about the spectacular event. We walked to a group where the police and Lieutenant Dickson were talking. Ivan stayed with us for a few minutes and then headed for the kitchen. There was a long table set up in the middle of the hall with plates and cutlery at each end. Then the kitchen staff came out with platters of food. Then Ivan came out with a large cake and placed it in the middle of the table. It was decorated with a large 'Farewell' on it.

On each side was placed a tub of ice cream. We all applauded and picked up a plate and walked around the table choosing what we wanted, we stood and talked and enjoyed the food and each other's company and after a while Lieutenant Dickson asked for quiet so he could speak.

"As acting commander of this operation, I would like to thank all of you for the successful conclusion to this operation. It has been a long hard and stressful job but a very successful one."

"I would like to thank the military police for keeping us secure. the local police for their cooperation. The engineers and epically the navy. Without their help we would be here until next year cleaning up this mess. Most of all I want to thank Sergeant Ivan Dorvick and his crew for keeping up the moral. This is the best food I have ever had in my years in the army. Also thank you for the great party."

There was a lot of cheering and clapping and the lieutenant held up his hand for silence.

"Today will be the last day here for a lot of us, so I would like to say goodbye and thank you all again. Finally (a groan front the crowd), without the expert help from our civilian consultant Dave Freeman we would have blown ourselves to hell and the operation would have been a disaster."

Sergeant Jones came up to me and said, "What does it feel like to be a hero?"

"Not very good. He didn't have to say that."

"Well, that is what everyone thinks."

"I only did what I was asked to do."

"The trouble is you will never get a metal because no one will ever know what we did here. By the way say your goodbyes because we leave here early this afternoon for Brisbane and take the evening flight to Darwin."

"We cannot drive from here to Brisbane it that time."

"We are taking a charter flight from the local airstrip at four o'clock."

"It will only take a few minutes to pack because I only have one bag."

I wandered through the crowd shaking hands and saying goodbye. When I got to the navy crew they were getting ready to leave so I walked to their vehicles with them we all shook hands and said goodbye. With the extra men there were no empty seats in any of the vehicles. I stood in the driveway and watched them leave. Then I went back to the mess most of them were gone when I returned. I saw Lieutenant Fitzroy and the Security Sargent talking so I went over with them.

"It was a great party," said Fitzroy. "When are you leaving?"

"Not long after lunch. We are going to Darwin to meet up with the colonel and who knows what he has instore for us."

"I am all packed and ready to leave. I have a couple of weeks leave before I start the next semester at college."

"What about you, Sergeant, where are you going?"

"Looks like I will be here for a while until they decide what to do with this place. I have signed up for NCO school and hope to start in the next class."

"At least you guys know what you are going to do; I have no idea what the colonel is going to do."

"It could be another great adventure," Fitzroy said.

We shook hands and said goodbye and they left.

I looked around the mess and saw Ivan. He signaled me to sit at a table and in a few minutes came over with a tray.

"The travelers last meal," he said. "When do you leave?"

"In a couple of hours."

"What about you?"

"I have two weeks left before my enlistment is up so I will stay here and organize the new crew and then take a few days leave, then end up in Melbourne. Why don't you come with me?"

"You know I cannot. I have been ordered to Darwin with the colonel and who knows how long I will be there. I have your address and will contact you when I can."

I was not very hungry but I sat there and ate and talked with Ivan. Then we said our goodbyes and I left the mess for the last time. I wandered around the area looking at the empty shed and remembering all the drama that had taken place here. When I arrived at the house a truck was parked near the porch. Inside the clerks were packing things away and loading them on the truck. Dickson was stuffing papers into a briefcase.

"There you are. We are finished here and if you are ready, we can leave here now and spend a couple of hours in town."

"That is a good idea. It will only take me a few minutes to pack. Where is Ian? Is he coming with us?"

"He is outside burning some classified wastepaper. He will be ready when you are."

In no time at all we were in the station wagon and headed down the drive. One of the clerks was driving, Ian was in the front with him and Dickson and I were in the rear seats and the back was full of our baggage. When we arrived at the gate I got out and said goodbye to the sentries.

"When we get to town Ralph will drop us off and wait for the truck and follow it to headquarters and we will take a cab to the airstrip."

"What about our luggage? Do we have to carry it around with us?"

"Good thought. Might as well take it to the airstrip? It is only a short distance from town."

It took about an hour to get to town and we drove to the airstrip. When we asked where we could leave our bags the pilot said.

"If you like we can leave right now and you can spend some time in Brisbane. There is a lot more to do there than here."

So, we packed our bags in the plane and took off for the big city.

WHEN the general, the cowboy, and Muller walked from the hire car office down the concourse to the main street Muller was looking for a way to escape. He knew he would be the next to get a bullet in the head. When the car pulled up to the curb, he saw his chance. He held the rear door open for the general and the cowboy walked around to the other rear door. He closed the door for the general and opened the front passenger door and said to the driver, "Let's go." He then slammed the door and turned and walked into the crowd and into the shopping mall. As he entered the mall he glanced around to see the car speed off in the traffic.

The general leaned back in the seat and rested for a few minutes. The cowboy was looking out of the window. They were well out of the city before either of them spoke.

"This great adventure did not turn out the way we expected," said the general. "We should get out of the country as soon as possible before they discover who we are."

"I agree," said the cowboy. "But we should go back to the depot and take a few nuclear cores with us. We have to make some profit out of this We have to pay Muller for his part in this operation. Isn't that right Muller? Muller? Muller are you asleep? Where the hell is he? He is gone."

"What do you mean he is gone?"

"He is not in the car, he is gone."

"That changes everything," the general said. "He will go to the police and they will hunt us down. We have to leave the country now."

"No, he will not go to the police, because he will go to jail too. No, he is afraid we would shoot him too. He will hide somewhere until he thinks it is safe and we have left the country. I think we still have time to get those cores and escape. Besides it will be two or three weeks before the next ship passes the coast so we might as well make use of the time."

"I hope you are right."

"We will rest in Brisbane for a day or two and then go to Darwin and organize a trip to the depot."

They were staying in the shipping company's private accommodation in Brisbane making plans for the trip to Darwin when the cowboy came in with a local newspaper.

"Look at this, we are in the newspaper. We are wanted for murder."

"That settles it we are getting out of the country now."

"Don't get all excited. They do not know who we are. They are looking for three men who left a hire car at an agency in Toowoomba two days ago. They only give a vague description of us and they have not identified the victim. We will leave for Darwin right away but we cannot fly or hire a car."

"How are we going to get there? Hitchhike?"

"No, I have an idea. Give me some money and I will be back in a little while with some transport. You pack our things and we will leave as soon as I return."

A while later the cowboy returned.

"Are you ready? Let's go."

At the curb was a rough looking Kombi Van.

"I got this from a backpacker. He was desperate to sell, we can go all the way to the depot in this and not have to stay in a motel so no one will see us."

They travelled without incident, sleeping at rest stops and eating and showers at service centers, until a couple of hours West of Mount Isa. When the Kombi broke down. They had to nurse it the rest of the way to Darwin.

"We will have to find another way to get to the depot," said the general. "This thing is junk."

In Darwin they stayed at the home of the manager of the Cowboys shipping company. He was not very pleased to see them. He told them that two inspectors from the immigration department had visited the office looking for illegal immigrants. They also checked his visa and they inquired about the cowboy. They wanted to know if he had visited that office recently.

"I told them that you have not been in this country for two years and there is no reason for you to visit because the business is doing well. They gave me a card and told me to contact them if you should arrive here."

"I am sure that you know better than to do that," the general said. "Remember you have family in Burma."

"We will only be here overnight," the cowboy said. "All we want is a little help from you."

"I will do whatever I can."

"Good. Get rid of that van and get us a vehicle that will travel over the back roads and not break down."

"I have a friend who has a car yard he will have something suitable."

"The sooner you get the car the sooner we will be gone and make sure that it cannot be traced back to you."

The manager returned a couple of hours later with an old beat-up four-wheel drive ute.

"It may not look like much but it is in good mechanical shape and will take you anywhere."

"It will do," the cowboy said. "But if it breaks down you will have to come out in the desert in your new BMW and rescue us. All we need now is a couple of jerry cans for fuel and a couple for water and we will be on our way."

THEY left Darwin late that evening and headed South towards the desert. The drive was uneventful until mid-morning the next day when the general started complaining.

"This thing is a piece of junk. It is noisy and rides like a tank and there is no air conditioning. We have another day to go to get there and two more on the way back. I don't think I will last another hour never mind three more days."

"Stop complaining when you were young you put up with a lot more than this. Just think of how much money we will make out of this."

They drove for another couple of hours in the heat and the grumbling from the general. The cowboy suddenly stopped the car and pulled off the road.

"What is wrong? What are you doing?" said the general.

"I have an idea and if I am right you will be able to travel in comfort."

There is a sign back there that says 'airport and charter flights'. With a little luck we will be able to fly there and back in one day."

The airport was a grassy paddock with a windsock and a tin shed. There were three small planes parked there, a Tiger Moth and two small Piper Cubs. They pulled up on the shady side of the shed and the Cowboy went inside. After a while the general was getting anxious when the cowboy emerged with another man who was also wearing cowboy boots.

"We are going to take that one," he said to the general. "It has a compass and we have a map of the district so we should find the property without any trouble."

After checking over the plane and getting instructions from the owner they climbed aboard, taxied to the strip and took off.

"I told him we were looking for a property to buy and we were lost and the car was playing up so we thought we would fly. He was not going to rent us the plane until he saw my boots, we talked about our boots for a little while, then he said I could rent the plane."

They had a good laugh while they got their bearings and headed towards the depot.

After about an hour the general said.

"We must be getting close by now. Is that the road down there?"

"This is the third time you have found the road. I hope you are right this time."

They banked and dropped down and follower the road.

"It looks like the one I remember, all those little hills. It cannot be far now. Just over that hill I bet."

They flew low along the road and climbed to get over the hill. As they passed over the crest they could not believe what they saw.

As they cleared the top of the hill looking for the entrance to the depot there were soldiers everywhere. Jeeps were crisscrossing the valley and men on motorbikes were riding up and down the hills and there was a helicopter parked a little way off. At the sight of the plane the soldiers were pointing at the plane and a couple of them started running towards the helicopter. When the general saw them, he started screaming.

"Soldiers, Soldiers! Get out of here quick before they start shooting at us."

The cowboy revved the motor and pulled up the nose and the little plane shuttered and nearly stalled. The motor roared and the plane banked hard to the right and dove over the next hill and down into the valley.

"That was close," said the general. "Those soldiers nearly got us."

"We are not clear yet. We have to get away from that helicopter. If they spot us, we are done for because this little plane cannot outrun it."

The cowboy flew low, nearly on the ground going between hills and even under trees.

"We have to find somewhere to hide; we cannot escape if they see us."

After what seemed like hours of acrobatic flying and near misses with rocks and trees they came through a small canyon and out on to the open plain.

"We have had it now," said the cowboy. "There is no place to hide. They will spot us soon."

"Look over there," said the general. "There is a small airstrip with a couple of planes parked there."

"It is our only chance. We will land and park next to those planes and hope they think we are just another plane parked there."

The plane banked hard and landed all in one maneuver.

"Get into the back behind the seats, lie there and don't move."

The cowboy pulled the plane up, turned off the motor and squeezed under the instrument panel. After a few minutes they could hear the thump, thump of the helicopter coming closer.

"Don't move," whispered the cowboy.

The chopper came closer and slowly flew over the parked planes and then flew on.

"Stay where you are," the Cowboy screamed. "They will circle around and come back for another look."

A few minutes later the chopper returned and flew over the planes again.

"This is it, they will either land to take a closer look or fly off and search somewhere else."

The helicopter did another circle of the airstrip and then flew off. As they left the cowboy looked out to see in which direction they were going.

"They are gone, you can get up now."

"I can't move. I am stuck here. I moved so fast, I can't get up."

The cowboy helped pull the general out and into the seat.

"Maybe now you will lose some weight."

"We will wait here for a few minutes and then head out in the opposite direction."

They took off and headed in the opposite direction from the chopper.

"According to the compass the chopper headed West and we are going East. We will turn North and head towards Darwin. We will soon have to find a place to land because we are low on fuel. Look for a landmark."

"I think I see a road over that way."

"I see it, we will fly in a tangent to it to save fuel. It looks like the road we came down on. We are probably somewhere near the airfield we took off from."

"Good, let's find it and get our car back and get out of here."

"No, we will use up our fuel looking for it. We will fly along the road as long as we can and find a place to ditch the plane."

"This is it we are nearly out of fuel. Look for a place to land."

"Look over there. There is a service station. We can land there and get some fuel."

"They will alert the police and we will be arrested. Over here there is a field and a grove of trees. We will fly on by over the hill and circle around and glide onto the field and hide the plane under the trees and walk to the service station and get a ride to Darwin."

They flew on past the service station and out of sight of the road then turned and flew low to the field glided on to the grass and stopped near the trees the plane taxied up to the trees and the engine stopped.

"How about that, we are out of fuel. Come on break off some branches and put them around the tail so it cannot be seen. Now which way is it to the service station?"

"We flew along there," said the general. "Around that hill and circled back and landed here."

"Are you sure? It did not look that far from the air. That is a good ten clicks away. Come on we have to get there before dark."

They were weary and tired by the time they arrived at the service station and were glad to get something to eat. They told the waitress that they had broken down and had to walk for a long time.

"You are in luck, the only bus that travels this road will be here in about a half hour. It only goes to Katherine but you can catch a mainliner there to Darwin."

They finished their meal, freshened up in the men's room and were ready to board the bus when it arrived. On the bus they sat near the rear got comfortable and promptly fell asleep. It was still dark when they arrived in Katherine. The cowboy found a pay phone and called the manager and told him the ute broke down. He was to come and pick them up right away. They found an all-night café and settled there to wait for their ride.

On the way back to Darwin they made arrangements with the manager to rent a holiday cottage owned by one of his staff.

"We will rest there until it is time to leave," the cowboy said.

"I never want to come to this place again," said the general.

They were two weary worn-out fellers. After resting for a couple of days the cowboy used his satellite phone to make arraignments for them to be picked up by the passing freighter. A few days later they were on their way back to Burma.

We did not realize how tired we were until we were in the terminal and booking our bags. We decided not to go into town but stay in the terminal, so we walked around for a while and then had a meal in a nice restaurant. Then we boarded our flight and settled in for the journey. I was a little restless and could not sleep. I sat there thinking of all that happened over the last couple of months and wondering when this weird situation would end. I must have slept because the next thing I knew we were preparing to land.

As we were retrieving our bags, two soldiers approached us and told us the colonel had sent them and they had transport waiting. It was late at night but it was a lot warmer there than it was on the farm. It wasn't long before we arrived at a rather plush motel. The soldier booked us in took our bags to our rooms and told us the colonel would meet us in the morning.

In the morning we made our way to the dining room. There were a few people there, all men and mostly solders. Even the cooks were solders.

"Looks like the army has taken over this place," Ian said.

We had no sooner sat down when Colonel Martin and Lieutenant Rodgers came in. It was all smiles and handshakes, just like old friends meeting after years of separation. We were all eating and talking at the same time until Allen asked to speak.

"It is good to have the gang back together all except for Captain Williamson who has been assigned to other duties. As you have observed we have commandeered this motel, there was not enough room at the local headquarters. All we are doing here is searching for the depot, all other activities are out of headquarters. Mr Fowler gave us the location of the depot and the troops arrived there last night. I am sure the search is well underway by now. We should hear from them later on today. When we do we will proceed there right away and take over the operation. That means you three can have a few hours to wander around the city. Don't go too far and be back here at noon.

Captain Williamson had a successful interview with Fowler. As soon as he heard his sister's voice he couldn't stop talking. The interview with Dawson did not glean any new information but did tie everything together. It looks like the depot operation will be a very large one and require a lot of manpower so Rodgers and I will get on with it and meet you here at noon, good morning gentlemen."

"I know what I am going to do," Ian said. "The bed in my room is the most comfortable I have ever slept in, so I am going to have another sleep. Who knows when I will get another bed like that. If I am not here at noon come and wake me."

We had a good laugh and headed for the door.

"Anything special you want to do?" asked Dickson.

"Not really, except I would like a good cup of coffee, that army stuff is hard to take."

"All right I was stationed here for a while so I will show you the sights, including the best coffee in town."

We returned to the motel and found Ian sitting in the lounge reading a newspaper.

"I only just got up and had a shower and came down here to wait for you. I took the bed apart and found the name of the mattress. When I retire I am going to get one."

"We had better have our lunch," I said. "We may not get another good meal for a while. I don't think they will have much in the desert."

We were nearly finished our meal when the colonel came in and sat down.

"They have found the depot. We will be leaving in a couple of hours; Rodgers is taking care of the details. It looks like we beat the general. About an hour ago while the men were searching the area a small plane flew low over the area. It flew away as soon as they saw the troops on the ground. Unfortunately the helicopter had just landed and by the time they were airborne the plane had disappeared."

"They have been very lucky," Dickson said. "Every time we get close they always seem to slip away."

"We will get them one day, the important thing is they did not get to the weapons."

"We will fly down there this afternoon and survey the situation. We may return today or stay we will not know until we get there. It is a couple of hours flying time so we will leave within the hour so we will have some time before dark. I have given orders for them not to enter the cave under any circumstances until we arrive. Get ready we will meet here in a half hour."

The colonel had a helicopter land at the airport instead of driving all the way to the air base. As we arrived there was an army truck near the helicopter and Dickson was supervising the baggage being loaded. We climbed aboard and found a seat and a crewman handed us earphones. Soon the door was closed and we were away. Darwin was soon behind us and we were travelling above the green, brown countryside. I thought to myself, here we go again a chopper ride into the unknown.

The time passed quickly and we were soon over rough hilly yellow, brownish country with nothing as far as you could see. Then the chopper slowed and began descending. Below there were trucks and men everywhere scurrying around like ants when they are disturbed. We were soon on the ground. The colonel had arraigned for the chopper to stay with us so there was no hurry to unload the baggage. While we were standing there three soldiers came to meet us.

After all the saluting and greetings, they introduced themselves. In charge was a Captain Benjamin Frazier. He was in his dress uniform, it was unkempt and dusty and he was sweating. It was easy to see he was way out of his depth, he was probably a desk jockey thrown into the fire.

Lieutenant Jacob Larson, nicknamed Joey because he was so young. He looked like he just left high school. Then there was Master Sergeant Scott McAlister. He looked like he came out of an English movie. You could see he was the real power in the camp.

All the captain could talk about as we walked toward the camp was the general's plane flying over earlier in the day. The colonel finally brought him into line.

"What have you accomplished so far today, Captain?"

"Well sir, it took a while to find the entrance to the cave. We found the bobcat first and one of the men figured that it could only travel on flat ground, so we back tracked and found a soft patch near the escarpment and dug there. We had been looking for an opening in the side of the hill not a hole in the ground. The entrance has been cleared. There are two large doors but we have not opened them."

There was a long slopping road leading down into the side of the cliff and at the bottom were two large doors. Some men were cleaning the last bit of sand away.

"Is this all you have done today, Captain?"

"Sir, it took a while to find it, also we had a camp over the other range about fifty clicks from here. The men are moving that camp here and setting it up for tonight. That is taking most of the manpower."

"Carry on with your work, Captain. We will have a look around the cave. Before you leave, Captain, I would like to inform you that from this moment on Mr Freeman is in charge of this whole operation. You sir will obey his every order instantly and without question. Do you understand?"

"I think so, sir."

"Captain, you will have command of the camp and your troops but everything else comes under Mr Freeman's control and his aides Lieutenant Rodgers and Sergeant Jones. Over to you Mr Freemen."

"Thank you, Colonel. Sergeant McAlister, could you spare a squad of men to help us go into the cave?"

"Yes sir. How many do you need?"

"How many are bunked in a tent?"

"Six, sir."

"That will do and Sergeant, they will probably be with us until dark or longer. I don't want them to have to set up their tent when they finish with us, Understood?"

"Yes, sir."

"Also, Sergeant, we will need some torches, electric ones with no flames. Have the men bring them with them. After we have had a look and decide what we are going to do we will have a meeting and explain everything to you."

We walked down the incline to the large doors. I asked Ian if he knew Sergeant McAlister.

"No I don't, he is obviously from England. Probably served in Nam and come over here for R&R and stayed. He looks like he can handle men and I am sure this outfit would be in a sorry mess if it wasn't for him."

"I figured the same thing. I bet the captain will spruce up now that the colonel is here."

"What are you talking about back there? Catch up with us."

"We were just admiring the Yankee ingenuity, look at this ramp."

The doors were a steel frame with corrugated steel sheets. They were each two meters wide and three meters tall. It took all five of us to push them open.

"I am sure Fowler could not open these doors on his own," I said. "There must be another entrance somewhere."

"Never mind getting the doors open," Dickson said. "He could never dig his way down here."

We peered into the dark cavern but could only see vague outlines.

The work crew appeared at the top of the ramp and Sergeant Jones went up to meet them. He escorted them down and introduced us. They were eager young men looking for adventure. I gave them a little pep talk.

"This cave is full of tons of old unstable explosives. If you see anything that looks it has explosives in it do not touch it. No running around and no shouting. Do any of you smoke? Make a place near the door and leave all your cigarettes and lighters there. One flame and this whole mountain would disappear. We are here to look and decide what we have to do so we will break up into groups. How many torches do we have? Four, then it is four groups. I am sure when we go in you will see some amazing sights."

We walked through the doors into a large cavern we could not see the end in the torch light. On the left side was a long-partitioned wall with windows in it. As we walked, we could see the end which was another wall coming out at right angles and nearly as long as the other one, with more doors and smaller windows. At the end of this wall was a large opening that went way back into the cavern.

"All right, we will split up here and look around. That front wall will be the office and orderly room. This back wall will be the barracks and kitchen. And down the end of this corridor will be the munitions.

Each group pick an area to explore and stick tougher and don't get lost. I will go down to check the munitions, who is brave enough to come with me?" The soldiers had a little chuckle amongst themselves and pushed one of them out towards me.

"Jack will go," someone said. "He is the brave one."

Another one said, "May I come too, sir?"

As we walked along the dark corridor I said,

"This is enormous, I wonder how it was formed?"

"It is a larva tube, sir. It was formed as lava flowed and cooled leaving a tube-like formation. There are more in North Queensland, but not as large as this one."

"How do you know all that?"

"My family went there on holiday years ago."

After walking for a few minutes, we came to the end of the partitioned wall into another large cavern. As we shone the torch around all we could see was a large wall of sandbags along the rear of the partitioned wall.

"Look at all those sandbags, there must be thousands of them."

"They are a blast shield in case of an accidental explosion," I said. "You will see a lot more of them soon."

We walked across the cavern and came upon another wall of sandbags. We walked along them and found an opening. Another long corridor. On the left side was an empty cubicle and another then in the third was a trailer with a canvas cover and the same in the next one.

"What in the world are they?"

"Large bombs," I said. Not wanting to frighten them too much.

"They stored them here and then forgot them. That is enough for now, let's head back."

"Are there more of them?"

"Shine the light down the corridor, can you see the end?"

"No."

"Well, that is how many are on this side"

"Wow."

We headed back up the corridor and when we got to the end I said.

"Let's turn left and look down the other corridor."

We turned left past a wall of sandbags and turned into another corridor. Just like the other one we could not see the end of it in the torch light.

"This one is parallel to the other one and would be just as long."

On the right side was a cubicle with a weapon in it.

"We will check a couple more of them head out of here." The next two cubicles had a weapon in each so we turned and headed back to the main chamber.

"How did you know that all of this would be here? Have you been here before?" asked one of the men.

"No, I have not been here before. It is my job to know about this. That is why I am in charge."

We soon reached the main cavern and met Jones and Rodgers.

"This place is enormous," Rodgers said. "We only explored little bit of the barracks and the kitchen. There is even a small hospital back there."

As we were talking alight came from the office area and we all headed that way. We met the colonel and Dickson as they came out.

"We have our work cut out for us here. It will take us weeks just to get this place in working order. We did not get very far in there the office is full of files many of them in locked cabinets marked top secret. I want them out of here as soon as possible before the yanks find out they are here. Rodgers, that will be your job. Get some men and trucks here tomorrow and put those files some where no one can find them."

"Colonel," I said. "It will not take very long to get this place in working order. Everything is already here. Look around, there are lights everywhere. All we have to do is find the generators. Are there bunks back there, Sergeant?"

"Yes, there is a whole barracks there."

"Good, Lieutenant Rodgers can order mattresses and bedding from the stores at Tindal and take the files away on the trucks when they bring the supplies. We can move in and save sleeping in tents."

"Sounds like a good idea. Let's get out of here and call it a day."

We came out of the cavern and closed the doors. At the top of the ramp, I said to the solders.

"Before you head back to camp, I want to mark a demarcation line along here. No one is to go past unless I say so and no smoking or flames anywhere near here. No one is to enter the cavern without my permission."

As we walked toward the camp I said to the colonel.

"It appears that only the two weapons were taken from here. The rest of the area appears undisturbed."

"That is good to know. We can scale down our search for the general now. I think we should all return to Darwin tonight. There is a lot of organizing to do and we cannot do that from here."

Captain Frazier was waiting for us when we arrived in the camp. The colonel told him we would be back tomorrow and I told him to set up a security patrol to prevent anyone from entering the valley.

"Why do we have to guard this valley? No one comes out here."

"Captain, we are not worried about our enemies, we know who they are. We are hounded by news and TV reporters. If the news got out, they would turn this place into a circus and we don't want that. Captain, no one comes into this valley, fly over or observes us from the surrounding hills, is that understood?"

"If that is what you want, yes I understand."

"We will have a meeting tomorrow and work out the details. We have to go now; the colonel is ready to leave."

It was a long flight back. Later at the motel we spent the evening deciding what we would need at the depot. It looked like a convoy of trucks would be heading down there tomorrow. The colonel was being called to Canberra for an important conference on the depot, Rodgers would be busy with the files and Dickson and Jones with procuring all our supplies and transport.

"Looks like I will be on my own tomorrow," I said.

"You are not the only one," Norman said. "I have to go to Canberra alone all my staff are occupied."

As we were retiring, I said to Dickson.

"Would you try to get some good coffee like we had at the farm. I have the name, Ivan gave it to me."

"No problem, we are organizing a field kitchen, the men need real food not field rations. We may even get a real cook. I thought we could turn the small mess in the cavern into a recreation area for the men to go after work for a hamburger and a beer."

"That is a great idea, it will lift their moral."

I was up early and met Ian at breakfast. He said he would come out with the first load of supplies and organize the barracks so we could sleep there tonight. He said we would not see Dickson or Rodgers for a few days because there was no communication out there. When I arrived at the helicopter there were a couple of trucks there loading supplies. The pilot asked if I was the only passenger.

"Then we are ready to leave. I will make another trip this afternoon so if you have any dispatches have them ready for me, I will also carry mail for the troops."

I climbed aboard and most of the cabin was full of cargo. I saw boxes of torches and batteries and two cartons of coffee.

The captain and lieutenant were waiting for me as I climbed out of the chopper. Some men came to unload the cargo.

"Good morning, Captain Frazier, Lieutenant Larson. We have a big day ahead of us and I would like to get started. There are a few things I want to do before we have our meeting so may I borrow your lieutenant for the day then we can talk later."

"Are you ready Larson? I am going to run your legs off you today. Firstly, I would like the same men we had yesterday, then I want a mechanic, a plumber and an electrician."

"Yes sir, right now?

"Yes, right now. I am sure there some here who have some knowledge of those trades so find them for me right now."

"I am on my way."

I went over to the men unloading the cargo and said, "I think most of this will end up in the cavern so load it on a couple of trucks and park them near the entrance until it is safe to take them inside."

The crew arrived and I had them carry the cartons of torches and batteries down to the cavern.

"We are going to look for the power plant and the water supply. The lieutenant is looking for a plumber and an electrician and I want you to escort them around so they can find the source of these things, so break out some torches and batteries and let's be ready when they arrive."

A few minutes later the lieutenant arrived with five men.

"I found you two electricians and three plumbers."

I explained about not smoking and no one was to go down into the munitions tunnel.

"You are to trace the wires and pipes and find the source of the water and power. These guys know their way around and will escort you. We will meet back here later. I will take Jack and the lieutenant with me; we will look for the other entrance."

The other groups moved off and we went into the barracks area.

"How do you know there is another entrance if you have never been here before?" asked Jack.

"A little over a year ago a man exploring this area found this place and I am sure he did not find the main entrance. So, he must have come in some other way and I think I know where it is."

We were standing in the main corridor of the barracks.

"Now Jack, you live in one of these rooms and when you get up in the morning what is the first thing you do?"

"Well sir, you go to the latrine."

"Right, where is the latrine? Now think a minute, you surely are not going to walk all the way to the main entrance and then up the ramp and off to the toilet. Let's look around."

After walking up and down the corridor and opening every door we could not find the exit.

"It would be easier if we had more light," I said.

Then Larson, who was shining his torch all over the corridor said, "Look up there."

High on the wall at the end of the corridor was an exit sign. We hurriedly walked to the end of the corridor and as we got close we could see a large sheet of plywood propped against the wall. When we removed it and daylight shone through dead branches piled in the doorway, we quickly removed the branches and walked out into the open. After congratulating each other we pulled the plywood outside and propped it against a shrub so we could easily find the opening again.

When we went inside again we could hear someone calling. It was the electrician.

"We traced the cable and it goes through the wall to the outside, we also found the main fuse box and it looks in good order."

"You don't have to walk all the way around to get outside," Larson said. "You can go out the side door."

"Good, we will look around and find the power plant."

As we were talking one of the crew came through one of the doors.

"We followed the pipe all the way through the cavern and it goes through the munitions area so I came back to get you so we can follow it to the end."

We all followed the soldier through a long corridor and came out in the cavern where the weapons were.

"The pipe runs along the top of the sandbags down that corridor," the plumber said.

"All right we will follow it. Now we will walk down the center of the corridor. Do not go into any of the cubicles and do not touch anything metal you could cause a spark and if there is any gas in here it would be the end of us all."

We walked along the dark corridor counting the weapons as they came into view in the torch light. There were thirteen in all along the corridor with two more cubicles. One filled with miscellanies boxes and the last one had two small aircraft tugs parked there.

"When we clear the gas out we will try to get them going, they will be very useful moving these things around."

The corridor ended into another large cavern. We followed the pipe to a low wall of sandbags and on the other side was the end of the pipe hanging above a concrete platform. Another pipe was at the other side of the platform. A little way along the pipe entered a large pool of water.

"Look at all that water, one of the plumbers said, there is enough here for a city. I wonder how deep it is?"

"Never mind that now," I said. "Where is the pump?"

"There is a hole in the wall and what looks like an exhaust pipe in it. It must have been a diesel pump."

"Can we get another one?" I asked.

"It has standard fittings; a five horsepower would fit right in there."

"I'll get one," I said. "One of you who can run, go see if the chopper is still there and hold it up until I can get an order made out for a pump. Let's go back and meet the electricians and see if they need anything."

The electricians were nowhere in calling range, so we moved on to the entrance. I told the plumbers to look around outside and find the exhaust outlet and I headed for the chopper. After the chopper left, I went looking for some coffee. I was drinking army coffee and eating toast when Lieutenant Larson came in with his crew.

"Get some coffee and we will have a conference," I said.

"They just gave me a funny look and a couple went looking for some cold drinks. They moved the tables and chairs and we sat around discussing what we had found.

"The electricians found the power plants. They were under an overhang and a lot of brush had grown around them."

"Clean it up and get the mechanics down there and try to get them going. The rest of you clean around the side door and where the pump exhaust comes out. Can you work without the lieutenant? I want to talk to him and the captain."

The captain and Sergeant McAlister were in the orderly tent. I let Larson tell them about what we found so far. Then the captain asked.

"What is this all about? I have heard rumors that there are some large bombs in that cave."

"That is true sir, but they are more than large bombs' they are *Atomic Bombs* dumped here years ago by the Yanks. Not only that, but they are also old and unstable and must be handled with the utmost caution."

The captain just sat there staring and the Sargent was shaking his head from side to side.

The sergeant was the first to speak.

"They did the same thing in England and I always figured they would do the same elsewhere in the world."

Then the captain said, "What is going to happen here? Will this become a permanent base or will you just bury the weapons and leave?"

"These weapons are unstable and must be dismantled and destroyed, they cannot be left here. For the next few weeks we will prepare this site for the work of dismantling and destroying them. We will be here for at least six months or more and there will be a lot more personnel involved."

"Six months in this hell hole!"

"Maybe more, even up to a year. Captain, your job was to find this site. If you wish to return to your old post, I can arrange that and find a replacement. It is up to you."

"A soldier does not desert his post. I will stick it out."

"Once we are organized you will have additional help to and decent quarters."

I have to get back to the men. We may have lights this afternoon and then you can take the grand tour. Also, a camp kitchen is on its way so the troops can have real food to eat. Do you need Larson? Good, I have a job for him."

As we walked towards the cavern entrance I said to Larson.

"After the noon meal I would like to talk to the men. Could you organize to have all of them gather here at the entrance, it is a good spot to give a speech just like an amphitheater."

WE could see the men working along the edge of the cliff face. They had the bobcat working and had cleared the brush away from the power plants and were building a path down to the side door and on to the pump site. As we approached the power plants some men were working on them.

They were large diesel engines enclosed in a large cabinet and that had protected them from the weather all these years.

"Two of them are in real good shape, we are not sure about the third one," said the mechanic. "We will start them as soon as the service truck arrives."

While we were watching the men the service truck made its way over the rough ground and pulled up. After a few anxious minutes the old engine roared into life with a large plume of black smoke. It was not long before the second one was going too. I was ready to go into the cavern to have a look in the light when the when the mechanic said, "We will let them run in for a while before we put a load on them. Come back in about an hour."

"In that case, let's knock off and have lunch."

The men assembled in front of the mess tent for roll call. Lieutenant Larson stood beside Sergeant McAllister while he called out the roll and the captain and I stood of to one side.

"I did not realize there were so many men here. There must be at least a hundred. Is this your command, Captain?"

"No, these men are a combat engineer company. They had assembled in Darwin to go to Arnhem Land to repair emergency air strips for the Flying Doctor Service when they were called out here. Their Captain is on leave and the Lieutenants wife is in the hospital. Their Sergeant stayed in Darwin with their equipment. I was called from my desk job and the lieutenant is fresh out of cadet training. We are lucky to have Sergeant McAlister, he can really handle men."

"These men are engineers and they have their equipment in Darwin?"

"Yes, they are trained to build roads and airstrips under battle conditions."

"Captain, when we finish here I want you to order that equipment here as fast as possible."

"All right but we do not have an engineer to supervise the work."

"Captain, by the time the equipment arrives I will have the best engineer in the whole army here to organize the work."

After roll call the men marched to the ramp and the lieutenant spoke to them.

"We are gathered here to introduce you to the civilian in charge of this operation. He would like to say a few words to you, men this is Mr Freeman, he is in charge and you will obey him as you would Sergeant McAllister. Men, Mr Freeman."

"Thank you Lieutenant, good afternoon, gentlemen. I would like to explain what is happening here to quell the rumors that are circulating among you.

I am sure that you are all familiar with the Commonwealth Secrets Act because what I am about to tell you is most secret so raise your right hand and say, 'I do', now you are sworn to secrecy and cannot tell anyone what you see or do here.

In the late fifties during the cold war the Americans somehow found this cave and turned it into a depot the hide some large bombs from the Russians. They hid it so well they forgot about it and it was not found until last year by a prospector who tried to sell the weapons to some foreign criminals.

Our job here is to get this site ready for a team to come and dismantle and destroy these weapons. Our other task is to keep this place secure, not from foreign gangsters but from reporters and TV newsmen. Those of you on patrol are to arrest and hold anyone found in this area. If you let them go they may have pictures of us and the story will cause enormous diplomatic trouble around the world.

Sometime this afternoon a convoy of supply trucks will arrive so we have to clean this place up to store the supplies. There is also a field kitchen and a latrine coming so you can have a good meal and a shower. I would like a detail to take the bobcat out along the dirt track and make it easier for the trucks to travel here. You are all experienced men and can work on your own because we do not have any supervisors to guide you.

We will have the lights on shortly and you can start in the big cave, but no one is to go into the rear where the weapons are. They are old and the explosive is unstable, so they are not to be disturbed. Also, absolutely no smoking or open flames anywhere near the entrance or in the cavern. One flame or spark and it is the end for all of us. There is at least thirty tons of very unstable high explosive in there. One last thing when the cave is secure and the lights are working I will take groups of you on a tour so you will all see what is in there. Thank you for your attention. Over to you, Lieutenant."

The lieutenant dismissed the men and I went over to the power plant. The motors were running smoothly and the electrician said, "We are ready to turn on the power, I will switch it on here then go to the fuse box and try the lights in the main cave."

When he threw the main switch the diesels growled and adjusted to the load. We walked into the cavern and it was twice as large as I thought it was. There were lights everywhere and every corner of the cave was illuminated.

"Man, this place is enormous," the electrician said. "You could put a football stadium in were."

We looked around for a few minutes and then I said.

"Check out the lights in the office and the barracks. Do not turn on the lights in the rear of the cavern yet, want to ventilate the area in case there is some residual fumes in there. While you are doing that, I am going to find the lieutenant and get started cleaning this place."

We divided the men into teams and set them cleaning the main cave and the barracks and the office. After about an hour a solider came up to me and said, "Sir, the helicopter has just arrived. When I arrived some men were unloading the cargo," the pilot said to me.

"I had a near collision with a jet fighter as I approached. Man, it was close."

"They are patrolling our air space. This is a no-go zone. I will have them set up a call signal for you. What did you bring this time?"

"I have your pump and two large blowers, a radio station and a bunch of dispatches for you."

"Very good we need the blowers and the pump, they will be a big help."

The items were quickly loaded on a truck and moved to the entrance of the cave while some men were setting up the blowers, I told the electrician.

"Put one at the entrance to the rear corridor and the other one in the back corridor and it will blow the fumes into the lake where they will disperse. Then in about an hour we will be able to drive trucks in here and unload them. Twice a day for at least an hour I want you to do this so we can work freely around here without fear of an explosion."

I went back to the truck and the plumbers were there looking over the pump.

"It is a beauty, top of the range; it will do the job without any trouble."

"Will it fit through the side door?"

"I think so, we will make it fit. Where is the tank?"

"I hope it is on another truck," I said. "Take it to the side door, then look for the tank."

I went back into the cave and found Larson.

"The men do not like working with the noise of the blowers."

"I will have them moved down into the lower cavern," I said.

"We can drive the trucks in here now and unload them."

"That will make things a lot easier," Larson said.

"Let's tour the barracks and the kitchen," I said.

There were ten rooms in the barracks, eight had four bunks and two had two bunks.

"Thirty-six bunks, which one do you want?" I said.

"Thank you but I will bunk with the men. I am just beginning to be accepted by them and I do not want to lose their trust by moving into the Ritz Hotel."

"You are a good man, soldier, you will go a long way with that attitude."

We walked along the hall into the dining area. All the tables and chairs were still there.

"Our lieutenant wants to turn this into a canteen for the troops. What do you think?"

"That is a great idea, it is perfect, they will really appreciate it."

Someone was calling so we returned to the main chamber.

A soldier came up to us and said, "Sir, we found something and we thought you should see it."

We followed the soldier into the office and into another room where a couple more men were working.

"Over here in the corner," he said pointing to a mess of garbage spread around the floor. "This stuff is new and there is no dust on it."

Spread around the floor was plastic drink bottles, candy wrappers and the tell tail cigarette wrappers and butts.

"This is where they camped, look at the mess. Good work soldier, go and find a clean bag and gather all this up. The colonel will want to see it."

"Where did it come from, sir?"

"The people who stole the two missing weapons camped here. This will help prove that they were here."

We went back to the main chamber and I told Larson to begin unloading the stores from the helicopter.

"Map out the area for the different types of goods. There will be a convoy coming soon and we will have to find room for that too. Don't block the entrances and leave the office until the files are cleared out. I am going to talk to the chopper pilot before he leaves."

At the top of the ramp I met one of the mechanics.

"Sir, we have only enough fuel for one more day. Can we get some more?"

"How much do you need?"

"A tanker comes once a week for our own vehicles. Those engines will easily use a tanker by themselves."

"I am going to the chopper now; we will have another load tomorrow."

"It is not that simple sir, we have nothing to store the fuel in except the small tanks on the engines."

"All right, we will get a trailer load and it can stay here and be replaced with another one."

"Yes sir, that will work but there is another problem. Those engines are old and are running close to their capacity. I don't know how long they will last."

"Looks like we will have to order a couple more then. Anything else you need?"

The pilot was about to leave when he saw me coming so he waited for me.

"Do you have a reply from those dispatches?"

"Bugger, I completely forgot about them. They will have to wait until tomorrow. I want you to order some more supplies."

"I am not caring any power plants it my aircraft," he said jokingly, after I told him what to order.

I went looking for Captain Frazier to take him on a guided tour.

"The captain is not here, sir," the clerk said. "He has gone to check on the men working on the track. You will find Sergeant McAlister inspecting the tents."

"Never mind. Where are the dispatches that arrived earlier?"

"Right here, sir."

"I think I will find a quiet place and read them. May I use the captain's desk?"

"I think so sir, as long as you do not disturb anything. He likes to keep everything neat in its place."

Most of the things I already knew but there was one envelope marked top secret. It was a detail of Colonel Martin's trip to the Sandia Corporation in the U.S.A. It seems that the Yanks have had a change of heart and are willing to cooperate in the destruction of the weapons. They have a portable factory in storage that will neutralize the explosive chargers. They will ship the factory and the personal to operate it in exchange for all the plutonium. The colonel is going over there to finalize the deal, he had taken Captain Williamson with him. Well, that makes life a lot easier for all of us. We will not be here for months blowing up the charges. But the yanks are going to come out on top, each one of the plutonium cores must be worth at least ten million dollars.

The captain came in as I was reading the dispatch.

"Sorry, I did not mean to disturb you."

"That's all right, I was looking for a quiet place to read these dispatches. By the way do you have a safe? There is one marked, 'Top Secret'. We have a couple of weeks to get this place in order then we will have a group of visitors from the U.S.A. They are going to bring a factory to dispose of the explosives."

"I was not going to ask what was in the dispatch but thank you for telling me."

"I came looking for you to take you on a tour. Are you free now?"

"Yes but I would like to wait for Sergeant McAlister he wants to come too. So why don't we have a cup of coffee, I have a percolator and make my own."

"That sounds great; I have some special coffee that I am sure you will enjoy. While we were enjoying a good cup the sergeant came in.

"How did the inspection go, Sergeant?"

"I had to be lenient, sir. The men have not had a decent shower for days and their clothes are soiled too."

"We can fix that soon as the pump is connected. The plumbers can make up a hose system and the troops can shower," I said.

"Mr Freeman wants to take us on a tour. Are you free, Sergeant?"

"Yes sir, I am ready. While I am there I will look into this shower system."

As we walked toward the cavern, I told the captain that we were way ahead of our expected schedule and in a few days he could roster some leave for the troops.

The men were unloading the trucks; Lieutenant Larson had everything under control.

The captain was very impressed with the layout.

"You can set up your orderly room in here and your office in the next room," I said. "We will leave the other rooms for the demolition team. I am sure they will want some office space. Would you like a room in the barracks?"

"I would give my right arm to get out of that cot and tent, but I will stay with the men. Their captain will return soon so I will stick it out."

I had the electrician turn off the fans and turn on the lights in the lower cavern.

"Let's go down the main corridor, I would like to count the weapons there."

"There are two parallel aisles, each with fifteen bays. The first two are empty. That is where the stolen weapons were. They used the bobcat to dig out the entrance and to tow the weapons outside and on to a large truck."

We walked past a couple more bays and I said.

"Would you like to see one of them? There is a light over this one, let's have a look."

I removed the canvas cover and the frame.

"It looks like it just came off the assembly line," the sergeant said.

"How many of these did the yanks have?" asked the captain.

"At least two thousand, maybe more. Who knows?"

We walked along to the end of the corridor, all the bays were full, so there are twenty-six weapons here.

At the end of the corridor there was a smaller cavern to the left.

"I will find the light switch and we will have a look."

Along the far wall was a long bench with some instrument cases along it.

"This is where I use to work," I said. "Well not in here, this is where the weapon is assembled. That funny looking crane is used to remove the fuse from the storage drum. It is hoisted out and placed on that trolley with the rails on it. It is then hooked up to these instruments and all the components are tested. Then two batteries are placed in them and plugged in then the trolley is wheeled to the rear of the weapon and the fuse is inserted. Then those overhead cables are plugged in to make sure everything is properly connected. The nuclear man bench is over there in the corner."

"Somewhere near there has to be a battery room because each weapon needed two batteries."

"There is a room over here," the sergeant said.

"This is a workshop and supply room," I said. "Someone has taken most of the power tools and the tools out of the supply closet."

"It was done a long time ago," the sergeant said. "Nothing has been disturbed in here for years."

"I bet it is the same person who took the pump."

We looked around a bit more and found another room at the end of the long bench. Inside were racks of batteries and two large chargers.

"I will have the electrician check this out. Come on, I have something interesting to show you."

We turned the lights off as we left and walked along the wall of sandbags past the other corridor towards the pool. We could see the plumbers working on the pump in the distance.

"The pump is nearly ready to turn on, sir. It was easy to hook up but the intake had sunk to the bottom and it took a while to get it repaired."

"Good work men," said the captain. "Sergeant McAlister has an idea he would like to try out, I will leave him here with you."

"But first I would like to show you something," I said. "Come over here."

I led them to the edge of the underground lake. They just stood there staring for a couple of minutes.

"This is remarkable," said the captain. "You could never explain it to anyone. It is awe inspiring."

The captain and I walked through the long corridor toward the main cavern.

"Dave, I know the shower was your idea but we are trying to keep a good rapport with the troops. Their commanding officer and sergeant are well liked and they resent being here and a new command."

"Ben, you are doing a great job under these conditions and I will go along with anything to keep up the morale. I asked for a load of cold beer to come in the convoy, if it arrives you may have the honor of distributing it to the men."

"Thank you, Dave, that will really put a feather in my cap."

The cavern was a hive of activity, there were men and trucks everywhere. Boxes and cartons were being piled in neat rows. Lieutenant Larson came up and said.

"We are working as fast as we can, there are ten more trucks out there waiting to unload."

"Looks like you have it well organized and under control," I said. "Here comes Lieutenant Rodgers, I will introduce you."

After introductions I said.

"Captain, the tour is over I am sure we all have things to attend to. One thing before we part, Lieutenant Rodgers, did the beer arrive?"

"I think so there is a refrigerated van out there with fresh food and meat in it and I am sure they made room for the beer. Also, the field kitchen is here so the men will have a good meal tonight."

"There you go Captain, another feather," I said with a grin.

Rodgers and I headed towards the office.

"I have two trucks ready to load the files in but it looks like all the men are occupied."

"What is the rush, do it tomorrow. What is the news from Darwin?"

"It is bedlam over there, both the army and air force bases are screaming. We have stripped them of their supplies the air force wants more money and personnel to handle all the extra flights over this area. Also, the mining companies are real mad because we confiscated all the available transportable buildings in the Northwest. Things are so bad they are sending a general from Canberra to tour the bases and calm the commanders."

"Another thing, all this activity has come to the attention of the press and they are gathering like vultures. Every available agent we have is in Darwin to control them. We have activated a company of Aborigine Reservist. They will camp around the area and stop anyone trying to observe what we are doing."

"I am glad I am out here in the peace and quiet. By the way did you get a copy of the secret dispatch from the U.S.A.?"

"No, I did not. What is it about?"

"It is in the captain's safe, you can read it tonight. By the way, about those files I want you to do me a favor."

"Anything, what do you want?"

"Many years ago someone broke into this place and stole the water pump and then cleaned out the machine shop. He knew where this place was and how to get in. I believe it was someone who worked here during the construction and then went back to America and later on returned here to live. I bet he bought a property around here and came here for the equipment."

"So, you want me to go through the personal files and find someone who immigrated here."

"Yes, he may still be around here. He could give us a lot of vital information about this place."

"Seeing you put it that way I will do it, but it will take a while."

"Did Sergeant Jones return with you?"

"Yes, he is in the barracks organizing the bedding."

"Let's go and harass him."

When we caught up with him Ian was in the barracks organizing the bed making.

"Welcome to the Jones Motel," he said as we came in.

"I found enough for ten beds. That is all they had."

"You did very well, at least we have a place to sleep tonight," I said.

"Which room did you choose?"

"It does not matter right now; we can each have a room until the other crew arrives. Are you finished here? Let's go check out the new kitchen."

"Always thinking about food," Ian said.

THE last of the trucks were leaving as we climbed to the top of the ramp.

"They will be back tomorrow," Rodgers said.

Down in a hollow some troops had laid a large tarpaulin out and they had two fire hoses spraying some of the men.

"Sergeant McAlister's shower," I said.

"The men seem to be having a good time," Dickson said.

The field kitchen was a new smaller version of the one at the farm. The smell of cooking food was floating around the area. We looked in the mess tent and there were a group of men eating.

"They are the night patrol getting ready to go out," said McAlister who had just walked up.

"They are drinking beer," I said.

"A couple of beers will not bother those fellers."

"Would you mind if I spoke to them? I want to give them some instructions."

McAlister got the men's attention and I said to them.

"Our little depot has caused a lot of commotion in Darwin and has caught the attention of the press. They are gathering like sharks at the smell of blood. Be on the alert if you spot anyone arrest them. Do not let them go. They may have already been here. If they try to escape shoot their tires, if you cannot catch them call the air force and they will use them for target practice, I can assure you that they will try to infiltrate this place so don't sleep out there stay alert. Thank you for your attention."

I said to the men with me, "We need a compound out of sight of this place to keep anyone we catch until we can transport them to Darwin for interrogation, Sergeant McAlister do you have a spare tent?"

"Yes sir, two in fact."

"Tomorrow we will setup a guard post somewhere on the other side of a hill out of sight of this place. It does not have to be manned, except when someone is caught."

Captain Frasier had walked in on our conversation and said.

"Surely we do not have to take such extreme measures, I am sure the Russians have known about this place for many years."

"Yes sir, and the Americans know about the Russian secret ones too but the public does not know. If the word gets out each other will have to protest and the protest turn into accusations. Then loudmouth politicians on both sides will fan the flames and we will spiral down into another cold war. That is why this place must remain top secret at all cost."

Nothing more was said so I said, "I am hungry, let's eat."

It had been along hard day and it was good to sit and enjoy a good meal of steak, eggs and a fresh crisp salad helped down with a couple of cold beers. We took our time and sat and talked for a while. When we finished the mess hall was nearly empty.

"The men enjoyed their meal and the beer really topped it off," said McAlister.

We were all tired and called it a day. Most of the lights were off and the cavern had an eerily glow.

"Kinda spooky in here, isn't it," said Ian.

"You will sleep all the better thinking there are ghosts around," Rodgers said.

Although it had been a long hard day I could not sleep, besides I had dispatches to get ready to send tomorrow with the helicopter. I was woken by a knock on the door, it was Ian.

"Are you going to sleep all day? You will be late for breakfast. No VIP treatment here."

"It is so dark and quiet in there I did not know what time it was," I said as we walked to the mess. "Are you going back to town this morning?"

"Yes, I will give Lieutenant Dickson a hand, he is swamped with paperwork. Order ten alarm clocks for the rooms. They will have to be battery ones because of the generators."

The mess tent was nearly empty and the cooks were cleaning it up.

"I really miss Ivan," I said. "I am going to talk to the cook and see if he will brew my coffee for me."

Ian smiled and said, "Now you know what it is like to be a real soldier."

After breakfast I went looking for Lieutenant Rodgers and found him loading files on the trucks.

"I am not supposed to tell where these are going but there is a small base near Alice Springs that is used for desert training. It has a large storage area and I can hide them there."

"What about the personnel files?"

"I will box them and ship them to Darwin for you."

"Let's box them now and save you a lot of work and time. Which cabinet is it? Is it on the truck?"

"Only the classified files have been loaded in case we run out of space."

"Let's find it and have a look."

"They are over here; I had them set aside until the others were loaded. See, they filed everything, equipment, expenditures, repairs, and here are the personnel one."

"*Holy Dooly,* it is full. They had a lot of people working here. You will never box all of this. I have an idea I will strap it and put secret on it and ship it on the chopper with Ian. He is going back to Darwin to help Lieutenant Dickson."

"You are the boss I wouldn't dare to do that."

"Almost forgot. Here is the dispatch I told you about. Sit down under the light and read it, it will only take a few minutes."

"That is going to make things a lot easier for all of us. I feel sorry for the colonel over there haggling with the Yanks."

"He is tough and can take care of himself, I said. he will give back as much as they give him."

"I have to go. When will I see you again?"

"I don't know, I have to safely store these files. I don't think I have to guard them. I guess about a week, but that is a long time in this game."

I stopped a passing patrol and loaded the file cabinet and dropped it at the helicopter landing pad. Sergeant Jones was talking to Sergeant McAlister.

"Sorry to interrupt but I have something important to discuss with Sergeant Jones."

I gave him instruction about the file cabinet and told him I had some dispatches to go too.

"Don't leave without them."

I went looking for Lieutenant Larson to plan the day's work.

By the time I found Larson I changed my mind the men had worked hard yesterday and would again when the supply trucks arrived so I scaled down my plans for the day.

"The men will work hard enough when the supply trucks arrive," I said to Larson. "All I want now is some of them to look for a road. There has to be a better way in here than that potholed dirt track. I am sure the yanks would not put up with that. Also, soon there will be some very heavy vehicles coming; we need a good road for them. When we find it, the engineers can clear it with their equipment when it gets here.”

Next stop was the power plant.

“About two hours of fuel left,” the mechanic said.

“Turn off everything except the main chamber and you will only need one plant working.”

When I found the plumbers, they were getting ready to lay a pipe so the kitchen could have sufficient water to work with.

“If it is here by noon, it will be operational by dark.”

The electrician wanted to know why the power was turned off.

“You will have to wait until the fuel truck arrives,” I said. “Later, when the power is on I want to show you something in the lower cave.”

Finishing my rounds, I decided to have a cup with the captain. I was on my way to his office when a patrol truck pulled up.

“Mr Freeman, please come with me. We just stopped a car full of trespassers and we do not know what to do with them.”

“Arrest them and take them to the interrogation tent.”

“They are not newsmen, sir. They are natives and they say we are trespassing on their land.”

There were four men standing around a four-wheel drive station wagon auguring with the two guards. One of the guards came up and said.

“Sir, they are demanding that we leave here right away. This is a sacred site and we are desecrating it.”

I went over and introduced myself and shook hands. The leader was Paul Mason the Reserve Ranger and Tribal Elder. We talked back and forth for a while but they were in no mood to talk or listen and they were getting all the angrier because we were white men on their sacred site, So I retreated for a few minutes to calm down and think. Another patrol vehicle arrived and at the same time the helicopter flew over preparing to land.

“Bugger, I forgot the dispatches again, I said to the guard, I have to get to the chopper before it leaves.”

Then I said to the natives, "I am sorry gentlemen but I must meet the helicopter. I will be back as soon as possible. You are to wait here for me. Please be patient. Out of respect the men have not arrested or searched you, but there are spies trying to find out what is happening here so the men will search your car and all of you for cameras. Please cooperate and it will all be explained when return."

I said to one of the guards, "Get their car keys and back off if they give you any trouble. I will return as soon as possible."

AS we pulled up at the helicopter pad, I said to the guard, "Go to the mess tent and get some cold drinks and sandwiches for all of us and a couple bottles of water. I will be ready to leave as soon as you return."

As I walked to the chopper Ian was shaking the hand of a soldier and talking excitedly. When the soldier turned, I knew why.

"Trooper, no Sergeant Larmarra. What are you doing here?"

Before he could speak, I said.

"Am I glad to see you? I can really use your help right now."

"May I get my bag out of the chopper first?"

We all had a good laugh. I gave Ian the dispatches and a quick explanation of what was happening.

"Good luck and a good flight."

"You are the one who needs the luck," he said.

The patrol pulled up and I said to Larmarra.

"Toss your gear in the back. I will explain on the way."

The guards were sitting in their vehicle and the natives in the shade under a tree.

"Let me do the talking," Larmarra said. "They will not open up if you are there."

He took some of the sandwiches and drinks and sat and talked with them. A little while later he returned and said.

"They are very upset. This is the most sacred site there is. So sacred, that no native has been near here for nearly a hundred years. When the last elder came here to talk with the spirits, he was told some pale men would come and chase them away from their homeland. No one has dared to come here since."

"Tell them some white men came from over the sea many years ago and built a camp here and we are here to remove that camp and restore the site and return it to the original owners."

Larmarra went back and talked and returned a little while later.

"That calmed them down a bit but they want a better explanation, so the elder Mr Mason wants to talk to you alone."

"I remember my father telling me about some white men looking for a cave and asked him to help them. Being young and foolish and enjoying the candy and beer they gave him he led them here. He never returned here and neither has anyone else. There was a drought on, so they stayed in the South near the waterholes," Mr Mason told me as we sat in one of the vehicles.

"Would you like to know what is going on here?" I said.

"Yes, I would, we are very concerned about this place."

"Have you been in the army?"

"Yes, three years in the navy."

"You know about the national securities' act then?"

"Of course, all service men do."

"If you want to know what is happening here, I will tell you after you swear to the act, agreed?"

"If I must, I will for my people'"

"All right step out of the car."

I called Larmarra and another guard.

"You are witnesses."

"Mr Mason raise your right hand. Do you swear that you have never been here and have not seen or heard anything about this place that you have never been to."

"Yes I do," he said with a perplexed look on his face.

"I have always wanted to do that," I said.

"We are going for a short drive. You guys finish off the sandwiches and drinks."

I drove Mr Mason to a hill overlooking the camp.

"This Is where your father brought the Americans all those years ago. Down there is a very large and deep cavern. A natural lava tube. It runs a long way back into the hill. There is a large pool of water in there. It could support a small town. The Americans built a large camp here and turned the cavern into a depot to store atomic bombs during the cold war. We found it and are now preparing to remove and destroy those weapons. When we are finished we will clear the site and return it to your people. It may take a little while to do this. Do you understand? Mr Mason?"

He just sat there dumbfounded, unable to speak. It took a few minutes for him to come around.

"I am sorry I came here. I am sorry you told me this. I now have the burden of my father's folly to bear. Also the concern of my people. What am I going to tell them?"

There is not much I could say except, "It will all be over in a few months and if your people can overcome the taboo of this place it can become a great asset for you, even a tourist attraction or meditation place where you all can come to renew you tribal rites."

"Take me back now I have seen enough. Thank you I know you mean well and are trying to help my people. I will think it over and talk to you again. How do I contact you?"

"Just like now, come up to a guard post and tell them who you are and you want to see me. I hope I have been of some help to you. Come and see me anytime."

The Aborigines left, followed by a patrol vehicle and Larmarra and I came back to the camp in the other one. On the way I said.

"What are you doing here?"

"I am enrolled in the next class of the cadet college and to fill in time they sent me here to liaison with the Aborigine Reservist who will be guarding this place. I gladly accepted when I knew your crew would be here. I met Lieutenant Dickson in Darwin. He is swamped with paperwork, hardly had time to say hi."

"I know, he is organizing supplies for us and controlling the influx of newsmen. They want to know what is happening out here. Sergeant Jones went back to help him."

"The colonel and captain have gone to America to organize a team to dispose of the weapons. We might catch Lieutenant Rodgers; he is shipping out some material today."

As we approached the camp Larmarra said, "What are those men doing walking around over there?"

"I have them out there looking for the road into this place."

"They are looking in the wrong place. That is the dry riverbed. The road is over there under that low hill. The river comes down through the valley right where most of the tents are pitched and down through the gully where the men are and on into the valley below. Good thing it is the dry season or the troops would get a wet surprise one morning."

"How do you know all that?"

"I saw it from the chopper as we approached. I thought it was strange to put the tents in the middle of the river."

"I suppose you saw the outline of the base too?"

"Yes, it is off to the left, where the tents should be. I could make out four large buildings, three in parallel and one opposite to them. I will pace it out later for you."

"You have just saved us many days of hard work scratching around looking for that."

We pulled up in front of the orderly tent. I told the driver to send the road party in for lunch.

"I will introduce you to the camp commander and his staff."

After introductions I told them about the episode with the Aborigines and then I said.

"Sergeant Larmarra found the lost road, tell them about it."

He told them of the river and the road and how the buildings were laid out.

"You saw all that from a moving helicopter? Amazing," the captain said.

"Yes sir, and there is something else further up the valley but I could not make it out."

"I have an idea of what it is," I said. "When the chopper returns this afternoon we will go up with a sketch pad and map out the whole area. By the way where is Lieutenant Larson?"

"He went out with the road detail. They should return soon."

"We will probably meet him in the mess tent," I said.

On our way to the mess, I said to Larmarra.

"Have a good talk with Larson, he just graduated from the cadet college. He could give you a good insight of the place."

We picked up a tray and moved down the line. Not much of a choice soup sandwiches and apples or grapes. We found a table and sat down.

"A lot different from the farm, Larmarra said, no VIP treatment here."

"I don't know about that, I have spoken to the cook and he is going to brew me a small urn of coffee every morning, and he has a hobby of making sourdough bread so he is going to bake me a fruit loaf each day so I can have coffee and fruit toast for breakfast."

"Maybe when I get to be a general I will have my own cook and I will make sure he can bake sourdough bread."

"Meet me here in the morning and I will give you some."

While we were talking Lieutenant Larson saw us and came over to our table. Larmarra jumped to attention and I said.

"Sit with us Lieutenant, I want to introduce you to our detective, he has something interesting to tell you."

After talking about the road and the visitors the two of them were in an earnest conversation about the cadet college and forgot about me so I sat there quietly because I knew how important it was to Larmarra a few minutes later Sergeant McAllister came in and told us the convoy had arrived.

"Time to go back to work," the lieutenant said.

On the way out I said to Larson, "There is a tanker of diesel for the generators, give it first priority because they are nearly out of fuel."

Then I said to Larmarra, "Get your gear and I will show where your bunk is, and then I will give you a tour of the site."

We walked towards the ramp where the trucks were lining up to unload and I said.

"This is a large lave tube and it runs way back into the hills. The yanks turned it into a storage site."

Larmarra looked around the cavern and said, "This is sure a creepy place."

"Come on the barracks are this way."

As we approached the barracks door Larmarra said.

"I am sorry Mr Freeman this place is taboo I cannot stay here I must get out before something bad happens to me."

He turned and swiftly walked out of the cavern and to the top of the ramp.

"Those local fellers were right, there is a strong spirit in there and he is very angry. No black feller will go near the place. I will bunk with the troops. Please do not tell anyone what happened because they will make fun of it and I cannot defend myself."

Larmarra walked off towards the camp and I went to check on the power plants. On the way I met Lieutenant Larson.

"I am going into the rear cavern, send someone after me when the helicopter arrives."

"We have plenty of fuel now," the mechanic said. "One of the drivers told me they are looking for a semi-trailer to transport two large power plants. They found them at the Naval base."

"That is good news. You will have to find a suitable site for them and have it ready when they arrive."

"I already have. We can move these two down into the camp for lights for the tents and the cook house and put the other two here."

"That is a great idea I should have thought of it myself. I will leave it up to you and the electrician to work out. Where is the electrician, I want to speak to him?"

"He is down in the tunnel changing some blown bulbs."

"Are you finished here? I want to show you something."

We walked to the lower cavern to the battery room.

"What do you think of this?"

"This is amazing; these are sealed lead acid batteries. How old are they?"

"At least twenty-five years old."

"Amazing they are just coming on to the market now. Look at these monster chargers I have never seen any this strong before. One thing for sure those generators could never handle this load. The two of them running at full capacity could only handle one charger charging half the batteries. Also, the wiring here is not heavy enough to handle the load. They would get a big surprise when they turned it on."

"I doubt if the engineers would make such a grouse mistake. Could there be another power plant somewhere?"

"Maybe, I will look for some heavy cables and they will lead to a power source if there is one. What are you going to do with all of this?"

"Eventually everything in this whole cavern will be dismantled and removed probably junked. Why, did you have something in mind?"

"Yes sir, our outfit could use those chargers and maybe some of those batteries may still be serviceable, we could put it all to good use instead of junking it."

"I have no objection. Get the mechanic to get the tugs going and find a trailer to take them out."

We walked around the area and I showed him the test station and the machine shop.

"After seeing all of this I think this whole depot is a fake. There is no way those two generators could have handled all the power needed to run this equipment and lights. Those power plants are straining just to keep the lights going never mind any of this back here. I will look for another power source but I doubt I will find one. It looks like someone pocketed a lot of money because they knew this place would never be used."

"You have stirred up a hornets' nest. I will ask for a search of the original specifications of this site. Lieutenant Rodgers is not going to like it. I will have to leave you and write a dispatch for the helicopter to take back to headquarters. Turn off the lights when you finish."

As I was finishing the letter to Lieutenant Rodgers and the other paperwork, I heard the helicopter coming in. I arrived just as it landed. The door opened and an officer stepped out. At first glance I thought it was Lieutenant Dickson but I got a surprise.

"Lieutenant Fitzroy, what are you doing here so soon?"

"Hello Dave, I was visiting my parents in Kununurra when I got the call to come here. I got a lift with a local pilot and landed at Darwin just in time to catch the chopper. The pilot was not going to let me aboard without a clearance but Sergeant Jones was there loading freight and he vouched for me."

"Don't go away we have a job to do. I have to talk to the pilot first and then find Sergeant Larmarra."

I exchanged dispatches with the pilot and told him I wanted to fly around the area to map it out.

"I can only give you fifteen minutes because I need the fuel to get back. Give me a half hour to unload."

I told Fitzroy what I wanted to do and we had time to meet the captain. A patrol truck came up to meet the chopper and I asked if he had seen Sergeant Larmarra.

"He is out with a patrol looking for campsites for his group who will arrive here tomorrow."

"Will you call him in I need him to go up in the chopper with me."

"Sorry for the poor greeting but we can talk later and I will show you around. Come on, I will introduce you to Captain Frazier. We may even get a cup of coffee." After introductions and a little chat over coffee, as we were leaving, Frazier said to me.

"I really like your coffee Dave, do you have any more?"

"I will bring over another pack and ask the pilot to bring a couple more cartons tomorrow."

I picked up a large note pad and a couple of colored pens from the orderly and we headed back to the helicopter.

The pilot was ready and Larmarra was just getting out of a vehicle. He and Fitzroy said their hellos and we climbed aboard.

"Where do you want to go?" asked the pilot.

"That is up to the sergeant, this is his mission."

As we took off I gave Larmarra the pad and pens and he quickly drew a sketch of the area.

"Let's follow the road first and then we will look over the campsite. There it is over there."

"Road, what road? I don't see any road," said Fitzroy.

"That is why Larmarra is here," I said. "Take a look because you have to repair it."

"It goes through that hill and down over the other side and along there to the riverbed. It looks like the river changed course and washed out the road. There it is again overt there. It is easy to follow from there so let's go back and look over the camp."

"Veer over to the right," I said. "I want to look at that flat area on the other side of the riverbed."

"If it was not way out here I would say it was a landing field, a big, long runway with a tarmac there at the foot of the hill," Larmarra said.

"That is exactly what it is," I said. "We will look at it later when we have time."

"Hover over the camp for a couple of minutes so I can map it," Larmarra said to the pilot.

"What is he mapping?" Fitzroy said. "I cannot see anything."

"You will when we land," I said.

"That's good, now move up the valley to that other site we saw earlier."

"You have only a couple more minutes," the pilot said.

"There it is a large round shape, I bet it is an underground tank. Could you circle around the top of the range on the way in? I want to check out some lookout sites for the men."

We circled the hill tops and landed Larmarra and Fitzroy got out and were in a huddle over the sketches. I thanked the pilot for his cooperation.

"That guy is a wiz, I couldn't see any of those landmarks down there. By the way on the flight here I was followed by two vehicles on the ground and asked for a different flight plan over the desert so they could not follow me. One of the fighter pilots called and asked me to go slow so he could use them for target practice."

"These reporters are giving us a lot of trouble. Half of our personnel are here just to keep them away. One more thing I have requested a standby tanker so you will not have any more fuel problems once it arrives."

FITZROY and Laramarra showed me the sketches.

"Let's go talk this over with the captain and maybe he will give us another coffee."

The captain was very impressed with Larmarra sketches.

"I will assign some men survey the area and they will draw a scale map then we can move the whole camp to better site."

"I can help them in the morning until my unit arrives," Larmarra said.

While we were enjoying the captain's coffee he told us that the heavy equipment was on its way and would arrive soon.

"Let's go and find this road," Fitzroy said.

"You will find Lieutenant Larson there with some men," the captain said.

We commandeered a patrol vehicle and found Larson and his men pegging the road. The men were glad to hear their equipment was on its way.

"Why would the Yanks put a road through this hill?" asked Fitzroy.

"They didn't," Larmarra said. "There is something under there and over the years the sand has piled up against it making this low hill. If you look at the contour of the other hills this one is out of alignment. The road follows the old river and it curves along over there behind us so this mound should not be here."

"It will be interesting to find out what is under there," Fitzroy said.

We followed the road along to where it was washed away.

"This can easily be repaired," Fitzroy said as we crossed the riverbed.

A little further along the road faded away into the scrub.

"Where does it go now?" Fitzroy asked Larmarra.

"The water runs into the low land around here and soaks into the ground and the grass grows. That is why there is vegetation in this area. Over time sediment would have settled on the road and grass would grow in it. My guess is that the road follows the higher ground along here and over that way. Look over there that is why the river overflowed and washed away the road."

We could see a long low mound stretching across the valley.

"There is a fence under there and the debris has piled up against it. Pull that out and the road will never flood again."

We followed what we thought was the road for a few more kilometers until in the distance we could see the main road.

"Look way down there and you can see a faint outline of the road where it meets the main one," Larmarra got out and said to us.

"Come over here. This a high spot and only a little dirt have blown over the road."

He kicked the ground with his boot and the pavement appeared.

"You have done my whole job for me," Fitzroy said. "I can finish my leave and go on to the university. I thought I would be here for months."

"It is getting late," I said. "Let's head back."

We met Larson and his men at the washout.

"What are you going to do here?" Larson asked Fitzroy.

"We will do what Larmarra said, move the road to along the edge of the washout."

"Won't it just washout again?"

"No, we found the cause over in the valley', all will be well. We are going in, are you coming?"

The first of the heavy equipment was parked on the edge of the compound when we arrived. Larson pulled up behind us and when he saw the large shovel, he looked at Fitzroy and they both said.

"We are going to dig out that mound tomorrow."

We were joined in the mess with Captain Frazier and Sergeant McAlister and we sat talking and enjoying a beer. Frazier had Larmarra doing most of the talking. He enjoyed listening to stories about the cowboy and the general. We finally broke up and headed to our bunks.

"Get your gear, Fritzie and I will take you to the Jones Motel."

"Where are they going?"

"They are gung-ho soldiers and sleep under the stars. We have five-star accommodations."

I told him about the situation with the captain and the troops and that Larmarra did not like caves.

"That captain is a very clever man."

Fitzroy just stood inside the cavern and looked around.

"This is marvelous, how big is it?"

"We really don't know it goes for a long way and we have not had time to explore it."

"I love caves, when things ease off let's go exploring."

As we walked towards the bunk room Fitzroy said,

"It is eerie in here. Do you feel it?"

"I have to live here so I ignore it. That is why Larmarra will not sleep here, it really had an effect on him."

I showed him the bunk area and the latrine and said, "Pick out a room I am the only one in here now."

"If you don't mind, I would like to sleep in your room with you until I get use to this place. Do you mind?"

"No but you are freaking me out now."

While we were settling down, I told him about the episode with Mason the Aboriginal Elder.

"Now I know why Larmarra would not stay in here. There is definitely something here."

"Thanks a lot. Goodnight and pleasant nightmares."

Fitzroy was coming out of the latrine as I was going in.

"Meet you at the mess."

When I arrived, Fitzroy and Larson were nearly finished their breakfast.

"Sergeant Andrews is organizing the men and we are going to dig out that mound."

"Who is Sergeant Andrews?" I asked.

"He came with the equipment yesterday. He is an engineer."

"Are you coming too?"

"No, I have a few things to do here, I will catch up with you later."

Sergeant Larmarra came in and sat down.

"You look terrible," I said.

"I didn't sleep last night. I don't like this place. I will be glad to get out in the hills today."

"Have a cup of my special coffee that will wake you up."

"What are you going to do this morning?"

"I am going to mark out the camp with the surveyors and then look at the mound, and by then the scouts should be here and I can get out of here. Thanks for the coffee it really helped. Come and get me when you are ready to go to the mound and I will go with you."

The first thing I wanted to do was to look at that tank on the other hillside near the side entrance to the cavern. I walked to the power plants and found the mechanic.

"I have prepared for the new generators but there is not any transport available to bring them here."

"There is now, there are five low loaders in the camp right now. Go down and take two of them and bring back the power plants."

"That is a great idea, I will go right now."

"First I have something to show you, it will not take long come with me."

We walked up the hill along the edge of the cliff.

"Here we are."

"Here what?"

I scraped the dirt with my shoe and stomped the ground. There was a deep hollow sound.

The mechanic walked around looking at the ground and said, "It's a tank a bloody big tank. And here is the manhole."

"Can you open it?"

"I will try." He kicked the latch a couple of times and we both pulled up the lid.

"Is it empty?"

"It is clean, never been used. What was it for?"

"Well from its location I think it was fuel storage for the power plants."

"Look over here, it is the inlet pipe and it is capped, it has never been filled."

"Thank you that is what I want to know. Let's go back to the camp."

We scrambled down the side of the hill to the bottom of the tank.

"It looks like they blasted a hole in the hillside and dropped the tank in it. Look over here this is the outlet valve, it is capped, never been hooked up."

"That puts paid to my theory."

"What theory is that?"

"I believe that the last group that worked here only did half the work and pocketed the money. It is beginning to look like they stole a lot of money and rendered the base useless."

"Wow that is treason. What would have happened if there was a war the yanks could have lost if they needed this base to win a battle?"

BACK at the camp I gave the mechanic the phone number for Lieutenant Dickson and Sergeant Jones.

"Call them from the highway so you will have clearance for the naval base and accommodation. Get some vouchers from the clerk for food and fuel." The helicopter would be here soon and I had some dispatches to send so I went to the captain's tent.

"Good morning, Ben. What is going on?"

"We are getting ready to move the orderly room into the cave as soon as I can find some help. The camp is empty."

"They are all out at the mound digging it out."

"There is no need for the whole company to do that."

"Sergeant Larmarra told them that that mound was not natural and something is under there and that caused the sand to pile up against it so curiosity has got the better of them. The worse ones are the two lieutenants."

"I will get them back in here, there is no need for all of them to be out there."

"Captain, the men have been working hard since they come here and there isn't much recreation for them. Let them have a little play. What is one day? We are ahead of schedule."

"I suppose you are right. I wonder what is under the mound."

"It has got you too. As soon as Larmarra said it was artificial I knew what had caused it."

"You are a clever one, aren't you."

"Not as clever as Larmarra."

"I bet you do not know what is under there."

"OK. How much?"

"A loaf of your fruit bread against my coffee maker."

"You sure about that? I hate to take your coffee maker from you, I will write it down and put it in an envelope and you go out and have a look then open the envelope and I will have a good coffee machine. Before you go may I borrow your clerk? I have some dispatches to do before the chopper arrives. May I use my new coffee maker now? I would love a cup."

I spent the rest of the morning writing reports Including one for Larmarra's exploits and how much help he has been.

Just as I finished the chopper landed.

"You are early today," I said.

"No freight today, just a package and a few dispatches. The package is for you, more coffee, I think. What are all those men doing over there in the valley?"

"They think there is buried treasure out there, you have lots of time would you like to have a look? I will get us a ride."

I saw a truck pull up at the captains' tent and went over to get it. It was Larmarra and the surveyors. I got there as the captain came out of the tent, I thought you were at the mound."

"No, I am just going now. Want a lift? Have you got room for the pilot?

We all piled into the truck. The officers in the front and the rest of us in the back.

The mound looked like an ant hill. Men and machinery everywhere. Lieutenant Larson came to meet us.

"It is unbelievable. We are just breaking through now."

We walked up to where the men were working and you could see the outline of a row of wheels and the shape of large vehicles. The men gathered at one of them and started to clear the sand away. It only took a few minutes. There was a large ten wheeled army truck. The side was clear shiny metal, the canvas cover was shredded, and the door window and the windscreen were opaque where the sand had blasted them.

"Well Captain, it looks like you will have to drink mess hall coffee from now on."

"What do you mean?"

"Read the note, sir."

He opened the envelope and read.

"Because of the length and height of the mound I think there at least ten large vehicles lined up along the road."

"Dam you Freemen. You are always right."

Another gang further along the line called out.

"Come and look at this."

They had uncovered a large ten wheeled crane vehicle in the same condition. I said to the captain.

"I was issued one of those. I used it to tow the weapon to the aircraft when I finished assembling and testing it."

We stood around for a while watching the men uncover more vehicles. Then someone pointed to the track and we could see a line of vehicles coming towards the compound.

"That must be the company of scouts," Larmarra said. "They are due about now. I should be there when they arrive."

The captain and the pilot also said that they would like to leave too. By the time we found a vehicle the convoy had already arrived.

The convoy consisted of eleven vehicles pulling trailers with their supplies and gear. As we pulled up there was quite a commotion. Men were shouting and running around and some of them were unloading motorcycles from a trailer. There was a roar as the bikes took off. Larmarra jumped out and ran into the middle of the milling crowd. The captain said.

"What the hell is going on? This is no way for soldiers to act, I am going to put a stop to this."

"Stay out of it," I said as I grabbed the captains' arm. "You will only make it worse."

"What do you mean?"

"I was afraid this would happen; this is a sacred aboriginal site and it has really spooked some of them. Let Larmarra handle it, he knows what to do."

"What do you mean, the men are spooked?"

"Look, some are still in the trucks, others are moving around waving their hands and shouting and some of them are trying to calm the others. I bet a couple of them took off into the desert and that is why the bikes went out. If you go in there you will only make worse."

Larmarra came up and saluted and said, "Sorry about the fuss, sir. Some of the men are spooked by this place so I am going to move out right away to calm them down."

"Where are you going?" I asked.

"You see that hill way to the north? That will be our main camp. It will take the rest of the day to calm these fellers down. We will start our patrols tomorrow."

"Do what you have to do soldier," the captain said. "I will send some food out in a little while and come out in the morning. Good luck."

THE convoy left and the helicopter took off and the camp was quiet again.

"Well that is enough excitement for today, come on Ben I will buy you lunch."

While we were eating I said to Ben, "I really do not want your coffeemaker. You may keep it."

"Thank you, a bet is a bet but I would really miss it. How did you know that the vehicles would be there?"

"They should have been in the cavern. They are needed for the operation of this base. I thought they had been stolen until Larmarra said the mound was not natural, I believe they were parked there ready to be taken away but for some reason they did not come back for them."

"What do you mean by things being stolen?"

"Ben this base was systematically looted. A great amount of supplies and equipment are missing. If there had ever been a war this place would not have been able to function. I am compiling a report of all the missing items and I don't think it is completed yet."

"This is serious, it could be considered to be treasonable."

"I will give the report to the colonel and let him decide what to do with it. To change the subject. What are you doing this afternoon?"

"With all the men playing in the sandpit there isn't much to do. What did you have in mind?"

"Would you like to come with me and explore the aircraft hangar?"

"What do you mean by an aircraft hangar?"

"Come along and I will show you."

"I have to check on the security patrols first. Really an aircraft hangar, this I have to see."

The captain left to check on the patrols and I rounded up a few men and a couple of vehicles and when the captain was ready we set off to find the hangar.

We drove to the mound which was gone and a line of vehicles were in its place. There were six trucks two cranes, two light trucks with trailers and two armored scout vehicles Lieutenant Fitzroy came to meet us.

"Those vehicles are loaded with weapons there are rifles, machine guns and the two smaller ones are field mortars. They were ready to defend this place."

"We are going to look over the airfield. Want to come along?"

Fitzroy got into the other truck.

"Hang on a minute, I want to speak to Lieutenant Larson."

"Jonathan, do you know the combination to the captain's safe?"

"Yes sir, I do."

"Before you move any of these vehicles, I want you to take a photograph of them just as they are. Also, I want a photo of each individual vehicle preferable from the good side with all the markings on them. Also, I want a complete description of each vehicle including serial numbers of the chassis and engine. Can you do all that for me?"

"Yes sir, I will photo them here and write up the description later in the camp."

"Later on, I want an inventory of all the weapons on board those vehicles. That will keep you busy for a while."

We followed the road but could not find the turnoff to the airstrip.

"It must have been washed out by a flood," I said.

"There it is over there the other side of the washout," said Fitzroy.

We drove on to the runway and I said, "Drive to the end and we will measure how long it is."

"Wow, five kilometers that is over two miles in the old measure."

"Now that we are here, where is that hanger?" asked the captain.

"This is the tarmac where they park the planes, so it would have to be over there in that hillside."

We got out of the vehicles and walked back and forth along the bottom of the hill.

"There is nothing here," Fitzroy said. "We are walking on gravel. The pavement ends way over there."

"Now don't give up, we have to think like Larmarra would. Look for something that should not be here."

After a few minutes the captain said.

"I see it now. Look at the top line of the hill. See how it goes along in an even line and just up there is a big mound."

"Yes, now I see it," said Fitzroy. "It looks like the tailings from a mine."

"The yanks built a large hangar there and then covered it over to hide it," I said.

"All this gravel has washed off it during the storms, Fitzroy said, we will have to get some equipment here to dig it out."

"Plenty of time for that," I said. "The road and the camp comes first, we will come back to this later."

"What do you think is in there?" asked the captain.

"If it is like the cavern in will be empty. Someone will have stolen everything. Otherwise, there should be a complete repair hangar in there with tools and spare parts."

"That would be a museum," the captain said.

The troops that came with us took some shovels and climbed on the mound and started digging.

"Over here sir, one of them shouted. We found the corner of the building."

"Dig it out a bit more and put a marker there so we can find it the next time," Fitzroy said.

"I think we have seen enough," I said. "Let's head back to camp."

As we drove by the mound some of the trucks were gone and we passed two of them being towed back to the camp.

"It has been quite a day," the captain said. "I wonder what the helicopter will bring this afternoon."

"Haven't you had enough for one day?" I said. "Speaking of the chopper I did not look at the report that came this morning."

As we pulled into the compound the men had the trucks lined up and were cleaning them with an air hose. Lieutenant Larson came up and said.

"These vehicles have never been used. It will not take us long to get them mobile."

"Lieutenant, you have the rest of the day to play. Then it is back to work tomorrow. Talk over with Lieutenant Fitzroy what you are going to do. The road is the main priority and also the survey of the campsite. You can work on the trucks in your spare time."

As we were talking a patrol vehicle came up and a soldier jumped out.

"Captain, we have been looking everywhere for you. Sir, we have captured some spies, the air patrol spotted them and fired at them to stop them until we arrived."

"Where are they now?"

"At the interrogation tent, sir."

"Have they been searched?" I asked.

"Corporal Jamerson is doing that now, sir."

"You return to the tent and send Corporal Jamerson back here. Do not talk to the prisoners, take them some sandwiches and water."

"I will go with you and interrogate them," Captain Frazier said.

"Captain, it would be better if you stayed here," I said. "Has headquarters been informed, soldier?"

"Yes sir, the pilot informed them and a Lieutenant Dickson is on his way in the helicopter."

"Thank you soldier, you have done very well."

When the patrol left, I said to the captain, "Ben, you do not want to get mixed up in this. It could get nasty. Lieutenant Dickson is from Army Intelligence. Let him take the flack. We have enough problems here without getting the big brass on our back."

A few minutes later Corporal Jamison arrived. We went into the captain's tent.

"Now Corporal, tell us everything from the beginning."

"We received a call from the air patrol that two vehicles were heading this way and when they were spotted they turned around and I gave the pilot permission to fire at them to stop them until we arrived. They said they were a German documentary team doing a series on Aboriginal life and had heard about a sacred site out this way and had come to explore it. We put two of them in one of our vehicles and the other two in one of their vehicles and took them to the interrogation tent."

"Did you search them?"

"Sir, there were only four of us and four of them, but I did find a can of film between the seats of their vehicle. Sir, my brother is a TV news cameraman and I have gone on assignments with him. He told me the first thing they do when an official approached them is to switch reels in the camera in case they confiscate the film. Also, their battery packs were low so they must have been filming for a while before we arrived."

"That is good thinking solider. Now the captain and I cannot get involved in this, so it is up to you to take our place. This is what I want you to do."

"Take a squad of men and return to the abandoned vehicle and search the whole area in case there is more film that they hid when they were discovered. Strip the vehicle and look underneath it, look everywhere. When you are finished let the air patrol know that they can use the vehicle for target practice."

"Yes sir, they will like that."

"On your way stop at the interrogation tent and instruct the men to strip search each one individually and to keep them separated, even if you have to lock them in a vehicle. One more thing. Put everything you find into bags or containers and seal it. We will give it to the intelligence officer when he arrives. Have you got all that?"

When the solider left the captain said, "You are right, this is serious I am glad you kept me out of it. The big brass will soon have the German ambassador demanding an explanation."

"Of course the brass would blame you. Now we have to prepare for Lieutenant Dickson's arrival. He will need transport to the interrogation tent."

It was not long before the helicopter arrived and the captain and I went to meet Lieutenant Dickson.

"Good to see you Jim, I wish we could have met under better circumstances."

"I wish I could stay out here, it is bedlam in Darwin and now I have to contend with this too. I hope Rodgers returns tomorrow I really need the help. We had to promote Sergeant Jones to warrant officer because some departments would not process requisitions signed by a sergeant. We got a call from a corporal asking for clearance to the naval base. Well, that started a war between us and the navy that took a couple of hours to clear up."

"Jim I am sorry but we only have the chopper and the radio to communicate with you and I am not going to use the radio. Come on, the captain will give us a good cup of coffee and we will bring you up to date on what has happened."

"Hang on, I brought something for you." He returned from the helicopter with a heavy suitcase. "These are all the dispatches I said I would send you, have fun."

While we were having coffee and bringing Dickson up to date an orderly came in and said.

"Excuse me sir, I have an urgent message for a Lieutenant Dickson."

"Well, this is all I need. One of the vehicles coming to take the newsmen to Darwin broke down and cannot continue the journey. They are trying to find another helicopter to transport the newsmen. It looks like I will spend the night here. Captain, will you arrange some bedding for the prisoners. Now I had better get on with it where are the prisoners."

We told Dickson about the interrogation tent and that we had a vehicle waiting to take him there.

When Dickson entered the interrogation tent he saw four men in their underwear each sitting in a corner of the tent and two guards sitting in the center of the tent facing them. When they saw an officer they jumped up and all started complaining at once as to how they were being mistreated and demanding their clothes and possessions to be returned. Just then Corporal Jamison came into the tent and asked to speak to Lieutenant Dickson.

Outside he showed Dickson the cans of film and explained, "Sir, we found two rolls of thirty-five-millimeter film in one of their underwear and later a camera with a telephoto lens hidden under the abandoned vehicle. We also found a mud map of this general area with a circle and the words army camp in it. We have everything bagged ready for you."

"Thank you solider, you have done a very good job and the colonel will hear of it."

DICKSON returned to the tent and told the men there was no transport to return them to Darwin and bedding would be found for them tonight.

"You will remain in your underwear because we do not have the manpower to properly guard you and I do not think you will attempt a fifty kilometer walk across the desert in your underwear. The guards are instructed to shoot if you do try to escape. I will leave you now and will escort you to Darwin tomorrow for interrogation that is if we can find some transport. Good evening gentlemen."

On the way to his transport there was a loud scream and a couple of explosions.

"What the hell is that?" he asked Corporal Jamison.

"Sir, that is the air force using the newsmen's vehicle for target practice."

"I bet I know who authorized that."

We put two tables together in the mess and sat around talking and enjoying our meal. I said to Dickson.

"Jim, Ben and I have a solution to your transport problem."

"Every day a convoy of trucks leaves here you can put your prisoners on them and return to Darwin."

"That is a good idea. It is nearly impossible to get a helicopter. But how is this going to help you?"

"We have a lot of men who are overdue for some leave time so we thought to send some of them along as guards and they could have some time in Darwin."

"Sounds good to me, I will send a message cancelling the chopper."

"That will give you a chance to relax here for a few hours," I said.

LATER, after dinner, I took Jim for a tour of the cavern.

"This is enormous and that lake is awe inspiring. This will be a big tourist attraction in years to come."

"I doubt that," I said. Then I told him about the sacred site and the effect it had on the aboriginal scouts.

"After seeing this place, I can understand that."

"It had a real bad effect on Larmarra, he only got to the middle of the large chamber and turned and ran out."

"Larmarra. Is he here?"

"Yes, he is in the hills camped with the scouts. I am going to visit him tomorrow morning. Want to come along?"

"I would like to say hello, I haven't seen him since the farm."

As we were retiring, I said to Dickson, "Have you read the dispatches you gave me today?"

"No, I do not have time to read anything. I am on the telephone most of the day."

"I was reading them while you were with the newsmen. We will talk about them in the morning. The guard will wake us up at seven. It is so dark and quiet in here you could sleep for a week."

"That would be wonderful, I cannot wait to get back here so I can do that."

The next morning they all met at the same tables in the mess.

"We all can have some good coffee but I do not know how much sourdough bread the cook has baked. But I am sure we can all have a piece."

As they ate they planned the day. Fitzroy and Sergeant Andrews would start on the road Larson would move the orderly room and organize the site survey. The captain and Mc Alister would organize the prisoners and their guards.

"I also want a grader to smooth the dirt track because the new generators will be arriving today. Lieutenant Dickson and I are going to visit Sergeant Larmarra and the scouts. We should be back before noon."

On the way to the scout camp Jim said to Dave.

"What do you have in that bag?"

"It is the leftover bread from breakfast Larmarra likes sourdough bread. Jim instead of you trying to read all those dispatches I will tell you what was in them. The main item is the yanks sent us the specifications of the chemical plant, as they call it. All I need now is the dimensions so you can take it with you and check that it is all there when it arrives."

"When will that be?"

"It is coming by transport planes and should arrive in about a month."

"That gives us time to prepare for it."

DAVE also told Jim about the looting of the site,

"That is going to cause a lot of trouble; it could even end up with someone being tried for treason."

"I will give the report to the colonel and he can decide what to do with it."

"It will give him a lot of bargaining power."

As they climbed to the top of the escarpment Dickson said.

"What a view, this is beautiful, rugged country. Look over there, that is what is left of the volcano that shaped this area. I wonder if that lava tube goes all the way to it."

"That is a long way for the tube to go," I said.

Sergeant Larmarra was glad to see them and thanked Dave for the bread. They went for a stroll and talked of old times. Then Dave said.

"I brought you some radios so you can keep in contact with the base and each other."

"Thank you, we were wondering what all the gunfire and explosions were yesterday."

They told him about the newsmen.

"I thought as much. We will patrol all along this ridge so no one will get in from this side. The men will not go into the valley after what happened yesterday. I doubt that anyone would attempt the long trek across the wasteland anyway."

They could see the convoy of supply trucks coming across the valley and said goodbye to Larmarra.

"We have to make sure the newsmen are properly guarded on the way to Darwin."

By the time they returned to camp the trucks were ready to leave.

"We are using all six trucks," Sergeant McAlister said. "One prisoner in each truck with five soldiers and two guard vehicles, one in front and one in the back. That gives thirty men a few days leave in Darwin."

Dickson said, "We will leave as soon as I get my gear."

There was a lot of cheering as the convoy left the camp to pick up the newsmen.

"Will this leave you shorthanded?" Dave asked Scott.

"Only a couple of days most of the men have a three-day leave, the married men a little longer and a couple have some leave time to use up. If it works we will send a few every weekend to keep up moral."

The camp was quiet for a while until the generators appeared moving down the track.

"These are beauties, sir," the mechanic said. "They are much stronger than the other ones and we will not have any more electrical problems. We did have a problem on the way back. We were followed by some cars all the way from Darwin. When we stopped at the service center they tried to talk to us and took pictures of the vehicles. I rang the number you gave me and soon after we were on the road again some police cars stopped them and one of them escorted us the rest of the way."

"Good thinking soldier, we caught some of them sneaking around here yesterday."

Every spare man spent the rest of the afternoon unloading the new generators. I met Larson in the cavern and told him that as soon as the generators were running he could open the recreation room because there would be enough power to use the barbeque grill and the men could have hamburgers and beer.

OVER the next few days the camp settled down to a routine and everything was running smoothly. The new campsite was laid out and the tents were moved a few at a time. The chemical factory layout was marked out as close to the entrance of the cavern as possible. The captain relaxed in his new office and we would stop by for coffee on a regular routine.

When the men returned from Darwin they said they were glad to be back. Darwin was crowded and noisy.

"I can understand that," Sergeant McAllister said. "I have never been in charge of such a group before. They are happy and do not complain and there are no arguments either."

"I have seen it too," the captain said. "But I cannot understand why."

"It cannot be the food," the lieutenant said. "This is regular army chow."

"I think I know," Dave said. "I may be wrong but I feel relaxed and content even though the workload is strenuous. I think it is the water."

They looked at me waiting for an explanation.

"It is simple. There was always something going wrong at the farm. The troops were always complaining about something, when the transport outfit moved out they had a party. Look at us we are sitting here relaxed and happy enjoying a good cup of coffee. It has to be the water."

We were about to start a discussion when there was a lot of shouting outside. We rushed out to find out what was going on.

Men were running around looking up and pointing. A soldier ran up and said.

"It is a hang glider sir, he is camouflaged we saw his shadow."

After straining I saw a dot moving against the clear blue sky.

The glider was colored light blue, just like the sky, and was almost invisible. The dot was the pilot's head. He was circling trying to find an updraft to carry him away from the valley. No telling how long he had been up there.

I grabbed a soldier and told him to alert the helicopter.

"Get him above the glider and force it down with the downdraft."

I ran into the tent and told the clerk to alert the air force.

"I have done thar sir and the scouts also."

"Good thinking."

I went outside to watch. The pilot was very skillful. He would circle trying to find an up draft. He had to come in close to the cliff face to catch one then he would soar upwards but when he passed the edge of the cliff the wind would blow him back into the valley. He was trapped but would not surrender.

Luckily the helicopter was unloading. Two men jumped in as observers. It went up high enough so not to crash into the glider. They followed the men on the ground until one of them spotted the glider.

It was hard because the top of the wing was the same color as the ground.

As the glider caught the up draft the helicopter pounced. It swooped in above the glider and the strong down draft forced the glider down.

It spiraled down neatly crashing but the pilot was able to land just in front of the men chasing it. The pilot was running trying to get some lift when the men caught it. A big cheer went up among the troops.

Some men were putting the pilot into a truck to take him to the interrogation tent. I told them to hold him here.

"Strip him down and put everything into a bag then dress him again."

When the helicopter landed, I asked the pilot if he had enough fuel to return to Darwin.

"That was excellent flying, dump your cargo, you are going to take this spy to headquarters. You two go with him as guards. You are not to speak to the prisoner."

"But sir, we do not have any weapons or handcuffs to properly guard him."

"If he wants to jump out in the desert let him. There will be troops at the field to take charge of him. Come back with the helicopter tomorrow."

Just as I finished talking two jetfighters roared across the valley and shot up into the sky.

A few minutes later we could hear a couple of faint explosions *They got them*, I thought.

The helicopter pilot waited until the jets were out of his air space then took off for Darwin.

The camp calmed down and returned to normal.

After talking with the Captain, I stopped a patrol and told them to take me to the scout camp.

I stopped outside the camp and the driver flashed his lights. Soon Sergeant Larmarra came up on a motorcycle.

"I do not want to be seen by the prisoners, I am not supposed to be here."

"There were six of them in three cars. They came in last night with no lights and camped in a creek bed."

"How did they get past your men?"

"They had a piece of canvas dragging behind the last car. There are five men and a woman. They got past us because two of them are locals. The woman and a man. I am sure they have been out here before. Also, they had a camouflage net to cover their camp. We would have seen their tracks if we had been walking but the canvas was enough to hide them from a bike rider. What are you going to do with them?"

"Can you keep them here tonight?"

"No problem, it will give the men something to do."

"Strip search them and their vehicles. Keep them separated and pack everything for the gang in Darwin. Do you need blankets for them?"

"They have sleeping gear. We will need food and water though."

"I will take care of that. Do you think the two locals are Aboriginals?"

"I do not know they will not talk but I am sure they know this area. We did not know that dry creek was there."

"Write that up in your report and anything else you can glean from them but do not interrogate them let the Lieutenant do that. One more thing, are you finished with their vehicles?"

"Yes, they were trying to escape when the air force stopped them."

"Call the air force and tell them you are finished with them then stay a safe distance away and watch the fireworks."

"You are joking, really. The troops will really love that."

"Have a good time. I will see you tomorrow when you bring the prisoners down."

I met Lieutenant Fitzroy in the mess. We talked about the glider then he said, "I am nearly finished here. All I have is the washout to finish then a couple of weeks leave before I start uni. I am going to remove the gravel from the hangar door to fill the washout."

"That is a good plan when the road is finished all we have to do is wait for the Yanks. Maybe I will be able to leave with you."

"Fat chance of that you will have to supervise the Yanks. Besides I am not leaving right away. I want to see what is in the hangar and I want to explore the cave. I have ordered a rubber dingy from the air force."

"Now I am sure it is the water you are addicted just like everyone else."

"What is this about water? Is this another one of your predictions?"

I explained the discussion we had earlier.

"I have to agree with you. I have noticed a change in my temperament now I know why. I am going to take a large bottle of water with me when I leave here."

I went to the tunnel and found the electricians. They were dismantling the batteries and the chargers.

They had lifted two weapons with a portable hoist so they could have the trailers. We were stripping everything except the weapons. I had to wait for authorization to do that. The trucks were returning to Darwin full of salvaged equipment. Even though it was thirty years old it was never used and as good as anything available.

Someone shouted from the tunnel entrance that the helicopter had returned. I went out to find out what was going on.

The two men I sent as guards stepped out of the helicopter with smiles on their faces. They had pistols strapped on and MP armbands and hats and a satchel full of handcuffs.

They handed me a dispatch envelope with, "Urgent," stamped on it.

"Dave, the glider pilot talked. He was hired by a large newspaper. Be alert, double the guard. Send the two locals back now. We will pick up the others tomorrow. This is serious. Ivan."

I told the guards and the pilot to wait in the mess then I went to the orderly room and gave the note to the captain. Then I called Larmarra.

"Have you written your report?"

"Just finished it."

"Bring it and the two locals down right away."

Captain Frazier wanted to know what the dispatch meant.

"I am not sure but if a major newspaper is backing an expedition to find out what is going on here that is going to involve the top brass. They will try again we will have to alert the men to be on guard. I suggest we keep out of it as much as possible. Let the colonel handle it."

"I think I should have left here when I had the chance."

"To late now you will drown with the rest of us."

I saw two Land Rovers coming down the escarpment so I sent a soldier to the mess for the pilot and the guards.

Sergeant Larmarra had separated the prisoners, one in each truck.

I directed them to stop at the helicopter. They arrived there just as the others arrived. I stayed out of sight in the orderly room.

"What is going on Dave?" Larmarra asked.

"I will tell you later. Do you have the dispatch?"

He handed me the envelope. I wrote, "We have taken you advice," on it and told him to hand it to the pilot.

"Aren't you going to read it?"

The guards handcuffed the prisoners then handed Larmarra the satchel then it took off.

I took two sets of handcuffs and gave the satchel back to Larmarra and said.

"Come on we will have a coffee with the captain and I will tell you all the latest news."

"You forgot I cannot go near that cavern. I am going right back the men do not want to be here."

I rode to the edge of the road and told Larmarra about the dispatch.

"They will not get past us. The only way they can get here is across the desert. I don't think anyone will try that. Come up tomorrow with the supplies and we will talk. The men want to get away from here."

I returned to the orderly room to bring the captain up to date. Lieutenant Larson and Sergeant McAlister were there.

I explained what had happened and told them what we had to do.

"Lieutenant Fitzroy told me that he was nearly finished repairing the road. So, I want to cut the work force in half and use the extra men to double the guard. I want to set up a roster for twenty-four-hour patrol using all the vehicles. We have to patrol the valley and the desert. I am going to order some night surveillance gear. The last group came in at night without lights. They may be foolish enough to try to cross the desert like that."

"I am sorry," the captain said. "The engineers are scheduled to leave here in two weeks. They have other things to do."

"The security of this base is the most important thing in the country. The engineers will remain here until headquarters can find another detachment to take their place."

"That is going to cause a lot of trouble," the captain said.

"Ben it will be a school yard argument compared the trouble that will be caused by a reporter printing a story about this place. Remember we are guarding against our own people trying to find out what is going on here."

"Surely you are exaggerating," Larson said. "This is just a small bomb storage depot."

"This small bomb depot had about a half a billion dollars' worth of plutonium and many millions of dollars of uranium here. Also, I am finding evidence that the Yanks built this depot without permission from your government. Another thing there was a disarmament treaty with Russia. Those weapons were supposed to be destroyed not hidden away. It will be years before the dust settles on this place and maybe another cold war if is found out. We keep our head down and our mouths shut and hope this all blows away."

They were silent so I said, "We will set up a roster tomorrow I am sure headquarters can find us another detachment to relieve the engineers. I have some dispatches to write so I will see you later."

I picked up a note pad then went to the rec room and sat at a table writing and sipping coffee.

"I hope the boys in Darwin can handle this."

IT was quiet all morning until the helicopter arrived. The two guards were there and the pilot and I exchanged dispatches.

Sergeant Larmarra saw the helicopter approaching and arrived with three Land Rovers with a prisoner and a guard in each one.

They stopped near the helicopter dropped off the three prisoners then two of them left. Larmarra stayed behind in the other Land Rover.

The prisoners were loaded in the helicopter by the guards but I told the pilot to wait until I read the dispatched in case I had to reply.

"I will return shortly with the supplies. Headquarters want these three flown to the air base because the newspaper is saying they were only looking for a lost tribe of natives."

The helicopter left then I had a chance to talk with Larmarra.

"My men are spooked they will not come down here again if we pick up any more spies you will have to send someone to pick them up."

"Come into the mess until I read the dispatches. They may include you. We have to double the guards and patrol the whole area, and headquarters are taking the engineers. We are going to be short staffed I asked for another detachment of troops and some night surveillance gear."

"We can use the night surveillance gear but I doubt if you will get any replacements."

"We cannot guard this place and work too. We cannot leave the weapons here they must be dismantled."

I was looking at the dispatcher and noticed one with Sergeant Larmarra's name on it. He quickly opened it and read it.

"They want half of my men down here to do guard duty to take the place of the engineers. There is no way that is going to happen. They are coastal tribesmen not desert tribesmen. This place is taboo to them they are afraid to look down from the escarpment. Also, they are longing to go home I was going to ask for replacements. They will desert if I tell them this."

Larmarra was talking loud and waving the paper over his head.

"Calm down, soldier. Stay here and write up what you told me and send it back with the helicopter."

"I should go to Darwin and tell them what is going on out here. I bet they do not read the dispatches."

"You are right I should go with you. There are only two lieutenants there. The other departments are pulling rank on them. We will have to get the colonel back things are getting out of hand."

We could not go to Darwin so I wrote a threatening letter to the lieutenants.

"If we cannot do our work and guard duty. I want a full complement of men or I will block the entrances and shut this place down and we will leave with the engineers. I mean it. Get Colonel Martin back here now."

Larmarra calmed down so we had a coffee and talked.

When he left, I decided to discuss the guard roster with the captain.

As I walked to the orderly room I began to wonder what I was doing here. I was not used to confrontation. When I was I in the air force I did my job and minded my own business. Now I am involved in military politics which is an ugly game that no one wins. That is the colonel's job not mine. I hate to think what will happen if I shut this place down. In military politics someone has to lose and I am the one with the short straw.

Just as I reached the tunnel a patrol truck came along sounding its horn.

Now what has happened, I thought.

"Mr Freeman, there is a Ranger Mason wanting to talk to you. He is in the Interrogation tent."

Ranger Mason stood up when I came in. He looked older and tired.

He started talking before I could say, "Hello."

"I am sorry to have to bother you but you are the only one I can talk to. I cannot sleep, I am having nightmares and hallucinations during the day. I do not know what to do. I hope you can help me."

"I understand what is happening to you. There are a company of Aboriginal scouts on the escarpment. They will not come down here. Their sergeant will not go near the cave."

"I am paying for the transgressions of my father. The spirits cannot get him so I am being punished in his place."

"I do not have any understanding of your dream time. All I can say is you have to confront the spirits and say sorry for what your father did."

"You do understand our ways. That is what I want to do but I do not know how. Do you have any suggestions?"

"Are you strong enough to go down into the cave?"

"I will do anything I cannot take this any longer."

We walked to the rear of the mess tent where I picked up two five-liter drink containers. Then I hailed a passing patrol truck.

"Take us to the orderly room."

The driver stopped at the entrance of the cavern.

"Take us down into the cavern," I told the startled driver.

"We are not allowed to go down there in our vehicles."

"You are if I say so. Now take us all the way to the end right up to the lake."

"Wow, yes sir. Can I tell the guys about this?"

"You can tell them anything you want but you are only allowed down here when I say you can. You are taking us to the lake so Ranger Mason can inspect it. He is an Aboriginal and he may be affected by the experience so we may have to quickly evacuate him. Do you understand that?"

"I think so some of the guys will not come down to the canteen they say it spooks them."

"How about you, can you handle it?"

"Yes sir, I was one of the troops that inspected this place when you first arrived. I like it down here."

We slowly drove to the end of the corridor and stopped at the edge of the lake.

"Turn around then wait here. We may have to leave in a hurry."

I looked at Ranger Mason. He had not moved or spoken during the ride.

"Are you ready? Can you handle this?"

He could only nod his head. I helped him out and led him along the edge of the lake to a spot where the light shown across the water.

He stood there staring out across the water. After a short pause I spoke.

"I understand that you have to greet the spirits. Can you do that?"

"I am trying to work up enough courage to do that, right now I am ready to run away."

"I have something to give you the courage to face the spirits. Trust me this works."

I took a cup out of my pocked, bent down and filled it. I drank it then refilled it again and handed it to Mason.

"We have found that this water has healing powers. Drink it then call on the spirits. I will wait at the truck. Take your time there is no hurry."

As I filled the first bottle, I could hear Mason calling the spirits. I looked towards him and saw him standing with his arms outstretched. When I finished filling the second bottle I looked out on the lake. Just at the point where the light ended, I thought I could a mist just above the water. It seemed to be moving and rolling.

I put the bottle away then looked toward Mason. He was laying on his back with his arms outstretched. I ran up and looked at him. He was breathing so I left him alone then after a few minutes he stirred and sat up. He held out his hand for me to help him to stand.

I brushed the sand off his back then we slowly walked to the truck without speaking. We did not speak until we reached the mess tent.

"Are you hungry?"

He nodded his head so we went into the tent and sat down. Shortly the cook served us lunch. After a few bites Mason spoke.

"Thank you Mr Freeman, is all I can say. I have made peace with the spirits. I will not bother you again and when you finish here I will return and listen to the spirits. I hope it will benefit my people."

We had a pleasant lunch then I rode with him to the main gate. When he stepped out of the truck he looked younger and healthy. Like he did the last time I saw him. I gave him the two bottles and told him to have one glass a day to keep his strength up.

ON the way back to the camp I told the driver to drive through the bush. I wanted to look at the condition of the valley I was dismayed. You could hide a thousand soldiers in this scrub.

I had the driver go back along the edge of the road and found a hole in the fence and tire tracks going off into the bush.

I asked the driver if he was armed.

"No sir, only the guards are armed. I stopped to have some chow, I am working on the road."

"Do you have a radio?"

"No sir, again this is just a work truck."

"Go back to the gate I will have the guard call it in. We are not going in there unarmed."

"Isn't that a bit over the top, sir?"

"What if we came on a camp of four or more? They do not want to be caught. I do not want to be beaten and tied up, or worse."

"We checked the fence yesterday, sir," the guard said. "I heard the helicopter go over. I will call it in."

"Good, be careful what you say others are listening."

"Yes sir, we have a code we change daily. We will take care of it."

As we drove back two Land Rovers full of troops went the other way.

We came to the work area there was no one there. I could see that they were nearly finished. We arrived at the camp just as the helicopter was taking off. There were two men sitting in the door.

"What is going on?" Fitzroy asked.

"They spotted some tire tracks in the bush so the hunt is on."

"Really, let's take your truck and join them."

"We are not getting involved. When this is over the newspapers will be looking for someone to blame. You would be a prime target."

Fitzroy laughed.

"There you go again with your dooms day predictions."

"The papers have been warned that this place is off limits but they have sent a group to spy on us. When they are accused of spying, they will claim we over reacted. They cannot blame the Intelligence Service so you are the only officer that took part so you will be accused of arresting innocent newsman looking for a lost tribe of natives.”

“You really think so? I suppose you are right.”

“I have not been wrong so far. Let’s talk of more practical things. As of tomorrow, half of your workers will be rostered for guard duty so you will have to slow down on your repairs.”

“What is happening? No one tells me anything.”

“I am telling you now. We have to double the guards. To combat the newspapers. Today is an example. Also, the engineers are being moved out next weekend. There will only be about twenty men here then.”

“I will be finished in a couple of days so that does not matter. How are you going to continue this operation without the engineers?”

“I cannot operate the generators and dismantle the weapons and guard this place without them so I will shut down and leave with the engineers.”

“You are mad they will blame everything on you.”

“I have asked for the colonel to come back, he will take care of everything.”

“That is the greatest doomsday prediction of all.”

“Come on we are going to discuss the guard roster with the captain.”

“What is all the fuss about?” Captain Frazier said. “We have captured everyone so far.”

“I found a break in the fence a small army could be coming through the scrub right now.”

“That is silly we are not at war, no one is going to attack us.”

“If word of this depot gets into the newspapers it could start a cold war worse than the last one.”

“I doubt it. Larson you are in charge of security, do whatever Mr Freeman asks, Sergeant McAllister and I have enough to do keeping this outfit running.”

Outside Larson told me he was doing all the work keeping the depot running.

“Don’t worry, I will take care of everything just go along with what I do. Come on we are going to the operations tent to find out what is happening.”

We arrived just as Corporal Jamerson reported.

"There were four empty containers and nothing else in the immediate area."

"Check inside the containers for any clues as to what was in them."

"There are no clues. Shall I have them removed like the others?"

"Record the serial numbers then remove them. Report to operations soon as you have done that."

"Understood, out."

"What was that all about?" Larson asked.

"There are four deserted cars in the scrub. Jamerson is going to record the license plates then call in the air force to dispose of them."

"I wish we could watch the fireworks," Fitzroy exclaimed.

"You cannot destroy other people's property," Larson said.

"That is the penalty for trespassing. We have done it before."

"Really, can we watch the air force in action?"

"We have more important things to do, there are a group of reporters loose in the scrub, we have to find them before they get too close. I want you to assemble the troops as soon as you can so I can talk to them."

The helicopter was landing so I told the radio operator to alert Sergeant Larmarra then went out to meet it.

"We did not see anything," the pilot said. "We skimmed the tops of the scrub and would have seen anything hiding in there."

"Thank you for trying. Can you stay here for the rest of the day? I need you to keep searching."

"I am at your disposal I will refuel and be ready in about a half hour."

"Thank you, have something to eat before you fly."

"I'll do that. Did you get your dispatches? I left them with the orderly."

I picked up the dispatch and asked the orderly if they had any maps of the area.

There was only one note in the envelope. It was handwritten in large letters with a felt pen.

"Dave, don't panic and do something foolish. We have contacted the colonel he will be here in a couple of days," Said Dixon.

Larson, Fitzroy and I were looking at the map.

We are in a valley formed by an ancient river. The escarpment on one side and rough rolling hills on the other. The desert is all around us then spreads out to the west and south. The eastern side was rough scrubby hills except for the riverbed where we were. It was very inhospitable, hot dry country. Miles and miles of nothing.

"They have to be somewhere near their vehicles," Larson said. "They could not survive without them."

Just then Corporal Jameson came in.

"We looked everywhere but there isn't even a rabbit out there."

"Did you find anything in their vehicles?" I asked.

"No sir, they were clean. Funny though I saw one of them when I was in Darwin on leave. It was a backpacker car for sale. I remember it because of the cartoon painted on the door."

"They must have dumped the cars," Fitzroy said.

"Why cut the fence and driveway in there?" Larson added.

"You are right," I said. "They dumped the cars there. It is a diversion to have us look in the wrong place."

"Is this another one of your theories?"

"I know what they are up to look here on the map."

A convoy of adventures were travelling along the outback road when they were startled by a low flying F 114 fighter crossing the road ahead of them.

They were even more startled when it fired two rockets then shot up at a steep angle with a deafening roar. They stopped when they heard the explosions in the distance. Then another fighter roared low parallel to the road and fired two rockets then blasted high into the air.

They were in a group excitingly discussing what happened when one of the jets flew low above them wiggled its wings and disappeared in an afterburner roar.

"Here is what I think is going on. A special built four wheeled vehicle stops at the fence. Someone gets out and cuts the wires then four junk cars drive in. The drivers run back to the road and get in two or more like vehicles. They drove fifty clicks down the road then turned off into the desert drive along another hundred clicks to the edge of the hills then head north up to us.

I figure they left those old cars there to divert us while they sneak in the other way across the desert."

"No one could be that desperate," Larson said. "They will perish out there in one day. Besides someone would see them."

"Not if they drive all night and camp in the daytime. The fence was checked yesterday afternoon. They arrived after dark then drove all night. I figure they are camped somewhere in the hills waiting until dark to sneak in here."

"That is a wild story," Fitzroy said. "But it does explain why we cannot find them."

"I will organize a search party," Jamerson said.

"Your Land Rovers cannot handle the desert. We will catch them when they come here."

The helicopter pilot came in and said he was ready.

"Stop on the escarpment and pick up Sergeant Larmarra."

"I would like to go too," Fitzroy said.

"Take Corporal Jamison with you."

"What are we going to do?" Larson asked.

"We are going to talk to the troops.

The troops had just finished lunch and were lined up in front of the operations tent.

"Have you taken roll call, Sergeant?"

"Yes sir, all present and accounted for."

"We have been ordered by headquarters to double the guard but they haven't assigned any troops to help us.

You saw and heard the jets earlier, we found four cars and destroyed them but we have not found the occupants and we do not know how many there are, so it is up to you to find and capture them.

They could be dressed in army clothes and wander around here unnoticed so we are going to start the 'Buddy System'.

You will pair off in twos. You should know each other by now so stop anyone you do not recognize and ask for identification.

Now in order to carry out our orders the work force will be cut in half. You will work a half a day and do guard duty the other half. The regular guards will continue as normal but the rest of you will be rostered for a half a day or night of guard duty. Lieutenant Larson has made up a list. He will assign you a post after we finish here.

Also, we have some night surveillance gear that you will learn how to use.

This is not a picnic. This is serious and I hope you all understand this. The newspapers have hired expert former service men who know how to infiltrate this depot so take this seriously and be alert. This project is the most important security operation since the World War. Now Lieutenant Larson will explain the roster to you. Thank you for listening and I hope you understand the seriousness of what I have said."

THE pilot picked up Sergeant Larmarra then headed towards the desert.

"Fly along near the edge of the desert," Larmarra told the pilot.

"How far are we going?"

"Not far, they should be about ten to fifteen clicks from here."

"How do you know that? Did you see them from your camp?"

"No, I figure that is as far as they could drive in the dark. This end of the desert is very rough."

Fitzroy was looking out towards the desert and Lamamra was looking along the edge. Jamerson was up front with the pilot.

After a while Larmarra said.

"Mark this spot but do not stop. Go a couple of more clicks then turn into the desert then return to the base."

"Did you see them?" Jamerson asked.

"Yes, there are three vehicles camped in the scrub at the edge of the desert."

"Why didn't we land and arrest them?"

"We cannot land in the desert and by the time we found a spot they would have bolted. We were just a patrol that did not see them."

"How do you know that?"

"They think they are clever and have outsmarted us. We will wait until they come in closer then capture them after they leave their vehicles."

"I do not understand we should have taken them by surprise and captured them."

"We might have caught a couple of them but we cannot chase their vehicles across the desert our Land Rovers would be bogged as soon as we hit the soft sand."

"Land Rovers can drive in soft sand."

"Their vehicles are designed for the desert. The Rovers would have to stop and deflate their tires and then drive very slowly. We could never catch them. We will get them tonight."

"They are camped here," Larmarra said and pointed to the spot on the map. "I will have the helicopter drop two men off on this hill to watch them. We will catch them when they move."

"That is a good plan," I said. "But what if they listen to our radios?"

"No problem, the boys will be talking all night in their own language. Even if they hear them, they will not understand what they are saying."

"That is a good plan," I said. "But we will continue the other patrols in case that is a decoy."

I gave Larmarra some night survey equipment then he went off in the helicopter.

I went to tell the captain our plans. There was nothing else to do until the intruders made their move.

EVER since I was told that the colonel was returning, an idea had been forming in my mind so I decided to see if it would work. I went into the tunnel to think about it.

I found the two electricians removing the last of the battery equipment.

"This stuff is amazing," one of them said. "Even though it is thirty years old in is good as new. All the batteries work and the chargers are top of the range, as good as anything available now."

"You can imagine how much they cost thirty years ago. I bet each of these weapons cost a couple of million each."

"Come with me, I want to discuss something with you."

We went into the last corridor where the two tugs were stored.

"I want to get these running. Then I want a couple of A-frames to lift the weapons off the trailers."

"That is an engineer's job, we are electricians."

"The engineers are busy repairing the road. I have an idea to get out of here in a couple of weeks, so I need these tugs and a couple of trailers to do it. We will put a platform on the trailers then start removing the sandbags. Then if the colonel approves, we will begin stripping down the weapons. The toughest job will be removing the barracks and office."

"You cannot do all that in a couple of weeks, a couple of months maybe."

"We could easily do it if we did not have to do guard duty."

"It would be a lot easier to remove the battery rack and the chargers with a trailer," one of them said. "I will find a mechanic to work on the tugs."

I knew I could get into trouble with the colonel but I was tired of this silly game and wanted to go home. I was going to strip down the weapons the take the spheres into the desert and blow them up.

The whole plan went through my brain in a flash and when I looked around I was anxious to get started.

I was working with the men until someone called me. When I went outside it was dark

It was Corporal Jamerson. "We just got a call from the scouts. The vehicles are moving."

We ran to the operations tent.

"Where are they now?" I asked.

"They are behind the hills. They will come out into the open desert soon."

We waited with anticipation then the radio operator said,

"Sir only two of them have been sighted."

"It is a trick, I exclaimed, where is the map?"

I looked at the map then told the radio operator.

"Call Larmarra. Tell him to send the scouts to area B 6."

"What is happening? Jamerson asked.

"The other two vehicles are a decoy."

"I do not understand."

"They assume that we will only spot two vehicles and chase them. They do not realize that we spotted them earlier. The other one will sneak in here while we are capturing the decoys."

"I will pick up the vehicles in the desert."

"Let the patrol do that I want you to find the third vehicle."

"Yes sir, how do I do that?"

"Get ready to move Larmarra will call as soon as his men spot the vehicle."

I told the radio operator to make a lot of noise when they spotted the two vehicles. "I want the third vehicle think their trick worked.

ABOUT a half hour later there was a lot of noise on the radio they had caught the two vehicles. They were taken to the detention tent and their vehicles were searched.

Larmarra came down to help.

"We have not spotted the third vehicle," he said. "Show me the map I will try to figure out where he went."

While Larmarra was looking at the map I got a report from Lieutenant Larson.

"We thoroughly searched them and their vehicles. They were clean no cameras or maps and they only had a bottle of water each and some fruit. They are trying to say they were only joy riding in the desert."

"They are trespassing on government land which is a prescribed Aboriginal reserve. Arrest them and ship them to Darwin. Send them to headquarters not the local police. They are a decoy for the third vehicle that we cannot find."

"What third vehicle? No one tells me anything."

"You are a lieutenant, you are supposed to know everything."

I looked at the map with Larmarra.

"The vehicle must have turned off here. That is the only area it could drive through but it did not come out over here where my men would spot it. They must be hiding in here somewhere waiting until they think it is safe to move."

"There are still four hours of darkness," I said. "He will have to move a lot closer or walk all night then take some pictures and wait until dark to return to his vehicle."

"He would have to be a very fit person to do that. I think he will move closer when he thinks it is safe. I will tell the men."

"Another thought," I said. "What if the third vehicle has not moved? It would be easier and quicker to skirt along the edge of the hills then hide."

"He would be quickly spotted. My men have night scopes."

"What if they quit after they spotted the other vehicles.?"

"I will check both lookouts."

"I want you to get the two vehicles ready in case we have to chase the other one. The Rovers would never catch them. Get Jamerson to help you."

"That is a good idea, I should have thought of it."

NOTHING more happen, and the first rays of the new day were shining over the edge of the hills. We had been up all night and were thinking of retiring when the radio operator called Larmarra.

"They spotted the vehicle," Larmarra shouted.

He talked a bit then showed us on the map.

"They spotted the heat from the vehicle. He is a long way off. He must have got lost in the dark. He seems to have broken down. He has not moved for a few minutes."

"Go get him," I said. "Take some ropes to tow the vehicle."

All thought of sleeping quickly vanished.

We were in the mess when the orderly came in.

"They have them, sir. The vehicle bogged in some bull dust. It will take both vehicles to pull it out."

"Tell Larmarra to leave it for the air force."

"He wants the three vehicles for his troops, they are expensive desert vehicles. He will be back at noon."

This episode had messed up my schedule. I was tired but I wanted to be here when they brought in the newsmen.

The helicopter arrived, it took all my persuading powers to get the pilot to transport the four decoys. I had to convince him that they were harmless tourist. The two guards went with them.

While they were organizing their departure I wrote a note to Lieutenant Dixson explaining what had happened and wanted to know what to do with the others. I smiled when I thought of the reaction it would cause.

I went to have a coffee with the captain. He was surprised when I told him about the reporters.

The men had the tugs going they were riding around the corridors.

"Like everything else," the electrician said. "They are like new. The mechanic has a couple of A frames. He will be here this afternoon."

We removed the canopy from two of the weapons. I showed him how to disconnect the trailer and then to put sandbags under it.

A plan was forming in my head to put bins on the trailers then load them with pieces of the weapons as we dismantled them. I hope the colonel goes along with the idea it will take a long time and a lot of work to render the explosive material.

To keep busy until Larmarra returned I decided to record the serial numbers of all the weapons, so I picked up a notepad from the orderly.

Each weapon had a record of maintenance. I used to fill them out when I worked on them. They were missing from these. I wondered if I had worked on any of them. I doubt it because there were so many of them. I estimated I loaded more than a hundred of them. At least two or more a week for three years. I do not know what happened to them they never came back and I never unloaded one.

They were replaced by a much smaller and more powerful one that did not need any maintenance and anyone could put them in or on any plane. The new ones had arrived at the depot just before I left.

That was a long time ago. What do they have now?

The men were heading for the mess hall, so I went with them.

A little while later Larmarra arrived.

He dropped off the two newsmen at the interrogation tent. They left them in their underwear with a guard for each of them.

"What a mess," Larmarra said. "Instead of stopping when they hit the bull dust, they tried to drive through it. We needed both vehicles to pull theirs out."

"For those who do not know, bull dust is fine talcum powder like sand that moves along with the wind. It is deposited in shallow depressions and looks like the surrounding area. You must be alert when you hit it or be swallowed. It is dry quicksand."

"They had planned for a long campaign, the vehicle is crammed full of water, fuel, food and camping gear. The two of them could have stayed out there for two weeks. What are you going to do with them?"

"I am sure Lieutenant Dixon will be here soon. I sent a note with the other four. Maybe you should take those vehicles away before he arrives."

"That is a good idea, I will leave right now."

"Separate all their personal gear the, lieutenant will want to examine it."

"I already have. We thoroughly searched them and the surrounding area when we caught them. They did not try to run away because they knew they would not survive without their supplies. Let me know what happens."

"I will bring you some bread in the morning."

Not long after Larmarra left the helicopter arrived. I was there to greet Dixson.

"Peace and quiet at last," he exclaimed. "Hello Dave, I envy you being out here with no telephones."

"Why don't you stay overnight and get a good rest."

"I would not wake up for a week besides I cannot leave Jones and Rodgers on their own."

"Come on, we will have a good cup of coffee I cannot offer you any Danish pastries but the cook does bake a good sourdough bread.

"Dave it is a crazy circus in Darwin. We not only have the local brass on us now the big newspapers are claiming we are censoring the news. There must be a hundred reporters in town. All of them asking questions."

"I know we sent four of them to you this morning and there are two more for you to question."

"That is why I am here the four you sent are not reporters they are American tourists claiming they are, desert explorer."

"That is serious, the Yanks must be spooked and are sending spies over here to check on our claims."

"That is what I tried to tell the colonel but he thinks they do not want to admit they built an illegal base here."

"They would never admit that anyway. I think it is more than that. It is an enormous racket and some big companies made an enormous amount of money here."

"Is this another one of your predictions?"

"It is not a prediction it is fact. This depot would have never been able to function it there had been a war. The diesel tank was empty and not connected and there isn't a fuel tank for the airfield. I am compiling a document of all the missing equipment and another for all the stolen items. This place was systematically looted by the builders and the big contractors."

"I know, I have been searching through the names of the workers. I found two. One has died but the other one sold his property and moved away. We found the missing water pump and the tools you had listed. I have someone looking for him.

Another important thing. The Yanks deny any knowledge of this depot but they are demanding the return of all the nuclear material. Also, they cannot find any trace of the so-called rendering factory they promised us. The colonel is worried that it will be years and an enormous cost to dismantle the weapons ourselves."

"When will the colonel arrive?"

"He is in Canberra now discussing this problem with the top brass who think he is mad."

"Can the colonel organize a large plane? At least a caribou?"

"I suppose so, why?"

"I have a plan to clean out this place in two weeks but I need the Navy boys. Call the colonel tonight and tell him to pick up the plane and the Navy Crew then he can return with twenty-six nuclear cores to hide where the yanks cannot find them. Then he can come back in two weeks to take the navy crew and two plutonium cores back and declare the site clear. Also have the navy crew bring some explosive bullets and at least twenty C-4 timed fuses."

"Dave, you are either mad or a genius."

"One more thing my plan includes finding three or four helicopters with night searching gear."

"I don't know about that. What do you want them for?"

"They will take the place of the hundred men we I need for my plan to get out of here."

"That is a wild plan but I can see what you want to do. I think the colonel will agree, what else can he do? Now I have to get back into the turmoil. Where are the tourists?"

I said, "Goodbye," to Dixon. He went in the helicopter to the interrogation tent.

I stood there watching the helicopter disappear over the hill wondering what I was going to do when I realized that I was extremely tired.

"I am going to bed."

I woke up with a start wondering where I was. I took a minute for the rest of my brain to wake up. It was pitch black, as usual. I laid there thinking of all that had happened and the weird mess I was in. *How did I get mixed up in this international intrigue?* I wondered.

I turned on the light and looked at the clock, six-twenty.

"Is it six-twenty in the evening and I have only slept a couple of hours or is it six-twenty in the morning and I slept all night?"

I dressed then walked to the entrance. It was dark only a few lights in the cavern. *It is dark at six-twenty at night,* I thought and I looked around.

This is weird, am I cracking up? I know I will go to the mess tent if they are serving breakfast, I will know it is morning.

On the way I reasoned with myself that I was tired and stressed and not going mad.

I could smell the bacon before I entered the tent. I smiled and realized I had a good long sleep.

A quick coffee woke me up and cleared my head.

I saw Corporal Jamerson sitting alone so I sat with him. He told me how they captured the Yanks.

They just sat near their vehicle with their heads in their hands.

I learned a lot from Sergeant Larmarra. He showed me how to survey a crime scene. He found a backpack they had hidden.

"Always look for something different or odd," he said. "When someone hides something, they always hide it near a marker so they can find it again."

I was about to leave when Fitzroy came in. I sat with him while he ate.

"Today is my last day," he proudly announced. "The last of the gravel will be removed from in front of the hangar. We will have the grand opening this afternoon."

"Congratulations but do not plan on a vacation just yet."

"What do you mean? I am finished here, it is six weeks before the next term starts. I am going to relax till then."

"I have one more small task for you."

"I do not want to hear what you are going to tell me."

"It is not that bad. The runway has to be repaired so a large plane can land here and it has to be done now."

Fitzroy thought for a few seconds then said.

"That is not too bad unless there has been some damage done by the floods. Why didn't you tell me this sooner?"

"Because I only thought of it yesterday. The colonel is coming in a big plane."

"Have him land at Darwin and drive here I want to get out of here."

"So do I, that is why the plane is coming so we can all get out of here."

"All right I will get the men started then look at the runway. I could work faster if I had more men. This guard duty thing has slowed me down."

"Take all the men you need. We caught the spies I doubt if anyone else will try to sneak in here. That reminds me I have to talk to Larson to change the roster. See you at the grand opening."

I picked up all the spare bread as I left then hitched a ride to Larmarra's camp.

"Thanks for the bread. The men are pleased to get those vehicles. They are eager to take them home and put them to work."

"I have a plan and if it is approved you can go home in a couple of weeks."

"I really hope so, I am afraid I will miss the next course at the academy then they will reassign me and forget me."

"You are a worse doom prophet than I am. After what you have done here they will make you a captain."

Larmarra laughed then said, "Tell me about your plan."

He was pleased to hear my idea.

"That is remarkable. You thought that up all by yourself? They will make you a general."

We both laughed.

"One bit of advice, set the charges off a long way from the cave. Whatever you do you must not upset whatever lives there."

"I agree," then I told him about Mason's visit and the specter I saw on the lake. It upset him.

"Please do not talk about that if the troops hear that, they will desert."

The helicopter was coming. We could see it in the distance. To calm Larmarra down I asked him if I could drive one of the new vehicles back.

"I want you to come too incase there is a dispatch about the grand plan."

On the way down I asked Larmarra if the valley could be cleared of scrub.

"I want the men working full time so we can get out of here. You can see the desert side but a hundred men could hide in that scrub."

"I will send down a crew to burn it. Will you feed them?"

"Of course. How are you going to get any of your men to do that? The fire will be seen for miles and cause people to investigate he smoke."

"Don't worry. Not all the men are initiated but they will not go near the cave that is why you have to feed them. The way we burn there will not be very much smoke."

"I will have to watch that."

The pilot handed me a fat envelope. The two guards told me the two me did not cause any trouble. This is the best assignment they ever had.

"I am sorry to have to tell you that it is finished. Have a coffee then go to the tunnel for reassignment. We have caught all the spies."

Larmarra and I went into the mess to read the dispatches.

The fat envelope was a summary of the colonel's visit with the Yanks. I would read it later. The big news was a handwritten note.

"Dave, I spoke to the colonel as soon as I returned. He was all excited. He called me this morning and told me he stayed up all night planning the most important operation he has ever done.

You are to start immediately. He will be here with the navy as soon as he can organize the plane. Good one Dave."

"That is great news," Larmarra said. "I will send the men down as soon as I get back."

"Before you leave will you drive me out to the hangar so I can tell Fitzroy the news."

"OK. I can say, 'Hi' to Fitzy."

"I was just about to send someone after you we are ready to open the hangar doors. You may have the honor."

"Thank you but it is your project so you do it."

"OK. But I want you to tell me what we will find in there."

"That is easy, nothing. Maybe a few odd spare parts like tires and instruments for the planes."

"There has to be more than that in there maybe even a B 52 Bomber."

I laughed.

"The hangar will be stripped just like everything else here."

The rollers were rusty but moved easily once they were freed.

The hangar was bigger than I thought, it went way back into the hillside.

Except for a row of tires and some packages of instruments the only other things in the hangar were two enormous airplane tugs. They were the old-style ones. The wheels were larger and taller than we were, and it had a ladder to climb up to the cabin.

I remembered driving one when I was in the service. It was parked near where we were working on a B 52. The driver was standing nearby smoking. I asked him if I could drive it and he said OK as long as I did not hit anything.

It was amazing climbing up into the cockpit but I was surprised when I sat in the seat. There was only a steering wheel and one floor pedal.

I think the driver thought I would not figure how to drive it but I soon figured it out. The foot pedal was an accelerator, brake and gear shift all in one. You pressed forward with you toe to move. Pressed backward with your heel to reverse and straight down to stop. It was practical because it only moved at walking speed.

It was quite a sensation driving it because of the large wheels it rocked and swayed like a boat in a storm. I soon had enough and only did a circle on the tarmac.

It all came flashing back when I saw the big old thing.

"You were wrong," Fitzy said. "Look at those tugs."

"Where is your bomber?" I smiled.

After a quick look around, I told Fitzroy to start on the runway after lunch because the colonel would be here soon.

"It shouldn't take long maybe just this afternoon."

"Start right away in case you find something wrong. The colonel has to land here."

I had Larmarra drop me off as close to the tunnel as he dared to go.

I had a coffee with the captain and sergeant to bring them up to date. Then I began to organize the men to start dismantling the weapons.

"We will start after lunch. Gather up all the tools you can find. We are going to turn the trailers into work vehicles so scrounge some plywood for bins. We will dump all the scrap here in the main chamber then load it on to trucks. At the same time we will remove the sandbags and dump them somewhere convenient."

"That will take a lot of manpower," someone said.

"I know you are all relieved of guard duty. We have caught the spies and I doubt if there will be any more."

The men cheered.

I had one more thing to do before lunch. I had to find Larson to tell him to revise the guard roster.

I found Larson in the mess tent talking with Fitzroy. I did not have to tell him anything Fitzroy already had.

"This is crazy," he said. "I just finished the guard roster it took me all morning now You have changed your mind."

"That is how the army works, damn the torpedoes full speed ahead."

"You are mad that is navy lingo."

We all laughed.

After all the strain and tension, it was good to have a laugh.

Four of Larmarra's men came into the mess looking for me. I told them to have some lunch then I would show them what to do.

I was pleased with myself my plan was working we would soon be leaving here.

We went in a convoy to the runway. I showed Lamarre's men what to do then Fitzroy, Larson and I road along the runway.

"I will have the two graders scrape off the sand then the sweeper will clean it. I do not have to stay and watch so I will leave on the helicopter this afternoon."

"Why are you in such a hurry to leave," Larson asked. "I like it here no one bothers us."

"There is someone I want to spend some time with before I start my uni course. Maybe I will have time to convince her to go to Canberra with me."

"You will have to wait a little longer because I have another job for you."

"I thought you were my friend, what else have you dreamed up?"

"I want you to build another road for me."

"What, that will take weeks, get someone else. The regular engineer should have returned from leave by now get him. I am going back to school."

"I just want your advice. I have to build a road into the desert. About ten miles long, that's all."

"You are mad a road that long will take a month or more to build."

"It will only take a day or two we will look at it after you organize this job pick me up at the cavern when you finish here."

When we arrived at the cavern, I told Larson to have the captain and the sergeant come out so they would know what was going on.

I had the men gather in the large arena.

"We are going to dismantle the whole area. The sandbags and weapons first then the barracks and office. We need the trailers to do this so we will lift the weapons off the trailers on to sandbags then pile other sandbags on the trailers then haul them away. We will dismantle the weapons and pile the scrap here until we have enough to haul away. A navy demolition team will help us do that. You will see some interesting fireworks as we dispose of the explosives.

I am hoping we can do all of this within two or three weeks at the most. Then you can resume your usual duties.

Any questions?"

The captain spoke up.

"Mr Freeman, you cannot possibly dismantle all of this in three weeks. Two months maybe but not in that short time."

"Sir, I have a hundred men to do the work plus a navy demolition team, I am sure it can be done in that time."

One of the men put up his hand.

"I heard you mention, 'Explosives', I did not know there were explosives here."

"That is what this exercise is all about. There are enough explosives here to demolish this whole area and turn it into a desert. About thirty-five tons of the most powerful explosive known. We have to get rid of it in case someone came in here with a flame."

The men were slightly alarmed then Sergeant McAlister spoke up, well he shouted.

"Attention! Fall in!"

He walked back and forth in front of them then he turned on them.

"You are supposed to be soldiers.

It is your duty to be blown up for your country. That is what you signed up for. You will work hard and fast all day every day until this dirty job is finished and you will smile while you are doing it or you will do the demolition instead of the pussy navy men. Understand… What?"

"Yes sir!" They all shouted.

"You will do whatever Mr Freeman tells you to do. Now form into teams and pay attention to Mr Freeman."

"Thank you, Sergeant McAllister. We are going to start on this near wall because the navy team are going to dismantle those two weapons first. Remove all the sandbags then lift up the weapons and remove the trailers. Your supervisors have their instructions. Sergeant, dismiss the men."

I was about to have a coffee with the captain when Fitzroy arrived.

"I will not be long," I told the captain. "We will have coffee when I come back."

I took Fitzroy to a weapon the men had sat on sandbags. I removed the side panel to show him the core.

"We are going to haul these into the desert and blow them up. That is what I need the road for."

"That will take forever to do all of these."

"We are going to blow the whole core not a segment like we did at the farm."

"The whole thing? How much explosive is in there?"

"A ton and a half, approximately three thousand pounds."

"Holy crap! That will be one hell of an explosion."

"That is why we are going to do it in the desert. No one will see or hear it."

"I would like to see a ton and a half of explosive go off."

"I thought you were eager to get out of here. What about your lady friend?"

"That is only a 'May be', this is real."

"Come on I will show where the road is going."

I drove out of the cavern and around the long way towards the desert.

"Why are we going this way? It is much shorter around the other side."

"Larmarra told me to go this way, so we do not drive over the tunnel."

"The tunnel is deep enough to take the weight of our vehicles."

"We have to go this way and way out into the desert so not to disturb the spirit in the tunnel."

Fitzroy laughed, "I am surprised that you would fall for that hocus pocus."

"I can feel its presences and I have seen the specter on the lake. Believe me, it is real."

"We drove into the desert then stopped in the middle of nowhere."

"You chose a good route," Fitzroy said. "The ground is hard all it needs is leveling with a dozer."

"I thought a run out and back would do it."

"You have it figured out so you do not need me but I will stay anyway because I want to see the fireworks."

On the way back we had coffee with the captain.

I went to check on the men. They were using Fitzroy's vehicle to tow a trailer. The tugs were not strong enough to climb the incline. Most of the sandbags along the wall were gone. The two weapons were sitting on sandbags ready to be dismantled.

"Start removing the opposite wall. I have to get my camera to record everything."

"I had been recording all the thieving and taking pictures of everything we were doing. I had one of the men take a picture of me beside each of the weapons. I made sure the serial numbers were in the picture."

"Before we start dismantling these things, I want all the markings removed. Use the air grinder to do it because all of this is going to a scrap yard."

The air compressor was parked way down the tunnel because of the fumes.

The best tool of all was a pneumatic pipe cutter. A smaller version of the Jaws of Life. It cut through the struts like they were toothpicks.

But some of the tools were electrical so I had to close the canteen or the orderly room because of the power drain. The canteen lost.

We quit when the two spheres were sitting on sandbags next to the wall. I sat with the electricians and the mechanics in the now opened canteen. While we were enjoying a cold beer I explained how we would proceed.

"I want to use the far corridor to dismantle the weapons so tow them there. Take them apart just like the others. The navy is coming to dispose of them."

"What is the difficulty of disposing of them that the navy has to do it?" one of them said. "We are just as good as the navy."

"The two we just worked on are special. They are full of highly dangerous radioactive material that has to be handled by experts. When they finish with them, they will dispose of the other spheres."

"How are they going to dispose of all those spheres?"

"They will be towed into the desert then a block o C 4 will be inserted in the sphere then, 'Boom'."

"We can do that just as well as they can."

"I understand that but they are here. I know you will help them then become certified explosive handlers."

I was trying to calm them down. I guess it worked because another of them asked a different question.

"Mr Freeman, what is that round ring on the back of the sphere? It has what look like gold fingers all around the inside of it."

"That is the contact for the fuse. Yes, the fingers are gold and the same thing is on the end of the fuse. All the contacts on the weapon are either gold or silver. The gold is to make sure the contacts do not corrode. I am not sure if they are real or only plated."

"Can we have them? The fellow asked, real or not gold is worth money."

"You can have them all as long as you do not fight over them and share equally."

They were eager to get back to work.

I stayed behind when the men went to the mess tent. I wanted to arrange things for tomorrow. I had to make sure they did not get the two plutonium spheres mixed up with the others. It would be a disaster if they were detonated by mistake.

I wrapped, 'Do Not Cross Tape', around them.

It was dark when I finally quit. I stood at the entrance looking up at the stars wondering what I was doing here.

"I do not want to think about it. I am glad it is almost over." The two little men on my shoulders were laughing. A faint smell of smoke lingered in the air.

I had breakfast with Lieutenants Fitzroy and Larson. Fitzroy told me the runway was finished and he would start on the desert road as soon as he organized the men. When Fitzroy left Larson told me he had been talking with the men last night.

"They want to have a go at blowing up a sphere. They think they can do it as well or better than the navy. I would like to see a big explosion so why not let them have a go?"

I didn't like the idea, besides the navy men were experts but these men had been working hard and not complaining so I decided to let them, 'Have a go', as the Aussies say.

"All right I will listen to them. If I approve, they can set two of them off late this afternoon."

"That is great, come on let's tell the men."

There were smiles and back slapping when Larson told the men I had approved their detonating the spheres.

"Hold on a minute," I said. "I do not know what you plan to do. I may not like it."

"We are trained to remove obstacles with explosives," Sergeant Anderson said. "We have all the equipment and Garry has a fool proof idea so there is no reason not to approve it.
I will rig up one of the detonators to our control, simple."

"All right try it out with a detonator."

"I already have we set two of them off last night. They are more powerful than our detonators."

The men were smiling and nodding their heads.

"All right we will dismantle two weapons then take the spheres into the desert to set them off."

The men cheered.

"We were going to detonate one of the spheres last night but when we saw them wrapped in no go tape we decided not to."

I was shocked. I gathered all the men around me then said to Lieutenant Larson.

"Did you know about this?"

"I saw no harm in exploding a detonator but I stopped them from taking a sphere."

I had trouble controlling myself. I took a deep breath then casually said.

"Do any of you know what plutonium is?"

No one answered.

"What about you, lieutenant?"

"I know it is some sort of dangerous radioactive material."

"Pay attention," I said in a loud voice. "If you had exploded one of those spheres last night we would all be dead now."

They looked at each other wondering what I meant.

"Not only that the radioactive cloud would be over Alice Springs by now killing everyone there."

I was having a hard time controlling my voice.

"Then it would drift on to Broken Hill then on to the coast killing a lot of people and making the rest very sick. Then it would drift to New Zealand and make a lot of them sick."

I had to stop I could hardly control myself. The men could see I was upset they were getting nervous too.

After a few moments I calmed down.

"That is why the navy demolition team is coming here. They dismantled one at our last job. Just exposing the inner core of those spheres is very dangerous. There is enough material in there to set off a full atomic explosion. That is why the aluminum chain is in the sphere to prevent a full atomic blast.

I cannot trust any of you any more so from now on no one will enter the caverns unless I am here. Other than the Orderly Room and the canteen the rest of the area is off limits and I will show no mercy to anyone who disobeys that order. I will consider that you are a saboteur and ask for the full penalty. I mean it.

Now before we start work we will go through the full routine on dismantling and I will not stand for any more cowboy antics. You are dealing with a ton and a half of the most powerful explosive there is. It makes dynamite look like firecrackers. Also, it is old and unstable. You have no concept of how close you came to another Hiroshima."

For the next hour I had a very attentive somber class listening to my every word.

Then I had two weapons brought in.

I had not employed the strict safety methods we had at the farm because these weapons had not been move and the atmosphere was not dry in the cavern. We did earth the weapons before they were handled. That was all that was necessary.

The men worked quietly and efficiently. Larson watched for a while then wandered off.

I was surprised when someone said it was time for lunch.

On the way to the mess tent Garry, the electrician, apologized.

"I only wanted to show you that we are as good as the navy."

"You may be by the time we finish here. Just remember the navy boys are pros they do not play with explosives."

I sat by myself thinking I had trained a good crew and we would easily finish on time. Then it dawned on me. I am trapped in the cavern. If I leave the men have to leave too.

I told the men to wait until I returned. I walked around to the edge of the valley to see how the burning went. I could see all the way to the fence. The fire had cleaned all the rubbish off. Then I went into the operations tent to find out if I had any dispatches. There was only one so I took an envelope with me in case I had to reply.

I sat on a sandbag reading the note from Dixon. It was more than a note there were three pages.

The major has a plane but cannot find a pilot and crew. No one wants to fly into the desert and the navy crew have to finish a job.

The tourist turned out to be army SAS personnel. There is a secret war going on. We can shoot them as spies. The Yanks have a lot to own up to. The newspaper people have calmed down after some tourist reported jet fighters firing rockets close to the road. It upset the air force so they grounded all flights for a week.

What is going on there? You have been very quiet.

I wrote a quick note, "We are blowing up spheres come and watch the fireworks."

BY midafternoon two spheres were sitting on trailers ready to be towed to the desert.

There were a couple of minor setbacks.

Garry showed me his detonator. It was off the sphere. He had used one of the detonator terminals to connect the wires of the control to.

"Very clever but how long is the cable?" I asked.

"Thirty meters."

"When we exploded the single segments from the core, we had to be two hundred meters away. This is a whole sphere. Five hundred meters or no explosion."

"There is a full coil in the supply room. I will get it."

"The mechanic told me the bolts holding the spere together were very expensive high tensile tungsten steel. It is a shame to waste them."

"You can remove half of them as long as the sphere is still held together. You can have all of the ones the navy remove from the two special spheres."

Fitzroy came looking for me to tell me the road was finished.

I showed him the two spheres. He wanted to go right away.

"We need some transport. Have some lunch while we get ready."

"You can use my trucks. This is too good to miss."

Before we hooked up, I had the spheres covered with the canopies used for the weapons.

"Just in case someone is spying," I explained.

By the time we were ready to leave the whole base was going with us.

There wasn't enough transportation so there was a lo loader full of men in the convoy.

I stopped everything then said to the troops,

"Someone has to stay here. I want a patrol and someone manning the radio."

There was a groan from the troops.

"There are going to be a lot of these explosions. Those who stay can see the next one."

A Rover pulled out of the line and the clerk walked back to the operations tent.

Someone called out, "Wagons ho," then the convoy moved out.

Being engineers they thought of everything including A-frames to unload the spheres so they brought along some wooden blocks so they would not sink in the sand.

We found the perfect spot, a dip in the sand.

The spheres were placed about two hundred meters apart. Then I said to Garry, "Give me the control."

He was going to say something but he didn't.

"I will show you the proper way to set up the explosion."

Garry and I walked to a sphere. Two men followed us with the coil of wire.

Garry had attached the detonator to the wire so I said to him.

"On a long run like this you usually attach the wire to something so it will not separate from the detonator."

Garry disconnected the terminal then wrapped the wire around the lifting brace.

I told the other two to run the wire out. They had a stick to roll the coil on as they walked back.

"I can understand what you are showing me," Garry said. "I should have wrapped the wire on the lifting brace then attached the detonator."

"Your wire should always be secure in case there is a misfire. You would not know if the wire came loose or the detonator failed. Another thing, why did I take the control?"

"I really do not know."

"Simple, what if someone at the other end was playing with it? You would die when you attached the detonator. The one who sets the charge attaches the control. Come on the men have signaled."

There was a large crowd standing around waiting.

I held up my hand and said, "No one knows how powerful this explosion will be so we will move back to that mound over there."

There was a moan from the group.

"You may be able to get closer for the next shot. Now move back."

I signaled a driver to bring his vehicle with a trailer on it up to where we were. Then I had some men tip the trailer on its side. I gave Garry the control then left with the others.

"You can watch the next one."

When I joined them they realized I was serious.

Garry signaled then we all shouted, "Fire in the hole."

There was a tremendous explosion, the shock wave hit us hard. Some stumbled backwards.

There was an almighty cloud of sand that took its time dissipating.

When we recovered and looked around there were bits of aluminum scattered in the sand.

The trailer was tipped on top of Garry. We ran to see if he was all right. Some men lifted the trailer off him. All he could say was, "Wow."

When we looked at the trailer the plywood floor was peppered with bits if shrapnel and one tire was blown.

The outfit had a resident medic who checked Garry. He was shocked but all right.

I gathered the men around me then told them.

"Never take explosives for granted keep in mind that it is dangerous. You saw that today. We were safe because the explosion took place it the depression if it had been on that mound some of us would have been injured from shrapnel. If Garry has another coil of wire we will move to the next shot otherwise the wire will be too short."

"I have an extra hundred meters in my truck."

The men cheered.

The second sphere was further away so there was not any danger. Garry did it right this time and I crouched behind the trailer and set off the shot.

All the drama was forgotten. The men were smiling and cheering.

Before they could disperse, I called Lieutenant Larson to police the area then told the men on the lo loader to police around the where the trailer was. I was surprised they did not grumble. It did not take long with so many men. The wrecked trailer was loaded on to the other one. Nothing was left except our tire tracks.

There was a party in the mess tent. The meal was late because the cooks went along too.

THE next day the men worked steadily and quietly. Most of the sandbags in that area were gone.

I thought I could take a break and have coffee with the captain.

As I was walking towards the orderly room a patrol vehicle came down the ramp.

What has happened now? I thought.

The driver ran up to me and handed me a dispatch envelope marked, "Urgent."

"Wait till I read it."

The page was folded all I could read at first glance was, "Hold the fireworks," in bold letters.

I am in big trouble now, I thought.

I opened the page and it said, "Until we get there."

I smiled and told the driver to tell the pilot to be here at four this afternoon.

"He is invited too. Also call Sergeant Larmarra tell him his friends will be on the afternoon flight."

The captain was still excited over the explosions.

"Dave, I am a desk jockey. I have never seen an explosion in all my years in the army. That was the most exciting thing I have ever see.

Dave, you are dancing with the devil handling that powerful stuff. How do you handle it? I would have had a breakdown years ago."

"I respect it. I worked on a hundred or more weapons while I was in the air force then I worked in the mines for a time. If you treat explosives right, it will be good to you."

"I could never do what you are doing."

"I bet you could. I will prove it to you. Would you like to set off the spheres this afternoon?"

I could see his eyes bulging, he was so excited.

"I don't know I never thought of doing anything like that."

"Think it over, you have the rest of the day or you can wait till another day. There will be lots more explosions."

I thought I would burst his bubble before he burst so I said as I was leaving.

"By the way, the colonel will be here in a couple of days. He may stay for a day or two."

I thought two spheres a day was a good safe schedule. Maybe the navy boys would change it. So, when the spheres were ready I told the men they could quit for the day.

Garry and Sergeant Anderson hung around.

They showed me the pile of contacts they had removed from the sphere rings.

"They are eighteen carat gold," Anderson said. "We will have a fortune by the time we finish. Can we use one of those small drums to store them in?"

"You can have half the drums when the navy is through with them. They contain a segment of the explosive core."

"They are full of explosives," Garry asked. "We can set them off as well as the navy."

"Relax Garry the navy is bringing some explosive bullets so you can have some target practice. I assume you all have rifles."

"Yes sir, we are a combat unit. What do you mean by target practice?"

"The segments will be lined up and you can shoot at them. The explosive bullets will set them off."

"Man, oh man that will be something."

"I thought you would like it but you have to control yourself for now."

"What are in the other drums?" Anderson asked.

"The small ones with the pressure gauge on them contain the nuclear cores. The large ones contain the fuses. I suppose a crew can start dismantling the fuses."

"Are there some more gold contacts on them?"

"There is an identical contact ring on each fuse."

"Wow, we are really rich. I will get a crew on it right away. We can use a large drum to store the contacts in."

I had to smile.

I had lunch with Lieutenant Fitzroy.

"I am finished here, I have seen the explosion. The rest will be the same. I could leave but there is one more thing I want to do. I want to explore the lake in the cavern. May I have Lieutenant Larson and Sergeant Anderson? They said they would go with me."

"I think you are being foolish. Ranger Mason almost ended up in the psychiatric ward after his short excursion there."

"He is a native. I do not believe in that mumbo jumbo."

"I saw what happened to Ranger Mason and I saw the specter on the lake. Mumbo Jumbo or not there is something out there. Larmarra told me to set off the charges a long way away from the cavern. That is why

I put the road on the far side so not to disturb the spirit. Besides Larson and Anderson are busy dismantling the weapons.”

“This place has spooked you just like the men on the escarpment. You can spare the men for a half a day.”

“I do not know about that. It really messed up, Mason. I do not want them messed up I need them they are experienced.”

During lunch, Sergeant Anderson rounded up a squad of men to dismantle the fuses. They were eager to get started.

I was trapped I wanted to meet the helicopter and spend some time with Rogers and Dixon.

“We have seen the explosion,” Anderson said. “We would rather work all afternoon dismantling the fuses.”

“I do not know about that. I want to meet the helicopter then I have to go to the site to supervise the shots.”

The men were disappointed they wanted to harvest more gold.

“Would you allow Lieutenant Larson to supervise us so we can work all afternoon?” he pleaded.

“I suppose so, will he do it?”

“He will if you order him to.”

When the men mentioned gold Larson readily agreed.

I spent some time showing them how to dismantle the fuses. They were amazed at all the intricate expensive instruments inside it.

“That is the most intricate switch I have ever seen,” Garry exclaimed. “How does it work?”

“It is a failsafe system,” I explained. “There are two of everything. When the weapon falls from the plane, that brass wire pulls out then all those switches turn on. That arms the weapon.

Then the alternators turn on and charge the capacitors.

When the desired altitude is reached either the radars or the barometers close then the charge from the capacitors fire the detonators. A simple safe system.”

“It may be safe but that is not simple.”

“To a scientist it is. Two of everything times three different switches means it has to go off.”

“It seems like a lot of extra expense for nothing.”

"During the war ten percent of the bombs dropped did not go off. They made sure that that did not happen to these. Not only that they added a piezoeic switch in case everything else failed. It would go off at six hundred feet."

Garry shook his head.

"That is why technicians like me had to test every weapon before we loaded it. Now they are much smaller and come sealed just hang them on or in a plane. That takes away the chance that a technician could make a mistake."

"Did you ever make a mistake?"

"I never got a bad report."

I watched the men work for a little while then went to meet the helicopter.

I had planned to have a coffee but the helicopter was coming in as I neared the mess tent.

There was a lot of smiles and backslapping because they were excited about seeing the explosions.

I was surprised to see Ian there and even more surprised when Captain Williamson stepped down. Larmarra soon arrived on a motorcycle.

We sat at a table in the mess tent and caught up on the latest news.

Captain Williamson told me the top brass have given Colonel Martin complete control over the project.

"Things are so bad they have dumped it all on the colonel then he dumped it on me so in true army protocol I am dumping it on you."

He sat back and smiled.

"Thanks a lot. You had better watch me closely because if I go down you will go with me."

"I am not worried I know you know what you are doing. Seriously you saved all of us with your idea. It was too much for the brass so they were going to surrender to the Yanks. Now we have a ton of uranium to bargain with. You saved the day."

"I only wanted to get out of here. Speaking of, 'Getting out', we had better move it is getting late."

The convoy was about a third the size it was yesterday. There were plenty of spare seats, so it headed out as soon as we arrived.

I sat beside Captain Williamson in the rear seat.

"Would you like to set off a charge?" I asked.

"No thanks, I hate explosions I will just observe."

The spheres were set further away than the first ones for safety reasons. The same team went with me but one of the others set the detonator while the other two paid out the wire.

I handed him the detonator and watched his hands shaking as he tried to attach the terminal.

"There is nothing to be afraid of. I have been handling explosives since I was your age and I am still here. As long as you go by the book nothing will go wrong."

"I know that but I keep thinking it will go off."

"So, what if it does you will never know it so relax."

He gave me a funny look then began to laugh.

Walking back, he said.

"Thank you for telling me I would not have known if there was an explosion. I realized I was worrying for nothing. I will not be afraid of explosives from now on."

The destinations went off without any mishaps. The captain was impressed.

Back at the mess I had to explain to Captain Frazier that the captain and the others had arrived just as the convoy was leaving so there was not time for introductions.

The others left but Captain Williamson wanted to be brief on what was going on here so he bunked with me for the night.

When we settled down he told me he joined up just as the war was ending and witnessed two of his mates blown up a few days before the war ended.

THE next morning, I convinced the captain to have breakfast before he inspected the cavern. He wanted to leave with the morning helicopter but it took until lunch to finish the inspection because we had coffee with Captain Frazier.

The two captains joined the detonations and each of them set off a charge. They were very proud of their accomplishment.

On the way to the helicopter Captain Williamson said to me.

"Dave, I will stay in Darwin there is a lot to do. I have a lot to tell the colonel. If you had not devised this plan we would all be summoned before a bord of inquiry and blamed for this evil plot. All I can say is thank you."

The pilot gave me the mail and the only dispatch. It was from Dixon.

"The colonel will arrive Friday about Noon. He will refuel at Alice Springs. The navy will be with him. I found a junk dealer not sure about the helicopters. We are still talking about the fireworks."

I had to ask the clerk what day it was. It was Tuesday. I only had two days to get ready for the colonel.

When I told Fitzroy and Larson the colonel would be here on Friday at breakfast the next morning Fitzroy exclaimed.

"You can object all you want but we are going to explore the lake this morning and I will be on the afternoon flight to Darwin. I do not want to be suckered into any more projects. I am going back to finish my degree."

Larson jumped in and said.

"We will start right away and be finished before the detonations are ready. You have enough men you do not need us."

I knew better than to argue with them so I just nodded my head.

I walked down into the cavern into the corridor past the barracks. Everything had changed. There used to be a long dark corridor now there was a large open chamber with the two spheres and the nuclear canisters on the side wall. The rest of the area was a large work area with two weapons ready to be dismantled on one side. A row of trailers, packed with sandbags, were lined up ready to be towed outside.

The work had just begun when a Land Rover came into the area with a large rubber dinghy tied to its roof. All work stopped so we all went to the lake to watch the launch.

I stopped the launch until one of them came back with a large coil of rope. I had insisted that a line be tied to the dinghy in case they were rendered unconscious by the spirit. They grumbled but did not argue.

The dinghy had two seats, some oars and a small electric motor mounted on an add mount on at the rear.

Fitzroy, Larson, Andrews and Jamerson were dressed in shorts and T-shirts. They had flashlights and cameras just like tourists.

Everyone but me was excited and cheered as they pushed off. I was surprised at how well the little motor pushed them along.

They waved then settled down for their adventure.

We were watching the camera flashes and the torches flickering at the ceiling and in the water.

As they approached the edge of the light, I was watching intently for the mist I saw the last time.

Nothing happened for a few minutes then they disappeared.

They disappeared completely. No lights or outlines or shadows. They had vanished.

Then someone shouted. The line had become taunt and was rapidly running off the spool. One of the men grabbed it but it burnt his hands.

The Land Rover was parked at the edge of the water, so I ran to it and flipped the rope over the trailer hitch. A couple of men realized what I was trying to do so they grabbed the spool and used it to flip the rope over the hitch a couple of times.

The rope stopped then stretched and the Rover was being dragged into the water. One of the men jumped in and started it to drive it out.

The wheels were turning in the sand it was not moving but it was not going backwards either. I thought the rope was going to snap at any moment. Then the Rover started moving. Then it lurched forward. I shouted to the driver to keep going all the way up the ramp. We were all staring into the blackness. Then the dinghy appeared. We all gasped there was no one in it.

When the driver reached the top of the ramp he stopped. The dinghy was about ten meters out so it was quickly pulled in. To our great relief the four men were lying in the bottom. We soon realized they were unconscious. They were quickly checked and found to be breathing. We sat them up and gently slapped them to wake them up.

Jamerson was the first to wake. He began screaming. Two of his mates comforted him the other three were groggy so we took them to the cafeteria. I figured we should get them out of the cavern away from the influence of the spirit.

I was right, they quickly revived in the fresh air so we took them into the mess tent and fed them black coffee.

Fitzroy quickly left and went to his tent and packed his kit. I found him waiting near the helicopter landing pad.

"I am sorry, I did not heed your advice. I only hope I am all right. Do not ask me what happened. It was too horrible and I want to forget it if I talk about it I will remember and have nightmares. I have two weeks before the term starts. I hope I can recover by them. I do not want to talk any more. Goodbye Dave, you were a good mate thank you for everything."

He took my hand and vigorously shook it then he turned to look for the helicopter. I knew he did not want me there so I walked away. It was hard to leave a mate in distress but that is what he wanted.

The other two had recovered quickly. They both said the same thing, "Everything went black then they woke up on the shore."

I was worried about Jamerson so I stopped at his tent. He got up when I came in. He told me he did not know that he was part Aboriginal.

"I was punished because I did not acknowledge my heritage. How was I to know? My parents never told me."

"I will have Sergeant Larmarra talk with you when he comes down. Rest until then."

That is about all I could do. I was thankful that it did not turn out being a tragedy.

BACK in the cavern all work has ceased for the day. I inspected the dinghy. It was a miracle they survived. It was a wreck. The motor and its mount were gone. So were the oars, flashlights and cameras.

There had been a rope tied to a tab on the bow I guess that is how the spirit had pulled the dinghy because the tab and front of the bow was torn away. Because the motor was on the back and the rope was tied to tabs on each side, they were torn but held. The dinghy had two chambers a top gunwale and the lower body the gunwale had deflated. How would we have explained the disappearance of four men?

A few men were dismantling the fuses.

"There are only four left," Garry said. "But we still have the remaining rings on the weapons to do. I bet there will be nearly fifty kilos of gold when we finish. That is a lot of money."

"Don't get your hopes up remember it is only plated."

"I realized that but it is still a lot of gold."

"We will do two more weapons tomorrow then we will have to clean up the area the colonel will be here Friday noon.

"We can do four weapons tomorrow and clean up Friday morning," Garry said. "That way we will catch up."

He was not eager to catch up he wanted the gold contacts on the rear of the spheres.

That was all for the day. I hated to waste the day otherwise tings were moving along at a good rate with on mishaps, so far.

I helped with the dismantling as we easily had four spheres finished in time for a late lunch.

Sergeant Larmarra has asked if his men could set one of them off so I sent him a coded message to meet at the bottom of the hill. He had to tow them up the steep incline with his new vehicles it would put a strain on the Land Rovers.

"We will set ours off after lunch then I will come up with the control and detonators to do the others."

Only two vehicles towing trailers left for the site. The others have seen enough explosions. So had we but someone had to do it.

We rolled the spheres off the trailers into the soft sand then set them off. I returned with one vehicle while the others policed the area.

I dropped the trailer at the cavern entrance then drove to the scout's encampment.

Everything was ready. The spheres were in the dry riverbed where the reporters had camped. A good safe spot.

I let them do everything but kept the control until the detonation.

The scouts had watched the explosions from a long way off. They were thrilled to see it up close.

I asked Larmarra to ride back with me so I could tell them what happened on the lake.

"Dave, that was a very foolish thing to do. Why did you let them do that? You may have angered the spirit. Neither I nor any of my men will come down here again. No telling what will happen to them."

"I would have had to discipline Fitzroy and Larson to stop them. I was ready in case something went wrong and was able to rescue them. They are shaken up except for Corporal Jameson. He discovered he was part Aboriginal. The spirit really scolded him. I told him you would talk to him. Shall I bring him up here."

"No, I will come down even though I do not want to. The men would want to know what he was doing up here."

"You have to come down anyway because Colonel Martin will be here on Friday at noon."

"I will bring him up here to inspect the camp it will give the men a boost. Thank you for the demonstration. The men will talk about it all night."

"As long as they keep a keen lookout. There are only you and your men and the night patrol. I have everyone dismantling the weapons so we can get out of here."

"I will tell them that. See you tomorrow."

I dropped off the trailer and told one of the men to pick up the other one I was finished for the day.

SERGEANT McAlister was in his glory. An inspection by the colonel. Every soldier, except the guards, was busy cleaning and shining everything in the camp.

I was in the cavern checking on the barracks then I inspected the work site. I had the dinghy buried so no one would see it.

One more thing I wanted to do is inspect the air strip. I had a guard drive me the full length. Then I looked in the hangar.

The whole company was assembled on the tarmac. They were in full dress with flags and rifles lined up in formation. I felt a little out of place but had put on a clean uniform and shined my shoes.

The plane was on time. Larmarra and his sergeant arrived just in time.

Colonel Martin received a formal military welcome.

I stayed out of the way and greeted the four navy crew.

Sam and Harry had two new apprentices with them. We kept out of the way during the ceremony. The pilots stayed in the plane.

I sat with the officers but did not get much chance to speak to the colonel. He spent most of the time talking with Captain Frazier.

Just as we were leaving to go to the Cavern the colonel spoke to me.

"I understand Sergeant Larmarra is here. Bring him along I will speak to him later."

"Sir, Larmarra is a coastal Aboriginal this country is taboo to him and his men. He cannot go near the cavern and is having difficulty being down here."

"I do not understand, he is a soldier."

"There was a riot when they arrived here it took all of the sergeant's skills to keep them here. They will not come down here."

"Are you serious? They are soldiers they go where they are ordered."

"This whole site is taboo. There hasn't been a native on this land for a hundred years and none of the locals will come here. Sergeant Larmarra is doing a miraculous job controlling them, also they have captured most of the reporters and the American service men. We would have a thousand reporters here now if it were not for their skills in finding them."

"All right you have convinced me. Where is he? I will talk to him now."

"He is here to invite you to inspect his men."

"Is that necessary?"

"You inspected the army? They are Just as important."

"All right, I understand. Find him for me."

Sergeant Larmarra and his assistant stepped up to the colonel, smartly stood at attention and saluted.

"Sir, I would like to formally invite you to inspect the northern coastal defense detachment here on special assignment."

"Thank you Sergeant Larmarra, lead the way."

They shook hands then Larmarra introduced the sergeant.

We rode in two of the new vehicles. The colonel and Larmarra in one and the sergeant and I in the other.

Our vehicle fell behind because the driver was frantically talking on the radio all the way.

It was a repeat of the earlier inspection. Full dress with flags and rifles. Colonel Martin walked through the ranks inspecting each man as he was introduced. Then he gave a short speech saying how important they were to coastal defense and thanking them for their response to an assignment they did not want to do.

After the formalities a fire was lit then some of the men dressed in their ceremonial clothes performed a smoking ceremony.

The colonel graciously declined staying for a meal of kangaroo roasted on an open fire. Larmarra accompanied us to the bottom of the hill then returned to his men.

The colonel inspected the cavern. The navy team was there unpacking their gear.

"You did not need to call us, Dave," Sam said. "You could have finished this by yourself."

"I had to call you so my doomsday prediction would come true."

"Thanks a lot. I hope you are not planning to keep us here for a year."

"You got me there. You will be out of here in a week. I am not always right, but I am never wrong."

The navy team joined us on the inspection. As with everyone else they were awed by the lake.

We ended up in the canteen and sat around catching up.

"The weapon we took with us caused a lot of excitement," Fred said. "We removed the plutonium and the explosive then put it back together. It is in out museum."

"We have twenty more to dismantle. You can take a few back with you. After we remove the explosive of course."

"Really, I am sure the war museum would like one."

"Ask Colonel Martin, he is in charge."

Then I explained how I was disposing of the weapons. They thought it was a great plan.

"Now, I know why you wanted so many explosive bullets," Sam said. "We brought them but they would not give us any C4."

Colonel Martin spoke to us.

"The Yanks have given us a very hard time and have denied that this depot exists. I like the idea of selling the remaining weapons. We could get back at the Yanks and make enough to pay for this operation. I will think about it and let you know."

"That will cause a rift between our countries," Sam said. "On another subject I was thinking if we start early tomorrow morning we can have the plutonium ready to go with the other material."

"I like that," Colonel Martin said. "Then I will not have to return here. I mean it took a lot of effort to requisition a plane."

We decided to quit for the day. I showed them the barracks. They were relieved that they did not have to sleep in tents.

Later, Colonel Martin and I had a long discussion. He told me I had saved the country from an international disaster. He said he tried to have them give me a reward but all they would do in give me a pension.

"You are now a colonel in the army reserve so you will receive a colonel's pension. You should get a million dollars, you deserve it."

"Thank you, Dave. I have a bit saved so the pension will give me a comfortable retirement which I will start as soon as I leave here."

The colonel had planned to leave early but I asked him to stan and observe an explosion.

"I have to review the troops then load the plane. I want to be at headquarters before dark."

"You have to wait for the navy to pack the plutonium. We should be ready just before lunch."

"All right, I thought I would miss it. I have never seen a large explosion."

We all sat and told war stories after supper then retired. It had been a long day for all of us.

I knew we had a long day, so I knocked on the others' doors. They did not want to wake up.

"That is the best sleep I have had in years," was the general comment in the mess.

The colonel had his inspection. The navy was working on the plutonium cores so I found a few men who had avoided the inspection and took them into the other corridor to dismantle a couple more weapons so we would have a couple of spheres for the demonstration.

Lieutenants Dixon and Rodgers were coming with the helicopter. They were going to confer with the colonel after he finished his inspection. This is the only chance they would have to speak with each other.

It did not take the navy long to pack the plutonium. They helped my crew so we finished it time to set off the spheres before lunch. As the column formed up Larmarra arrived with a few of his men. I thought he wanted to speak to the colonel.

Captain Frazier and Sergeant McAlister joined us. Otherwise, this was the smallest group so far.

Everything was ready so I asked the colonel if he would like to set off a charge. Just as I gave him the control Larmarra came up and exclaimed that his scouts had spotted something moving out on the desert.

I took the control from the colonel then sent Larmarra to investigate. He sped off with a couple of his men past the spheres and over the embankment.

We were standing there wondering what was happening when the other vehicle started to move. It stopped in front of us then one of the men told us.

"Larmarra has captured them. Two of them hired some camels. We will take them to our camp and Sergeant Larmarra will escort the camels out of the area. He will call when it is safe to continue the detonation." The vehicle sped away.

"Larmarra is really on the ball," Dixon exclaimed. "He knew exactly what to do."

"Well agreed."

"I hope this does not take much longer," the colonel said. "I want to be back at headquarters before dark."

A short time later the call came. I reconnected the wires and handed the control to the colonel. He was very impressed.

So was Sergeant McAlister when I handed him the control for the second shot.

We left right away because the colonel was in a hurry to get away.

Everything was ready, all we had to do is tow the canisters to the plane and load them.

The colonel had plenty of time so we had a final conference during lunch.

"Dave, I want to thank you again because I doubt we will see each other again. I want you to shut this down as soon as possible. Then you can retire."

"I will do that but then I have to spend some time with Lieutenant Rodgers in Darwin. We are going to summarize the condition of the depot. You can do what you want with the report."

"I will bury it in the desert. I plan to retire as soon as I file my report. That document of yours will ruin my retirement."

"Make Lieutenant Rodgers a captain then he can present it to the United Nations."

"I am planning to promote both Dixon and Rodgers but I doubt if your document will ever see the light of day."

We all drove to the airfield and helped to load the cargo.

The colonel shook everyone's hand and thanked them. He told the navy they could have four complete weapons as long as they gave one to the war memorial.

I was surprised when Lieutenant Dixon boarded the plane too.

"That is one great load off our backs," Captain Frazier said as the plane disappeared.

As we were leaving, I said to Sergeant Larmarra.

"Sergeant, how far into the desert can you see from the top of the escarpment?"

He looked surprised then smiled.

"You are clever. I am an Aborigine and need every boost available to get ahead. I am glad you did not tell anyone."

"No harm done and you planned it well. We are going to do some shooting this afternoon. Would your men like to take part?"

"There is nothing to shoot around here except a few desert mice and they only come out at night."

"The navy has a carton of explosive bullets. We are going to shoot some explosive cores."

"Really? We would like that but the men will not come down here."

"Take a trailer load of cores with you. Have a coffee while I get them ready."

Lieutenant Rodgers went to the cavern with me. He wanted to blow up a core. The men were waiting to go back to work.

"The colonel has gone so we are going to take the afternoon off and have some fun," I exclaimed. The men cheered.

We went around to the base of the escarpment with two trailers loaded with sandbags. The navy boys loaded two trailers with cores. Harry and an apprentice went with Larmarra and Sam and the other apprentice stayed with me.

We set the sandbags up a good distance from the wall then lined the cores along the wall. There were a lot more men than there were cores but I told them there would be plenty more cores in the next few days.

"We have two hundred bullets," Sam said. "But that should be enough because some will only need one shot."

"Will regular bullets set them off?"

"I don't know. We will start with regular shots and see what happens."

We all watched while Sergeant McAlister emptied a clip in a core. Then Sam gave him an explosive bullet. Everyone cheered when it went off.

The men enjoyed an afternoon of blowing up cores.

WHEN the helicopter arrived, I walked back with Lieutenant Rodgers.

"I have enjoyed my time here. It is much better than being in Darwin. Although things have eased since we captured the Yanks."

"Speaking of captors, you have two returning with you. Larmarra has them in his camp. Do you think you will need a weapon?"

"No, they can jump out if they want to, I will not stop them. One thing before I go. I found a junk yard that has a crusher. I will send a truck in the next day or two, our men will drive it."

"I want you to go to the crusher and make sure that every piece is crushed. We have kept this place a secret so far it would be a blow if someone discovered what was going on now that is almost over."

"It is an inconvenience but I understand, I will take care of it. Goodbye Dave, see you in Darwin soon. Hang on I almost forgot, I have a letter for you it is from your mate the cook."

He took a crumpled up letter from his inside pock and handed it to me then smiled, waved his hand and boarded the helicopter.

I stood there watching the helicopter. I felt good, soon all of this would just be a memory.

That evening, we sat in the canteen deciding what to do next.

"We like it here," Sam said. "So we are not in a hurry to leave."

"It is very peaceful and relaxed," Fred added.

"It is the water; the men do not want to go to Darwin on leave. Unfortunately, we cannot linger here much longer. The engineers have been reassigned. They leave in another week. We have ten days to finish here so enjoy it while you can."

"We will dismantle the four weapons then help you destroy the rest," Fred said. "That should take about a week. Ten days are enough."

"Come on let's retire," Sam said. "I want another good night's sleep."

I sat on my bed reading Ivan's letter. It was short and to the point.

"Dave where are you? You should be finished with the army by now. I am in desperate trouble and need you. The business is a success but I have lost control of it, I need you here to help me. Contact me as soon as you get this letter and tell me when you will get here."

I wrote a quick note telling him to hang on it would be at least a month before I could get there. I gave it to the pilot to mail.

SOON as the navy dismantled a sphere the cores would be loaded on two trailers and taken to the firing ranges.

By the time we finished, every man had exploded a charge. It was the most exciting thing they had ever done but they could never brag about it.

While this was going on my crew were dismantling the rest of the weapons and disposing of the spheres. The only interlude was when a large truck came from Darwin to pick up the scrap metal and the engineers began moving their equipment.

I walked out into an enormous empty cavern one morning and realized that it was all over. All that was there were the buildings and four trailers with the weapons on them ready to be shipped to Melbourne.

Lieutenant Larson had arranged the shipment of the buildings.

I just stood there for along moment until the reality sunk in. This could my last day here. I could leave when the helicopter arrived.

We gathered in the mess tent to talk about when and where we were going.

The navy boys were going to Darwin to detonate some WWII bombs found at a construction site.

I was going to Darwin to finalize my report. I would leave on the last helicopter this afternoon.

Then Lieutenant Larson said he would be the last one out. We told him to be sure to turn off the lights.

I walked behind the mess tent to find a bottle to take some water with me. I found two large milk bottles.

When I arrived in the cavern the apprentices were moving the four weapons outside and Fred and Sam were packing their belongings.

All I had was a change of clothes and some underwear and socks. Then I walked to the lake with my two bottles. I took off my shoes and socks and pants and walked up to my knees in the water to fill the bottles. I put them on the sand then walked into the water again reached down and scooped up a drink in my hands.

I do not know why I did what I did next. I put my hands together and scooped up another hand full of water. I held it up then slowly poured it back into the lake.

Then I shouted, "I give you back your home. Live here in peace forever."

Way out in the lake the water bubbled up and a ripple flowed to my feet I put my flat palms in it then rubbed my face with it, I turned and walked out of the cavern. I did not look back and I never came back.

There were only a few tents left including the operations and mess tent. I said, "Goodbye to the two men in the operations tent then headed for the helicopter which was just landing.

A vehicle came down the hill. It was Tony Larmarra.

"It was a great adventure and a good time," he said. "Goodbye Dave, maybe we will meet again for some more adventures."

"Goodbye Tony, I am proud to have met you and served with you. By the time we meet again you will be a captain.

He laughed then said, "Is this one of your famous predictions?"

"You never know. I have not been wrong yet."

I sat beside the pilot and watched the landscape slowly change from dull brown to soft green.

It had been a long time since I came here not knowing what was going to happen. It seems like a distant dream now. Did it really happen? I had the destiny of half the world on my shoulders. They all depended on me because they did not know what do. Well, neither did I.

The pilot dropped me off as close as he could to the flight office then he went to refuel.

I was walking across the tarmac with my bag in one hand and my briefcase in the other when a Land Rover pulled up. An MP asked me for some identification.

"I just got off a helicopter. I have been on an operation in the desert."

"There is no helicopter. You do not have any rank on your uniform and you have no badge or identification. Come with me, sir."

I was about to be dumped in the back of the Rover when Ian came hurrying along.

"I will take care of this, sergeant"

"Dave, I did not know you were coming. I came to check the helicopter when I saw you being arrested. Come on let's get out of here before they change their mind. They have been spooked since you caught the Americans and you have an accent."

The MP's followed us in their vehicle until they saw us get into an official army car. We drove to the same motel I left from all those months ago.

"Is the office still here?" I asked.

"No, Rodgers and I live here. They found an office on the base for us it cost too much to rent the whole motel. The downside is we have to drive to work now."

Ian took me to Room twenty-four. There were two beds in the room, a small table with two chairs and a sort of recliner chair facing the television. There was a bathroom but no kitchen.

"The army pays for our meals, so we do not cook in here. My bed is that one because the phone is there. I have to leave you now. We will be back about six. Come to the lobby so I can get you a key. Just show the key to the waiter when you want something. There is no room service. We have to eat in the restaurant or the bistro."

Ian left me in the lobby. I looked around and saw the Bistro sign so I wandered in there for a coffee.

I sat there sipping a coffee and reading a newspaper. Then it hit me. I had not read a paper for nearly a year. I have no money or identification. I decided not to wander outside so I sat there and read the whole paper.

When I returned to the room I tried to turn on the television but there were no knobs so I sat in the recliner to get my thoughts together. I had returned to a different world.

There was a pad of paper next to the phone, so I wrote down some notes to tell Rodgers.

All I had to do is hand Lieutenant Rodgers the brief case then I would be officially discharged.

I was confused, was I happy or sad?

What am I going to do now?

Then I remembered Ivan's letter. There was a phone here so I decided to call him. It was not a dial phone, it had buttons. I punched in his number but nothing happened. Just a dial tone.

After a couple more tries, I was getting frustrated so I punched the, 'zero'.

"Desk, may I help you?"

"I would like to make a call."

"All you have to do is press, 'nine'" then dial the number."

After a couple of tries I punched, 'zero' again.

"Yes, sir."

"I tried but all I got is a funny dial tone."

"Which number do you want? I will dial it for you."

"Thank you, I would like to call Melbourne."

"Sir, that is a long distance call you have to have permission from the army to do that."

"I am the army, would you put the call through for me?"

"I will connect you to the long-distance operator."

There was one ring then, *"What do you want now?"* came blaring out of the phone.

"Calm down Ivan, it is Dave, Dave Freeman."

It took a moment then, "Dave, is that really you?'

"Yes Ivan, I am in Darwin. I am finished with the army."

"Wonderful, catch the next plane down here I need you here. Everyone is on my back and all I do is shout over the phone all day."

"I know that. I have a few things to clear up but you will not have to wait a month, only a week."

"You have given me strength to hold on, please hurry."

I sat in the recliner then must have dozed off because the next thing I knew, Jones and Rogers were in the room.

"We thought you were going to sleep all night," Rogers said. "Get cleaned up we are going out for a meal."

"How does it feel being a civilian again?" Ian asked while we waited for our meal.

"I want to go back to the desert. I have been arrested, tried to make a phone call, could not turn on the television and hardly understood anything I read in the newspaper."

"Well, you will have to quickly adapt to your new life," Rogers said. "We are leaving for Perth tomorrow. Come on we are going out. This is our farewell dinner."

We did not go far, just around the corner.

"What are you going to do?" Ian asked.

"I suppose I will return to my house if it is still there."

"Don't worry," Rogers said. "It has been well looked after. I have arraigned your transport. We will go to the airport in the morning."

We reminisce about our adventures together over the past months. It seemed like old friends getting together after many years apart. I was not adapting well to my new life.

When we arrived back at the motel Ian went to the recliner and reached in a side pocket and picked up a rectangular box and presses a button. The television came on. He stood there pressing buttons and the channels were changing until he found the one that he wanted.

He saw the blank look on my face and smiled.

"It is a remote control. There is a thin wire from the TV to this box. Just press the buttons to select the channel you want. It also adjusts the volume."

IN the morning Rogers and I exchanged parcels. I gave him the brief case and he gave me a large, sealed paper bag with all my personal items. My clothes and wallet.

I gave him the note for Lieutenant Larson. That was the last official duty I had.

We rode to the airport in an official car. Their flight was ready to leave so we said, 'Goodbye' as soon as we arrived. I had to wait for an hour for my flight then another short one to the local airport and a long taxi ride to my house. It was nearly dark when I arrived home.

I did not pay much attention during the taxi ride and only noticed that the house was clean and the bed had been made.

I woke up with the sun shining in my face. For months I had woken up in the dark. It took a long moment to realize where I was. Then I was alone. I did not have to walk to the latrine and mess hall. I wandered through the house slowly reorientating myself. Finally, I realized I was hungry but the refrigerator was turned off. There was nothing to eat. I dressed in my old clothes then went to the garage to get the Harley to ride to Fred's coffee shop. I wondered if the Harley would start after sitting there for a year.

When I went outside, I noticed the porch had new floorboards. I remembered I was going to replace them but never got around to doing it. The latch on the garage door was new too. When I opened the door, I noticed the floor had been swept and the Harley looked like a new bike.

I liked the old bike but had not taken very good care of it. I had planned to have it serviced. The tank was full and the oil sump too. It started on the first kick. Now I realized what Rogers meant when he said the house had been well looked after.

Riding through the town was confusing too. There was a lot of new construction where the old cottages had been replaced by large multi apartment buildings. Many of the shops on the main street had been remodeled. On the road to the jetty there was a large sign proclaiming a large caravan park. The biggest shock was Fred's coffee shop. It was now twice the size called, 'The Jetty'.

I sat at a small table and watched the steady stream of people coming and going to or from walking along the Jetty. They would stop for a coffee along the way. This place was a 'gold mine'.

After coffee I decided to ride around to look at all the changes. I was amazed. In one year, the big developers had transformed the quaint fishing village into a full-blown tourist resort and they were not finished.

I remembered my launch, so I ended up at the marina. Another shock, the marina was ten times bigger with rows of piers jutting out into the lake. There were all sizes and shapes of boats moored there. I looked around but could not see my boat, so I walked along the long concourse to the office. There were people everywhere.

The office was a large showroom with new boats and jet skis on display. I spotted a man who appeared to be in charge.

When I told him what I was looking for he took me into an office.

"I brought you in here because I did not want a scene with all the other customers out there. I am sorry sir, your boat was sold for payment of leasing fees."

I was stunned and could only stare at him.

"The former owner explained to me that you had left suddenly and he was sure you would return so I kept your boat as long as I could but when we expanded and people were asking for moorings, it was in the way so I sold it. I had kept it for more than six months. I hope you understand."

By then I had recovered my senses and said.

"I am in the army reserve and was called away suddenly. I have just returned. Is there any chance of reclaiming my boat?"

"The person who purchased it was here on vacation. All I have is his local address. A large truck took it away when he left. If you can find him, you will have to deal with him. What I did was perfectly legal. I am sorry but I have a large business to run here and your boat was an inconvenience."

"May I ask what you got for the boat?"

"According to law, I have to sell the article for its true value and deduct what is due. I sold the boat for three thousand dollars and deducted storage fees of fifty dollars a week for six months. Twelve hundred dollars. I will not charge you for the paperwork because you are in the army."

"I lived here for many years in a quiet peaceful town. I use to take the boat out on the lake and sleep, fish and cruse around.

I come back to a bustling city. Everything has changed and all my friends have gone. I cannot get my old life back and do not want to live in a crowded city. I will reluctantly take the eighteen hundred and thank you for taking care of the boat."

"Thank you, sir, I wish all my deals were as pleasant as this."

THE next morning I was sitting on the back porch planning what I was going to do. I did not want to live here any more. The only thing I could think of doing was to visit Ivan. By then I should have adapted to a new life. I had to sell the house and motorcycle. I was pondering how much I would get for them when someone came through the gate.

He looked at me then said, "Hello, you are back. Welcome home. I am Ralph, the maintenance man."

"Hello Ralph, thank you for looking after the place for me. Would you like a coffee?"

"Thank you, I had planned to spend some time here this morning so we can have a chat."

We talked about the weather and those sort of things then Ralph said.

"I am the local handyman and was wondering if you want me to continue taking care of your property."

"You were doing a better job than I was but I am not going to stay here, I have decided to move on. The village has changed so much I hardly recognize it and all my friends have left. I have decided to sell up and leave. Could you recommend an agent?"

"I understand how you feel. I had to adapt to the changes. I use to cut a few lawns and play golf and fish. But my wife has a good business here. She has a real estate agency and is doing very well so I maintain her rental properties. No more golf or fishing. You will get a good price for this place because of the size of the block. A developer will put four apartments here."

"There goes all your good work."

"I am use to it, I have lost most of my lawn mowing business. There isn't any grass on these new places. Do you plan to keep the Harley?"

"No, I am going to Melbourne. Why are you interested in buying it?"

"I rode it a couple of times. It is a smooth quiet ride."

"I know there is a sweet spot around a hundred clicks. It will cruse all day. I hate to part with it but Melbourne is not a good place to cruse."

"I will give you a real good deal on both the house and bike. All you have to do is pack."

"That sounds great. I was sitting here thinking about what I was going to do and now it is all decided. I can be packed and gone by this afternoon."

"That is great, come on we will talk to my wife."

"What a surprise, Dave Freeman how nice to see you," Fred's wife said.

Of course, I did not remember her. I guess she was a former patient.

"Muriel, Mr Freemen is leaving us. He wants to sell his house. He wants to leave right away."

"That is a big block, you will get a good price for it. Give me a moment to make a call then we will talk."

Muriel went into an inner office.

"Muriel is all about business," Ralph said. "She is very successful."

She soon returned and said, "Mr Freeman, I will give you forty-five thousand for your house if you sell right now. I must tell you that you can get more if you shop around but you want to leave right away so I have to sell it for you."

"Forty-five thousand. I only paid six thousand for it ten years ago."

"Prices have skyrocketed since the developers moved in. If you haggle you can get in the mid-fifties for it but you will have to wait until it is developed and the units are sold. I am offering you cash right now."

"I understand and I am not destitute and want to leave right away. Thank you, it is a fair offer."

"There is one condition, the deed must be clear."

"I do not have any relatives and paid cash for the house."

"Wonderful, all I need is the deed and your bank account number. The money will be deposited as soon as the deed is registered. Within a week. It was a pleasure doing business with you and I am returning a favor. You fixed my torn shoulder that I got from playing volleyball."

"My dear I will take David home and pick up the deed. I can drive him to the local airfield too."

Fred drove home the long way. He stopped at his house to get the money for the Harley.

"I hope I am not rushing you," Fred said. "But if I hang around there she will find something for me to do. I am glad that you did not mention the motorcycle. Muriel would have stopped me from buying it. I will keep it in my work shed."

I gave Fred all the paperwork and signed the registration.

While I was packing, which only took a few minutes, Fred reserved me a seat on the commuter flight to Brisbane.

"We have plenty of time," Fred said. "We will have some lunch. It is on me."

I reclined in the seat for the long flight to Melbourne wondering what would happen. My new life starts when I land in a strange city.

CORPORAL Ivan Walinski left the army with dreams of a future financial empire. He had Dave's recipes and a promise from his uncle. Things didn't work out quite that way. His uncle had a few doubts that his bakery chain would not be viable. He also thought that the recipes were common, found in any cookbook.

Ivan was very disappointed and almost reenlisted but he was going to prove to his uncle that he had a good business idea.

Ivan found a struggling bakery in the area. He would help the proprietor build up his business.

There were two conditions, change the name to, 'Better Bakers', and Ivan kept ownership of the recipes.

In no time with Ivan baking a new line of breads and cakes they were doing better than the supermarket nearby.

The uncle was impressed he would finance Ivan but there was one condition.

The uncle had a niece who had two small children.

'Marry my niece and I will finance you'.

The uncle was a shrewd businessman. Ivan needed his money and influence and she was a pleasant, good-looking woman.

The uncle helped Ivan to establish his chain of bakeries then moved on to other things.

Ivan was not a businessman and soon lost control of the rapidly expanding business. He also found out that his new wife was a control freak. She tried to control his whole day, and night. Ivan was rapidly losing control of his life. He nearly jumped out of his skin when Dave called from Brisbane.

With only a carryon bag I walked straight out of the arrival area. Standing there with a big grin on his face was this, gangster looking character in a hand tailored light blue suit, shiny Italian long pointed shoes and an enormous gold watch glistening on his arm. A Fedora hat and a neat, trimmed beard toped it off.

"Dave, am I glad to see you."

There was another man with him. He took my bag.

On the way-out Ivan said, "I hope you are going to join me in the business. I cannot handle it on my own. I am really glad you are here."

The ride took about an hour to a high-class suburb with large houses. Ivan talked the whole way. The man, Thomas, was Ivan's chauffer and assistant.

We went from the four-car garage into what appeared to be an annex.

"This is the guest's apartment. Thomas lives upstairs. I know you must be tired so you settle in we will talk tomorrow. I am glad you are here, Dave."

The guest suite was well furnished. There was a bedroom with a large bed, a lounge and a bathroom. I was glad to be left alone after Ivan talking all the way here. It did not take me long to fall asleep.

When I woke up, I laid there thinking, *This is the first day of my civilian life. I had easily adapted to military life now I have to adapt to civilian life.*

After a shower, I dressed in my only decent clothes then wandered around the apartment. It was tastefully decorated.

When I walked into the lounge there on the table was a coffeemaker, a toaster and a plate covered with a silver hood.

There was a note saying, "Dave, turn on the coffee and put the bread in the toaster. See you at lunch. Dave."

There were two thick slices of sourdough fruit bread.

Later there was a knock on the door then Thomas came in.

"Good morning Mr Freeman, I see Ivan has taken care of you. He never stops talking about you. He has a big day planned we are going to meet him at his office then go to lunch. I think you will need to be dressed for the occasion, come with me."

Thomas opened a closet in the bedroom, it was full of new pants and jackets. Then he opened the next one, it was full of shirts and sweaters. The bureau draws were pack with socks and underwear.

"I am sure you can find a suitable outfit among all of this."

"There are more clothes here than in a store."

"Mrs Walinski buys Ivan something each time she goes shopping. I have not had to buy any clothes since they came back from their honeymoon. Take your pick, there is everything here except shoes. She does not buy him shoes and his feet are much larger than yours or mine."

ON the way into town Thomas told me that he and Ivan were school mates.

"We joined the army together. We were separated there. I did not like it but Ivan reenlisted. We have just recently met up again. It is just like it used to be. Ivan has the ideas and I do the work. I helped him start his first bakery. Now he has twenty-two of them and there are others waiting to sign up. The business is more than he can handle. He has a manager but I think it is more than he is capable of handling, he is always busy running around but nothing gets done."

"What about you? Why aren't you the manager?"

"I am content to hang around with Ivan and take care of him. All I did while he was in the army was odd jobs and drove a taxi."

The office was on the fifth floor in a large building in the center of the business district. It was very large and well appointed. The foyer was large with only a receptionist and a few brochures about the bakery on a long wall bench.

Ivan had an oversized office with a secretary. He jumped up when we came in.

"Dave, welcome to my headquarters. This is where all the big decisions are made," Ivan said with a smile.

"I am really impressed, it is much more elaborate than a mess kitchen."

"Come on, I will show you around. This is Sarah my secretary and this is Joan the receptionist and my manager, Barry Crozier is in here."

We went into the inner office where a man was sitting behind a big desk talking on the phone.

He was middle aged with a bald spot on the top of his head. He smiled and kept on talking.

"Last of all Alaine, Barry's secretary. We are all going to lunch as soon as Barry finished laying his bets on the afternoon races."

We walked along the block to a Chinese restaurant and sat at a large round table.

The food and wine kept coming until we could not eat any more. Then they sat and talked.

We sat there for about an hour and a half and most of the time Barry Crozier talked on the phone that a waiter brought to the table. Back at the office he returned to his office and picked up the phone.

"Come on Dave, I want to show you where I started," Ivan said. "We are going to my first bakery."

On the way Ivan told me how he had to convince his uncle to back him.

SANDRA and Michael Schultz were sensible hardworking people. The shop was large and well set out with the bakery on one side and the coffee shop on the other. There were three girls behind the counter serving the steady stream of customers. Sandra was the casher. Michael was in the back room preparing for tomorrow.

"I have a baker who comes in at four a.m. and starts mixing the bread dough. I come in at five to start baking then we do the specialty bread and cakes. The first customers come in at six for their breakfast bread or rolls. Some come in for coffee but they get yesterday's muffins or bagels. The fresh ones are ready for the ten o'clock break. Then I bake the special orders such as birthday cakes and that is where we are now. Sandra and I go home at about four and rest until the next day. We have good staff who like working here otherwise it would be hard to keep going."

Michael told us all that while we were looking around the shop.

As we left, Michael gave Ivan two loaves of sourdough fruit bread and six bagels.

We drove back to Ivan's home. All Ivan said along the way was that I was going to meet his wife.

I liked Fredricka the instant I saw her. I have never been much of a ladies' man, but Fredricka had the bells ringing. She was tall, well-proportioned and good looking. She was way above Ivan's class; and mine too. Her eyes were bright, she had a self-assured manner and a friendly smile.

All of that flashed through my brain in a moment.

Fredricka held out her hand and said.

"Welcome Mr Fisher, at last we meet. Ivan has spoken so often of you, I practically know you already. May I call you, Dave?"

We strolled through the house with Ivan showing me all of its finer points. We ended on the veranda then Fredricka served afternoon coffee. We sat and talked until the children came looking for their mother.

I could tell that Fredricka and Ivan got along well with each other just by the way they interacted. She looked at Ivan when he spoke and looked at him when she spoke to him. A rare trait in a woman. Ivan was a lucky man.

Later I learned that they knew each other as children.

The five Walinski brothers left the Ukraine soon after the first world war. They were loyal to the Czar. The five families are established in the Melbourne food industry. The uncle has a stall in the farmers market, Fredricka's father in the fish market and Ivan's father has a warehouse.

Fredricka's husband worked in the fish market.

"I was warned by others in the family that he was unsuitable," Fredricka said. "But was young and in love. I thought I proved them wrong we had a good life until the children came. He could not stay at home and be a father. he wanted to be a big boss like my father.

He went off one night and was found two days later in a burnt out car.

There were a few reprisals but there is no money in fighting so the family soon settled their disputes.”

“In our family a widow with children has to have a husband,” Ivan said. “So I was chosen. It started as a marriage of convenience but turned into a loving relationship. We were good friends when we were young.”

As we were talking Fredricka said to me.

“David, Ivan told me you were in charge of an army and he was your cook.”

I smiled and said.

“It was not quite like that. I was the advisor of an army detachment and Ivan cooked for the whole group. I admit I did receive extra special service from Ivan. That is where we met. I had a hobby of baking bread and pastries. We use to discuss different recipes. Just like a couple of housewives.”

Fredricka laughed.

When the children came in Fredricka introduced me as Ivan’s army mate. They were about twelve years old. The girl, Francesca, was older than Sheridan.

“Were you a cook like Ivan?” Francesca asked.

“No, I was an advisor for the project we were working on.”

“What does an advisor do?”

“I am an expert at blowing things up. I showed them how to do that.”

“Any soldier can blow things up,” Sheridan said. “Why did they need you?”

What do I do now? I was trapped.

“You have seen explosions on television they have a big blast and a lot of noise. Well, I do explosions with no big blast or noise.”

“How do you do that?”

“Have you ever seen a big building taken down? There is no big blast or loud noise. That is what I do.”

“That is enough children,” Fredricka said. “Time for your homework.”

The children went off with their mother.

Ivan and I went into the kitchen to prepare supper. I liked working in the kitchen with him, he was so smooth and efficient. While we worked Ivan told me.

"Freddie was alone with the children for lot of years. She is a good mother but children need a father to balance out their upbringing. I came along just at the right time they have accepted me and we are a real family.

We have a routine; Freddie takes the children to and from school then they play for a little while then it is homework time until supper. After supper we retire to our sanctuary upstairs. We spend time with the children then put them in bed and have a little time on our own."

"That is a perfect ideal life. You are a lucky man."

Thomas set the table then we all sat down for a delicious peaceful meal.

THE next few days I followed Ivan around so I could get an idea as to how his company worked.

I soon realized that Ivan had no idea of what he was doing and Barry Crozier was not doing anything either.

I decided that I had to step in or step out. Unless something was done the business would soon collapse. I had to do something I could not let Ivan down and I was part owner.

I started with the accountant. Thomas would drive Ivan to his office then pick me up. I spent two days there. A lot of money was coming in and the bills were being paid but the surplus money was disappearing. The accountant said he would look for it.

Then I looked into the supply chain, another mess. Instead of using his uncle's warehouse for supplying the bakeries, each proprietor ordered their own goods from different companies. That meant there was no standard of quality. They were specialized bakeries in name only.

Finally, I visited different shops, especially the ones that were not performing well.

I was very busy organizing a constant supply of essentials to the shops with the manager of the warehouse. The most important was the supply of flour. Ivan used high quality organic flour and I discovered he did not have a contract with the producer. The warehouse became the sole distributor of all their flour and yeast.

After nearly a month of constant hard work I was ready to present my program to Ivan.

I had just come in one afternoon when there was a knock on the door and Frederica came in. She had a briefcase in her hand.

"David, I would like to discuss the plan I have for the company with you. I have been following your progress. You have accelerated my plans by about six months."

I just looked at her and was about to say something.

"Let me explain. The family has been in the food processing business for nearly a hundred years. You have met some of the uncles. We are well established and prosperous in a very volatile business. My husband found that out when he tried to take over the business.

I needed a husband and after refusing a few of the family suggested suitors I was pleased when Ivan turned up. I knew and liked him. He needed a position in the family, so we went along with his bakery idea.

Ivan is a master chef and I dearly love him but he is a hopeless business manager. I am the one wo has been syphoning funds from the business, with the help of our accountant. Ivan would have wasted the money if he knew about it.

We are successful because we keep up with the trends and the bakery was a good idea. We thought Ivan could handle it but he cannot so we have devised another plan.

As I said the family is always ready to change and expand to keep up with the modern trends. I have been helping my father reorganize the fish market. That is what I did before I married. I soon realized there was a big gap in the catering industry. Customers were asking us to organize banquets for them.

We have a large building that we are converting into a kitchen and I am organizing a catering company. The overall plan is for Ivan to cook his delicious meals for the catering company. With you taking over the bakery business I can convince Ivan to cook for us. The catering company will deliver meals to the various locations. I have already signed up some wedding planners and other party organizers. Ivan can easily cook for a thousand people at a time. All we have is the kitchen and a few vans to deliver the meals. We already have all the food, so it is a winner. I know I am talking fast and confusing you but I am excited about this project, it is a real money maker with little effort. What do you think? Is it a good idea?"

I was stunned. Fredricka was talking so fast that I could hardly keep up to her and there was a lot of information to consider. All I could say was.

"Ivan is a good cook and with you organizing things it will be a success. Have you discussed this with Ivan?"

"That is the problem, I am worried that Ivan will think he is a failure because he cannot run the bakery. I am hoping you can convince him that this is a better business than the bakery."

"You are right, it is a lot better than the bakery. Less staff and overhead and a lot more profit. Ivan wrote to me about a month ago asking me to help him. He said he was losing control of the business and wanted me to help him. He offed me half of the business."

"That is a relief, now it will be easier to convince him to turn the business over to you but he cannot offer you half of the business because he does not own it. His uncle and I own it. We will offer you a very good salary and bonuses to run it."

"Fredricka, I do not want to run a business and I do not need any money. I will help you and Ivan and then retire."

"Must you retire? Part of the plan is for you to run the bakery otherwise Ivan might not agree to the catering proposal."

"I could stay for a little while until Ivan settles in."

"Thank you, David, I know you do not have to do this. The family is grateful."

"I don't mind helping out. I do not want to be tied down, that's all."

"We will discuss this again but now I want you to meet the uncles. The family gathers once a month for a general meeting. It will be this Saturday. I want you to meet the whole family. We will vote on the catering proposal. It has already been approved but someone will say we will need a chef. Then the family will ask Ivan to be the chef. He will say the bakery takes all his time then you will offer to take over the bakery. He will think he is helping the family and giving you a job."

I smiled and said, "I am glad you like Ivan, he has no idea what is going on."

"Ivan is family I gave my husband the same chance but he would not listen. He was not family. We are successful because we look after each other and adapt to the changes. We are a lot larger than anyone knows and are always looking out for new opportunities for the young one coming along."

"It is going to be an interesting weekend."

Ivan was driving his 1950 Buick Roadmaster. Fredricka was beside him and I was in the back with the two children. We were going to the family gathering. We were playing, 'I spy'.

We drove past the warehouse then into a side gate to a parking lot beside a large building. There were a lot of cars there.

Inside was set up like a banquet hall with tables and a small stage with four large chairs in a row.

Ivan led us to a table then he and Fredricka moved around greeting people. The children asked me what I would like to drink then came back with them.

The meeting was called to order and Ivan and Fredricka returned to the table.

Three men and a woman, all with grey hair, sat and watched the proceedings from the stage. There was a lot of discussion of various things then finally they came to, new business.

Finally, the catering proposal came up. There was a lot of discussion about it. I thought it was because not everyone knew about it. Fredricka made sure Ivan was paying attention.

Finally, it came to the question of a chef. They asked Ivan to stand up. He had no idea of what was going on.

"You do realize that this is a good money making business and needs a master chef to make it work?" the man on the stage said.

"Yes, I do understand that but I have a business now that takes up all my time. I cannot run two businesses."

"I understand that your friend is helping you. He can take over the bakery and you can cook for the new business."

"If that is what you want me to do, I will do it but what if my friend does not want to take over the bakery."

"He is sitting beside you, ask him."

I stood up and said.

"I will gladly help out my friend. I have been looking into the running of the bakery and have thought of a few things to improve its operation."

"Thank you, Mr Freeman. Ivan you will start immediately to organize the kitchen and hire the help. Mr Freeman will take over the bakery."

"Thank you, sir, I am here to serve the family to the best of my ability."

That concluded the business then the people prepared for the meal. The children went off with other children and Ivan was lost in the crowd of well-wishers. I turned to Fredricka and said.

"That turned out just as you planned."

"Not quite, Ivan was not paying attention to what was going on I thought I had lost him for a minute."

"I saw you with your head down, were you praying?"

She smiled then said.

"I should go to Ivan he is lost in the crowd."

"It is his moment of glory, let him enjoy it. May I ask you a question?"

She looked at me then nodded her head.

"I was wondering, how often does the family use this hall?"

She paused then said, "That is a strange question. It is hardly ever used, it is mainly for our monthly gatherings and the occasional birthday party. Why are you asking?"

"You told me people were asking you to cater for their parties. Here is a big empty hall. Dress it up and you can double your business."

She nodded her head then said.

"Thank you, David. Now I must rescue Ivan."

The party lasted until late. We left early because of the children.

Monday morning Thomas drove me to Ivan's office. Actually, it was my office now and I had Thomas as my driver because Francesca was taking Ivan to work with her.

The staff was just arriving when I got there. Barry was on the phone when I walked into his office. I pulled the plug on the phone then told the startled Barry to come out into the foyer.

"I have an announcement for you. Mr Walinski has been transferred to another department and I am now the manager of the bakery, I was chosen because I know all about the baking industry. There will be some changes made so we can operate more efficiently.

Firstly, we are going to move from this oversized office to a more efficient and cheaper rooms in one of the families buildings. You will like it because it will be closer to where you live. We will spend this week moving and settling in.

Sarah, I want you to have the phones transferred and Alaine you can organize a mover. Have a look at the new office first."

"Mr Freeman, there is nothing to move this office was rented fully equipped."

"Then check out the new office and furnish it."

"I am not sure as to what your tastes are."

"The office is like this only smaller. It needs desks, chairs and office equipment. Nothing fancy just practical. Now Mr Crozier, you and I have a few things to discuss."

We went into his office and before he could say anything, 'I chewed him out'.

"Mr Crozier, I have been going through the books and inspection various shops. I have found many discrepancies, the major one is there are twenty potential people waiting to sign up with us. We are going to expand throughout Victoria. I want those people in a shop right now before they get tired of waiting and sign up with a competitor. Do you understand? You have one month or I will find someone else. Also, if I catch you chatting on the phone instead of doing your job, you are gone. Now get to work."

I walked out of the office leaving a dazed fellow there.

Now he knows what it would be like to be in the army, I thought.

I spoke to Joan the receptionist.

"I haven't forgotten you, Joan. You will have to remain here until the phones are transferred. We will call you and you can pass on the information."

I started with the real estate agent I found in Ivan's notebook.

"Yes, I have found a few outlets for Ivan. I asked if he wanted to expand into the country towns but he was only interested in the metropolitan area."

"I have twenty prospective clients waiting to open a bakery and I am interested in expanding into the country all the way to Aulbry-Woonga. I do not want to be in a shopping center or next to a supermarket or another bakery."

"I have some good locations for you."

Next, I lined up the shop fitters and arranged to get five shops going. Then I helped Barry. He was good with the new clients but he was so slow.

Over the next few months we had most of the new clients settled in their shop.

Before I knew it a couple of years had gone by. I was only going to help Ivan establish his business and here I was running a major franchise organization. I decided I had enough. Age was catching up with me and even though I had no retirement plans, I was a loner and I wanted to be alone.

I was satisfied with my lifestyle before I was kidnapped into the army now it was time to return to a quiet peaceful life.

I took my time so not to shock everyone and leave on bad terms. I picked out a cousin who was eager to start a business and over a few months I trained him. At the same time I slowed down so when I announced that I was going to retire everyone accepted it. They gave me a 'Farewell party'.

Ivan was involved with the catering business and over the past year we did not see much of each other. Thomas was the only one who was sad about my leaving. We have spent a lot of time together.

THE weather was cold and stormy on the coast of Victoria so I headed back to the upper coast of New South Wales where I was before. I found a small beach town with a narrow hard to reach road that the developers would bypass. It would be many years before the road would be widened.

The other reason I picked the town it had a bakery that has sourdough bread and a coffee shop near the beach. I found a comfortable house away from the beach. I had thought of a retirement village but I do not like noisy neighbors.

Instead of a motorcycle and a boat, I bought a small four-wheel drive so I could go beach fishing. I settled down to a quiet life.

OLD age has finally caught up to me so I am writing this so the world will really know what is going on.

There are powerful mad people out there that only care about themselves and it is only for power and money. Patriotism and religion are only excuses to make more money. I have always said if the secret banks were closed down there would be no more wars because the warmongers would have nowhere to hide their billions. The dictator steals from the people they control and big business feeds off them by selling them guns and bombs.

Think of all the thousands of bombers, ships, tanks and guns that have been scrapped since the Second World War. Think of all the schools, hospitals and roads that could have been built with that money. Then think of all the new ones that are being built now. Those new ones have to be used so they can build more and make more money. Why did the Afghan war last for twenty years?

It is beyond understanding except when you realize these people care for no one but themselves and how much money they were going to make. Always remember generals do not start wars politicians do.

There can never be another world war because it would wipe out all of mankind. There will always be small wars so these greedy people can control others and make a lot of money.

The dooms day clock has been restarted and there are only a few seconds left. Remember all the major countries have a stockpile of atomic weapons and if one of them is losing the button will be pressed. The others will automatically retaliate. If it happens my advice is to go to the highest point and watch the blast. You will not see it but you will not have to suffer the horrors the few remaining survivors will have to suffer.

Money does funny things to man. He can never have enough. If he is poor and gets a little, he wants more, if he has a billion — he wants two.

It has always been that way and it always will be that way.

I have had a good life. I joined the air force not knowing what would happen to me. Many airmen died in Korea and other wars but I never left the country. I did my duty and assembled and loaded the weapons in the bombers not knowing where they were going. I never thought about it until I walked into the tunnel and counted all the weapons there. That was only one of many depots around the world. Those weapons cost millions and were destroyed and replaced by others that also cost millions. And so it goes and will continue to go on. All those millions end up in the secret banks around the world and the rest of us have to settle for second best or less.

More than half of the world's population go to bed hungry and sleep on the ground and most of the rest live in better conditions but the few wallows in luxury at our expense. From the time of the Pharaohs to the Romans to the Czars to the present billionaires, nothing has changed and nothing will. I do not begrudge the rich but I do their excess.

A billionaire wants two billion and when they get that they want four and so on. The rest of us can go to bed hungry. It is called, capitalism, and is promoted worldwide by the rich as the only real way to live and the poor accept it because they are brainwashed into believing that someday they will be rich too. Look back through history. It has never happened except in rare exceptions. Capitalism is the cancer of democracy.

Maybe someday this will be published and maybe someone will be inspired by it. Maybe, maybe not but at least I said something.